FAERIE MARKED

Fae Academy for Halflings Book 1

BREA VIRAGH

Faerie Marked ©Copyright 2020 Brea Viragh

Copyright notice: All rights reserved under the International and Pan-American Copyright Conventions. No part of this book may be reproduced or transmitted in any form or by any means, electronic or mechanical, including photocopying, recording, or by any information storage and retrieval system, without permission in writing from the publisher.

This is a work of fiction. Names, places, characters and incidents are either the product of the author's imagination or are used fictitiously, and any resemblance to any actual persons, living or dead, organizations, events or locales is entirely coincidental.

Warning: the unauthorized reproduction or distribution of this copyrighted work is illegal. Criminal copyright infringement, including infringement without monetary gain, is investigated by the FBI and is punishable by up to 5 years in prison and a fine of $250,000.

Cover Artist: Heather Marie Adkins, Cyber Witch Press & Graphic Design
www.cyberwitchpress.com

FAERIE MARKED

FAE ACADEMY FOR HALFLINGS BOOK 1

No one said escaping her bloodthirsty fated mate would be easy.

Half Fae and half wolf-shifter, Tavi Alderidge's only chance to dodge a dangerous and disturbing arranged marriage is to attend the Fae Academy for Halflings. There's just one problem: shifters aren't allowed.

Her hope comes in the form of a potion to suppress her shifter half while she works to earn her ticket to Faerie, the cost steep but one she's willing to pay for a chance to escape. However, surviving the Academy's cullings meant to weed out the weaker students isn't all it's cracked up to be when a murderer begins taking out the top students.

Soon, Tavi finds herself doing the one thing she swore she would never do: falling for another student. And when she discovers he's the Crown Prince of Faerie, she realizes the one person she thought she could trust is the last person who can ever learn her secret.

Fans of Sarah J. Maas, Bella Forest, and K.F. Breene will find themselves enthralled with this dark paranormal romance full of magic and betrayal.

Start reading FAERIE MARKED by USA Today bestselling author Brea Viragh today!

1

The empty picture frames lining my dresser were a constant reminder of what I didn't have. I'd thought about keeping the stock images they'd come with, but the idea of staring at the perfect smiling faces of couples and families was like a knife to the gut. *Everything* was a reminder of the fact: my parents were dead.

I furiously wiped at the tears trailing down my cheeks.

A Fae mother and a werewolf father…a forbidden romance doomed from the start, and a daughter left behind, destined to fit in nowhere.

I had no pictures of the two of them and none existed of the three of us together.

Happy birthday to me.

Normally I wouldn't risk the tears because Uncle William hated any display of emotion that could potentially show weakness to our enemies. He hadn't even cried when his brother died, or so I was told.

Besides, he was a defense attorney—one of the best—and kept his guard high. Whether this was a side effect of his chosen profession or a personality defect, I didn't know.

I sighed, pushing heavy red hair out of my eyes, dreading the next few hours. Tonight's party should have been a few stolen moments of joy, a celebration of epic proportions for my eighteenth birthday. "You only turn eighteen once," Uncle Will had said, and he had always made sure to give me whatever I wanted after I became his ward.

Even though he possessed more money than God—excuse the hyperbole—he could never give me the one thing I wanted. *My parents*. It was simply beyond his scope.

If he knew I was up here moping instead of getting ready, what a lecture I'd get. His words had the ability to strip me bare and leave me a shaky mess. It was a particular talent of his, and sometimes I felt like he practiced on me and the house staff so he'd be better prepared for court.

The door to my room burst open, shattering the precious silence. From the doorway where she stood, my friend Dawn de León stared at me with golden eyes, her hair a perfectly styled wave of sleek chestnut running along her spine. She'd set her standards to *stunning* for the evening, adorning her lanky frame in a dress made of pure sunlight. The golden shimmering ensemble complemented her eyes, and every detail down to the diamond earrings dripping from her ears was on point.

By comparison, I looked like a troll.

"I've been looking everywhere for you. You do know you can't be a party pooper if it's your own party, right? Stop sulking and get down there!" she insisted.

I tried to force a smile for my best friend and failed miserably. "I'm sorry, Dawn."

"Tavi Alderidge, please tell me *why* you're up here in the dark alone when there is food to be eaten and a hot boy waiting for you to grab him and kiss him?" Dawn emphasized the statement by miming me grabbing the *hot boy* by the shirt and dragging him up to my waiting lips and tongue.

She wouldn't tolerate my behavior for much longer, if pulling out the last-name gun was any indication. I'd used up my allotted "alone time" for the evening and the cavalry had come to rouse me to battle.

My hands, stiff from clenching them at my sides, were nearly numb and I tried to shake them out. The sun had already set outside and washed the world in hues of violet and navy. I knew whatever fleeting moments of stillness I'd enjoyed were now gone for good.

"Sorry. I was thinking," I told Dawn with a soft smile.

"Tavi!" Her gasp scraped past me. "Unless you were thinking about Jason Rutledge and how to pull him into a dark corner to be alone, then clear your mind because no other thoughts have a place there. Not today. It's your birthday!"

I knew Dawn wanted to cheer me up. And part of me wished I could tell my friend about the sadness. About the real reason why my eyes were a little red. "I'm fine," I insisted. "Getting my head in the game."

"You're going to have to do a lot more than *get your head in the game*, girl. What have you done to your hair? All those waves..." She clucked her tongue and moved forward, apparently to straighten me out.

Dawn had done her shining brown hair better than any salon could reproduce. Blessed with beauty and the money to back it up, she was a prize by the standards of anyone in the pack.

A few more pokes and prods from her ever-caring hands and I was deemed good as new, her thumbs wiping beneath my eyes at any trace of smeared liner.

I took a calming breath and stood at last. "Okay. Let's go have some fun."

Every word cost me and part of me still remained back on the bed, staring at those empty frames. But now, I'd insisted on my readiness, and Dawn would brook no further argument. She looped her arm through mine until we were linked at the elbows.

"You are not going to believe the kind of spread your uncle put together tonight. You haven't seen it yet, have you? I mean, I don't know when you last left your room, but you are going to die! It's amazing. So much better than the party my parents did for *my* eighteenth. You are so lucky."

I listened to her talk without any need—or room—for comment, one good thing about Dawn. Once she got on a roll, she did most of the heavy lifting in any conversation.

It didn't take long to navigate the winding white-and-black-veined marble staircase, then Dawn pushed me out the back door and into the yard. A lush green lawn stretched as far as the eye could see, only a small part of Uncle William's estate and kept in manicured perfection by an army of hired gardeners. Tonight, he'd erected a stage for musicians to play and the sound of the band echoed across the horde of people. My pack members.

Warmth stole over me. No matter my bastard heritage, these people were here for *me*. They were here to celebrate a significant milestone in my life. My uncle led our wolf pack, and as his niece I enjoyed a place of esteem within the hierarchy. No one understood the tenuous grasp I really held on the position of status. If they knew the truth about me, I wouldn't be allowed to stand here.

I wouldn't be allowed to *live*.

"Look, there's Jason." Dawn pointed ahead through the crowd. "I know he's been making eyes at you for the last three weeks. Is he still texting you?"

"Yeah, sometimes. It's been three weeks of flirtatious fun," I replied, then sent a silent wave ahead to the boy in question. Masculine blue eyes pinned me and held, drawing a smile from me. My first genuine one of the night.

Dawn gave me a nudge in his direction. "Why don't you go talk to him? Start up the conversation and see where it takes you. I mean, it's your party. He can't say no to you tonight. Have fun!"

"There are other people to talk to…" I began, then trailed off.

My night, my rules.

With Dawn's permission to release myself into the wilds of teenage flirtation, I crossed the lawn toward Jason, my footsteps silent and stealthy. The wolf inside of me took hold. Although only fifty percent of my genetic makeup, my wolf was everything I wanted to be but rarely felt: confident, strong, capable.

None of those things had ever described me. Not deep down where it really counted.

"Well, hello there, birthday girl," Jason began the moment I stepped within earshot. "You look great."

He'd slicked his rich dark hair around his ears, lending the appearance of classic boy-next-door. He had the sort of looks appealing to the masses and I knew he had his fair share of females sniffing around for attention.

I plucked at the simple black sheath dress bought specifically for this occasion. "Thank you."

"Everyone has been waiting for you to make an appearance. I'm flattered you chose to visit me first." His deep rumble came from his chest, a richer tone than his young face indicated. The beginning of a beard darkened his chin while the rest of his jaw remained spotless.

I pushed my hands through my hair and mussed the strands Dawn had meticulously put into place moments ago. "You looked lonely standing here by yourself. I figured you might want a little company," I said.

"If the company is *you*, then I'm in luck. I get to spend time with the prettiest girl here."

A little light back-and-forth play did the soul good, I decided instantly, *especially* when the guy on the other end looked like Jason. Yet instead of a quick return, something coy designed to get him to step closer or take my hand, I snorted. Not surprising to anyone who knew me. I rarely did well with praise.

"How about you and the prettiest girl get something to drink?" I suggested. "As long as you don't mind if *I* tag along."

"Tavi, you're crazy," he replied with a chuckle.

"I know. It's a gift."

He casually cupped my elbow as he escorted me back toward the throng of people. At least Jason didn't try to touch me excessively. He'd grown up accustomed to wealth, so he knew the protocol. Not just within pack society, but the unwritten laws of the upper class as well.

"Your uncle did an awesome job," Jason observed as we walked toward the refreshments.

I nodded my agreement. "He did. He always adores a good party. It's his bread and butter."

"I noticed guards at the gate."

"Precautions," I stated quickly, hoping not to scare him away. "Uncle Will always hires someone to watch the entrances and exits. He takes his job as alpha seriously. He does whatever he can to protect our people."

I'd noticed the wolves standing guard at the rear, of course. They didn't bother me anymore. Not when I'd grown up seeing the extra muscle around at events and meetings.

"It's good to keep the riffraff away," Jason said smugly. "I know how bright lights and shiny baubles tend to attract the undesirables."

The *undesirables*…?

My spine went stiff and I shifted my gaze toward his eyes.

"I'm not sure what you mean. There hasn't been a theft in the neighborhood in ages. Most people know to stay out. We have pretty good security in the area."

"I'm talking about Fae and their like. All their little pixie and fairy brethren falling under the Fae umbrella. They're fond of anything with glitz so I'm sure the display here is quite the draw." Jason tucked his hands in his pockets, staring around the backyard with a scowl. "Have you had any issues before?"

Jason had no way of knowing his insulting statement struck a chord inside of me. I'd heard the words before and knew I repeated them myself in public only because I had no other choice. Otherwise everyone would know there was something wrong with me.

My mouth went dry. Despite it, I didn't feel like having a drink anymore. "No. No issues," I said vaguely, knowing no matter how nicely I tried to discuss the politics surrounding the Fae, it would do no good. Inside, I flinched, shying away from the harsh reality of the world. The inherent prejudices between the two races went deep.

"Your uncle only wants to protect you from our enemies," Jason continued. "There are so many out there who would consider you a way to get to him. He's prepared for any threat, which makes him a great leader. He keeps us safe. I'm glad." Then he grabbed two glasses of whatever they were serving from the table ahead, holding one out to me.

I took a sniff. Nonalcoholic cider, no doubt, although I'm sure the adults had found their way to the hard stuff. Uncle Will always kept alcohol around.

"To you. On your birthday," Jason said sweetly, winking and touching his glass to mine.

My smile cracked around the edges. He didn't bother to confirm if it was real or fake. He didn't care. "Thank you."

I kept quiet. Taking a long sip from the spotless glass, I let

Jason continue the conversation, knowing better than to begin an argument I had no chance of winning. But I glanced around at the party and the shine he'd spoken of, the twinkling white lights strung through every tree and the opulence of even the small detail.

Yes, the bright lights were a draw for any creature dazzled by sparkles and glitz. But for him to suggest the Fae would bother to break in here because of a few strands of twinkling bulbs—

I took another swallow just as an interruption came in the form of Uncle William stepping up to the microphone and halting the band's music with a raised hand. His commanding presence did more than earn him the respect of our fellow wolves. It made him a feared opponent in the courtroom.

"Everyone, may I have your attention please."

The single statement in his powerful baritone drew a hush over the crowd though it did nothing to drown out the beating of my heart. I placed a hand against it knowing soon the attention would fall on me.

Yuck.

"Thank you all for coming this evening," William continued. "What a delight it is to see my people, *our* people, gathered together in one place for this celebration."

He stood tall, his muscular frame dressed in an expensive three-piece suit and a sky-blue tie to emphasize the interesting color of his eyes. Though in his late forties, his hair held only the barest minimum of gray shooting through the auburn strands. The color I'd inherited from his side of the family.

"If you would raise your glasses, folks, I'd like to propose a toast to celebrate Tavi, my bright and brilliant niece!"

With my name, the gazes of the collective slid to me surer

than any spotlight. Jason clapped lightly along with the rest of them as I stifled another snort.

Uncle William's dark eyes flicked to mine and held, a mix of rich brown and green. "There you are, my dear! Anyway, as you all know, Tavi has been with me from the time she turned six years old. Since then, I have had the pleasure of watching her grow into the smart and capable young woman you see today. Not to mention beautiful. Although I have to admit she's given me her fair share of trouble along the way." This drew chuckles from the assemblage, and I ducked my head to hide the slight blush. Not at his words, but from the weight of so many gazes.

"What you don't know," William continued, "is how Tavi has spent this summer working as an intern with my law firm. Something she had to be coerced into." The joke drew more laughter. "However, she has done a marvelous job of each and every task we've handed her."

He jerked his chin in my direction and the clapping grew louder. I forced my smile to widen in response to the noise level. Sure, I worked for him, and I did a good job, if everyone ignored my memory issues.

No one knew how much I hated it. No one noticed how I kept to myself. It wasn't the job itself, although the world my uncle frequented, the world he thrived in, held no appeal to me. It was how everyone looked at me that irked the most.

I did the work because Uncle William desired it of me, and as his ward, I owed him my gratitude, my life, everything. He'd taken me in when I had no one else in the world. When he wanted something from me, I did it. Familial obligation took on a new meaning for shifters.

"She's a rising star no matter what room she walks into, and a guiding light for the future of our pack. When her father was murdered by those Faerie *pigs*—" William paused to shudder, and some of the crowd of shifters took to hissing at his words. "—I wasn't sure what to do with a child. I'm not the kind of man who gets along with children, generally speaking. But I believe we've managed well with each other. Tavi, I am so proud of the woman you have become. Your kindness, your generosity, your courage, and your work ethic. There is no one like you in this world."

He had the last part right. Only the others could never know the truth about me.

"I cannot wait to see where your future leads," William stated, gearing up for a big finish. I could tell from the way his gestures broadened, his eyes gleamed. "No matter the darkness in your life, you shine. You will be the one to lead our people into tomorrow. You will be the bridge for the canyon between the Alderidge pack and the Grimaldi pack. Lucky, lucky girl!"

Wait a minute, what?

My stomach curled with dread as William's smile went supernova. "Because the elders have determined that *you*, my dear niece, are the fated mate for Kendrick Grimaldi. Surprise! Please, everyone, give her another round of applause. What a gift."

A bomb went off in my head. I was suddenly sick to my stomach at the mention. Kendrick Grimaldi, the bloody alpha of the Grimaldi pack—and my sworn enemy.

2

My fated mate, the man I'm meant to be with, is none other than the alpha of our rival who had risen to his status not by right but by *might*, uncaring of who he brutalized on his rise.

No. God, no, it can't be.

Luck? No, this wasn't luck. This was suicide.

Uncle William couldn't be right. It was *impossible*.

An icy wave of revulsion threatened to bring me to my knees and my stomach heaved, sending a stream of acidic nausea to coat the roof of my mouth. Shivers ran along my limbs and the tiny hairs along my forearm stood on end. I almost dropped my glass.

Around me the pack erupted, cheering at what they would only see as good news. They viewed Kendrick as a leader, one who wasn't afraid to do what needed to be done to bring the wolves under him to order. To keep them safe and structured.

The Grimaldi and the Alderidge wolves had never been close. After my father's murder, the divide between the two packs grew even wider. We went our separate ways when we could no longer come together on issues such as a female's rights and inheritance, to mention a few.

I felt lightheaded. At once the vision of my uncle standing on stage blurred and the rest of me went hot and scratchy. *How could you do this to me? How do you know you're right? Who are the elders to decide* my *fate?*

I opened my mouth to respond but snapped it shut again. If it weren't for Uncle Will, I'd be dead. The pack was unkind to orphans like me. *Half-breeds.* I couldn't question him in public. Not without potentially damaging his position with the others and outing myself for a fraud by blood.

"Give it up for *Tavi*, everyone," William repeated, clapping his hands together. "She deserves it!"

Jason clapped, but he'd gone quiet, and I looked over in time to see him crinkle his nose with a sniff. "Congratulations," he said when he noticed me looking. "Not everyone is lucky enough to find their fated mate."

Fated mate. And again with the luck.

Fated mates were rare in this world, two souls who were destined for each other, their lives together written in the stars and their fates dictated by the universe itself.

Me…and Kendrick Grimaldi?

No.

I might have been looking at Jason when he spoke to me. But I wasn't at the party anymore. I wasn't sure *where* I was, honestly. The sting in my chest from the news had migrated lower to an ache in my gut and I felt untethered in the worst way.

Kendrick Grimaldi was about seventeen years older than me and a seriously bad dude. His pack and mine had been at each other's throats under the guise of peace for years, and Kendrick came into power with blood and betrayal on his hands. It had been a fight to get there, to seize the throne from the elder Grimaldi alpha and destroy him.

The man was damn near a legend in pack lore.

Jason stepped closer to run a hand down my cheek. "Hey, where did you go?" he asked with a dry neutrality I'd never heard from him before.

I took my time coming to, swallowing back the words I wanted to scream out at everyone, the tears threatening to give me away, about how I would rather die than spend the rest of my life chained to a man like Kendrick.

"I'm, ah, I'm here," I managed to get out. The smile I flashed Jason was anything but sincere. "I think I need a little bit more to drink. My throat's dry."

"You still have some sparkling cider left." Jason gestured toward the glass dangling from my limp fingers.

"I don't want cider." My lips felt two sizes too big.

"Come on, let's take a walk," he suggested.

I didn't want a walk, either. Did I have a choice?

Jason kept one hand lightly on the small of my back and it was obvious how his flirty facade had disappeared entirely. He kept his touch casual the way any wolf may have while escorting me, all hints of his earlier interest gone. I didn't blame him. One simple speech from Uncle Will and everything had changed.

If anyone else noticed how I wasn't over-the-moon thrilled by the news, they didn't mention it. I kept a fake smile plastered on my face even as it felt like hot pokers were stabbing at me.

My future—*gone*. Whatever choices I'd wanted to make, chances I'd wanted to take, ripped away from me with two little words.

Kendrick. Grimaldi.

I was as good as dead but no one could see it.

My cheeks flushed but not from happiness. Fear had me walking stiffly away from the refreshment table to make a loop around the lawn with Jason. Finally, when he couldn't take my silence anymore, he brought me into the house, trying not to stop for all the well-wishers stepping forward.

Congratulations!

You are one seriously lucky pup.

Thank you, bless you.

Bless me? No, *damn* me. I glanced up at all of them through dark lashes damper than they had moments ago.

"I can't believe it," Dawn said with a pout, having cut through the crowd to stand at my side once Jason left it. She took my hands in hers. "Did you know your uncle was going to spring this news on you?"

My jaw clenched. "No, I didn't," I said, trying to calm my breathing. "I had no clue. He took me completely by surprise."

"I just can't believe it," she repeated. "You and Kendrick Grimaldi. He's drop dead gorgeous! You are one of the luckiest people I know." Dawn shook her head. And if I didn't know any better, I thought I detected a hint of jealousy in her tone.

I huffed. "You can't be serious right now—" But I stopped myself from going further.

No one would understand my reservations. Fated mates were few and far between. To the rest of them, yes, I was fortunate, blessed, not only because I'd found mine—*supposedly*—but because he turned out to be a handsome, powerful wolf. A leader in our community.

Deadly and violent.

It wasn't until much later, after the party ended and the guests had gone back to their own homes, that my uncle stumbled into the kitchen, with the sounds of the cleaning crew winding down behind him. I'd been waiting for him. I knew where he kept the good scotch, and it wasn't in his office.

"We need to talk," I said the moment I had his attention.

Then I slammed the bottle he wanted down with enough reverberation to have his eyes widening at the sound.

His brows narrowed. Sometime during the evening he'd undone his tie and left it loose around his neck. "I wondered where you'd been hiding," he told me. "I hadn't seen a hint of you since my speech."

"Yes, your *speech*. We have a few things to talk about."

But William was already walking toward me, his hand outstretched for the bottle and frowning at me as though I'd run away and ruined his night on purpose. Only one of those things was true.

I slid the bottle away and he growled, flinging off his outer jacket before tossing it onto one of the stools lining the massive kitchen island. "You know I don't approve of you touching this stuff," he warned.

It was all I could do to keep from collapsing. *Be strong. Say what you need to say.* I'd never spoken up to Uncle William before. Then again, I'd never had any reason to question him.

Things had changed.

"If you think you can so nonchalantly sell me off to the highest bidder without asking me first, then with all due respect, you've got another think coming." Bracing my arms on the granite countertop, I shook my head, ignoring my nerves. "What were you thinking, announcing an engagement in front of everyone? Why didn't you come to me first?"

William's brown eyes narrowed. "I'm thinking about how you are my ward, and eighteen or not, this is not your decision to make. You have a fated mate, Tavi. The pack elders divined the match. The divination *means* something, despite your feelings. It's a gift."

I went hot and cold at the same time. My finger tapped against the booze bottle. "A fated mate. I'm calling bullshit, Uncle Will. I don't think Kendrick Grimaldi and I are fated at all. We don't even know each other. I think you auctioned me off like cattle behind closed doors so you can gain control of the Grimaldi holdings and land. Pack elders? No way."

The moment I said it, I knew I should have approached this with a little more finesse.

No reaction or hint of alarm showed on his face. He cocked his head. "Is that what you think I did, Tavi?" Then suddenly Uncle Will's fist slammed down on the countertop. "Answer me!"

Wow, he was pissed.

But I would not be cowed. "Yes! It's exactly what I think!"

His unrelenting steel and grit had helped both me and the pack survive—*thrive*—until this point. He alone maintained our status and had brought the Alderidge wolves to new heights, especially after the problems with the Fae. With my mother's people.

"Do you have a problem with your fate?" he asked icily.

My jaw seized from clenching it too hard.

William shifted, blinking, and grabbed the scotch from between my hands, knowing I wasn't foolish enough to face him if it came to a fight. "You should be pleased with the match, Tavi, considering your tainted bloodline and the nasty influence from your mother's side. Not everyone is as gifted as you are. Kendrick Grimaldi is certainly one of the most eligible alphas around, with great wealth and power. This match between you two will strengthen the relationship between our packs. You're marked for greatness. It is destiny. It is *fate*." He stressed the word. "And therefore, it is out of my control. I want you to remember before you sling accusations at me."

I couldn't take any more of his cool indifference. Not when inside I wanted to rage. I drowned out the urge to scream at him by storming off and slamming the kitchen door behind me hard enough to rattle the dishes. Heels and fancy dress and all, I ran. Out the front door and down the street. Into the darkness.

Nothing about the night had ever scared me. Not when I knew I could handle whatever threat came my way through strength and wits.

I could handle anything except what my uncle asked of me. *Demanded* of me. I swallowed the urge to give in to tears. They were there, ready to come flooding out.

The park up ahead, a community green space where the rich moms took their toddlers in our exclusive community, had become my escape. The lateness of the cool evening meant the area was empty. Thank God.

I slowed my steps to a methodical march, the black iron fence around the park positioned like silent sentinels.

"Elfwaite?" I called out.

My voice echoed back to me without an answer.

Despite the hush of night, I finally relaxed. The tension in my shoulders eased the farther I walked into the park. Large oak trees shaded the paths during the day, but tonight, with the moon high and casting shadows, I stepped through random pools of buttery light.

Here, I didn't have to pretend anymore. I didn't have to protect myself against judgment. Elfwaite was the only person in the world I truly trusted with my truth. She didn't care about my blood. She only cared about me.

A flutter of wings caught my attention and instead of preparing to run, I smiled. This time, I meant it.

The pixie's nostrils flared delicately as she crept between the leaves of a bay laurel bush. All four inches of her tiny, purple-skinned supernatural self. "You're supposed to be enjoying your birthday party, young lady," Elfwaite gently scolded, her voice a mere whisper of sound. "You told me you were going to have fun."

"And it was fun, for the first five minutes."

"Somehow I doubt things went downhill fast without a good reason. It wasn't an unruly guest throwing food around, was it?"

I shook my head. "No, definitely not."

Elfwaite's family had left Faerie a hundred years ago, during the great Pixie War. She was born and raised in the human lands and knew no other life. Yet she had been my best source of information on Faerie so far, the only connection I had to my mother's people, of her life before coming here.

My pixie friend had returned to her homeland multiple times once the war ended to visit family. She'd simply never wanted to stay.

We met by chance when I was jogging one day, a passerby knocking into me and sending me flying into the laurel bush where Elfwaite happened to be napping. Her kind didn't normally associate with wolves, even half-wolves. But she'd been kind. So had I. It made an impression.

I knelt down on the soft grass, uncaring of what happened to my dress.

"I...I need to talk to you," I began haltingly, holding out my palm for her to rest on. This was followed by an embarrassed cough, glancing back along the empty path. I knew I could say whatever I wanted to Elfwaite without fear but it took me precious moments to let my guard down. "I need to talk to someone who won't judge me. Or, heaven forbid, be happy for me."

"What's wrong?" Elfwaite pressed her palm to mine and magic sizzled between us.

Laying my free hand flat on the grass and resting upon it, I raised my gaze to meet her slanted pupils. Why did this seem so difficult? "My uncle found my...my fated mate."

Her wings fluttered. "This is not good news for you."

Not a question. A true statement. She understood better

than most. "No, it's not. Uncle Will announced it at my party." The rest of the story spilled out of me faster than I'd anticipated and I ended up telling Elfwaite everything.

I told her about the first time I'd seen Kendrick at a rather explosive pack meeting at my uncle's estate. I'd seen the gleam of desperate violence in his eyes when he spotted me. Like a starving hunter spying a rabbit warren. Like I'd be easy pickings because I was pretty and weak.

I'd never killed anything outside a few deer, let alone another wolf shifter. Seeing Kendrick all those months ago, I'd wished for something to defend myself against him, and I would have used a weapon if necessary. Now I wanted nothing more than to bury the memory and never think about it again.

I stared at my friend. "I don't understand what's happening. I really don't," I continued, swallowing hard. "Worse, I don't know what to do to get out of it. I'm not strong enough to fight the will of two packs by myself. No one will listen to me."

"Oh, Tavi." Elfwaite kept her tone comforting and quiet, fluttering forward to hug me. She was only a little bigger than my nose, and she moved there to soothe me.

"There's no way I can let my uncle marry me off. I would rather die than spend the rest of my life chained to someone like Kendrick, someone people say revels in the misery of others. How can he be my fated mate? He's not a good man."

"I would rather you *not* die. There is always another option, though…you can run away to somewhere you would be safe from your uncle's reach."

I was desperate for a solution when it seemed there was none, and clung to her words. "Where?"

"To Faerie, of course."

Unable to help myself, I laughed. "Elfwaite, I would never

be allowed in. I'm half werewolf. The gatekeepers would throw me back into human lands on my ass."

The pixie moved back to stare at me, frowning. "There is another way," she insisted.

My laugh turned into a snort. "It sounds almost as ridiculous as Kendrick Grimaldi being my fated mate."

But her gaze held steady and strong. A being so small, one would think the expression laughable on her face. I knew better. She packed a world of power inside her minuscule body.

"There are places in this world standing apart," she said. "I've told you this before. Places the lucky few know about. You happen to be in the correct position to travel to one of them."

As if I'd been struck, I leaped up from the ground, an electric current in my blood at her words. "Tell me."

"You could apply for a spot at the Fae Academy for Halflings. It's located in the mortal realm, a school for halflings like you who want to earn a place in Faerie."

"How far away?" And how would I get there?

"Not far. It's located on the east coast. Massachusetts, if I remember correctly. A few hours if you travel by car."

It was strange to hear her melodic voice say the word *car*. "I've never heard of such a school."

"Because it's hard to hear about Fae dealings when you're smack dab in the middle of a wolf pack, having to hide your truth," she replied, her eyes narrowing and her smile revealing sharp white teeth. "Your people are good and kind in many ways, but they can also be wild beasts without the ability to see both sides of an argument. Someday, Tavi, you are going to have to learn. This world is not just black and white. We all exist on a spectrum of shades of gray and you choose where you fall on the spectrum."

"You of all people should understand. I know those lessons," I replied bitterly. "Better than most."

Elfwaite inclined her head in agreement. "In some respects, yes. I will not lie to you. You know this. Your best option in this case is to apply to the halflings school, because it's the first step toward freedom. They will test you for Fae blood, and if you test positive, you must compete to earn the right to stay. If you do, and you graduate, then you are permitted permanent access to live in the Faerie realm. It is one of the only options for halflings like you. Fight for your freedom, Tavi."

"They'll know about my shifter nature," I argued. Still, the idea had taken root inside of me. A place to escape, not just from my future but from the expectations going along with it. "What am I going to do about my life here?"

It seemed a moot argument at this point. I no longer had a life here, or I wouldn't after Kendrick came to claim me.

I needed this hope and gathered it close to me. For the first time this evening, I imagined a better life for myself when I'd been taught only to stay in my lane and obey someone more powerful than me.

Elfwaite pointedly cleared her throat. "Your life will change irrevocably whether you apply to the school or not. And if you get accepted, then you would have to hide your wolf. I have a friend who can help, if you decide to go through with it, though her help will come at a price. You must be willing to pay the price."

"I'm willing to pay," I insisted quickly. *Anything.*

Her mouth quirked to the side. "Be sure before you commit to it. You never know what may be required of you. I'd hate to see you give up something you truly love in order to get what you think you want."

3

I had to formulate a plan to get out of Kendrick's clutches. Even without talking to him face to face, I felt him around me, felt his influence like invisible fingers tightening around my neck. Or maybe a chain.

I stayed in the park talking with Elfwaite until well after midnight, if the arc of the moon overhead was any indication. Sneaking back home, I kept my feet silent, my breathing even, and my focus on what lay ahead for me.

My fingers curled into fists as I walked through the front door. There was nowhere to run once inside the sprawling two-story mansion. I stared at familiar marble and bronze fixtures, the paintings belonging in a museum rather than on a civilian's wall. When I looked toward my uncle's study, my gaze hardened further.

Funny how things could change in such a short time. My life had been altered with my father's murder and my mother's public execution at the hands of their enemies. Things seemed to straighten out, and I'd been given a stable place to hide here with Uncle Will, yet now I stood at what felt like a final dead end.

Unless Elfwaite was right about this school.

At least the party was over and the house emptied of guests. From the silence and the slender dark space beneath the office door, I'd guess my uncle had gone off to get drunk with his high-ranking pack buddies at their favorite bar. It was a Friday and Saturday night tradition for them. Five or six males staying out until the sun crept over the horizon sharing stories and dirty jokes over expensive alcohol. I'd learned not to expect him home.

Admittedly, I'd been banking on tradition. I didn't want to face him again. I didn't want to hear him tell me again how wrong I was to fight this. Or how I should be grateful for a match at all, let alone a match with a fated mate. A match with Kendrick Grimaldi.

Gag.

Shoulders tense, I took the steps two at a time and pushed through the door to my room. My laptop lay on the desk beneath the windows, surrounded by papers and collectables, odds and ends I knew I needed to organize yet couldn't bring myself to. Yet.

A glance at the clock told me it was 12:30. Grit and exhaustion had my eyes closing and wanting to stay shut. Even so, I needed to know more. I *had* to know more about the Fae Academy for Halflings.

Elfwaite had told me about their online application process. Someone had brought the ancient institution into the twenty-first century and made them more accessible to my generation. They were very progressive.

Now if I could find the link to their website…

It was the one thing my friend hadn't been able to give me. Although she'd seemed to know enough considering she didn't have access to the internet. The pixie knew more about the world than most humans I'd met.

I lifted the laptop lid and clicked the power button, giving the machine time to wake up. The screen glowed blue in the dim hush of night. I had work to do.

Thirty minutes later I still hadn't found the right website. There were a few links that seemed promising at the time but led to something either completely different or a blank page asking if I wanted to purchase the domain name.

So yes, someone had updated their online application process, but then made it insanely hard for any normal person to find.

A way to weed out the weak before they even applied?

It took me another thirty minutes to get through enough false starts and leads to fill a ship. *I'm never going to find this damned site.* Fatigue and frustration went hand in hand, and another glance at the clock assured me it was hours past my bedtime and my birthday was long over.

No wonder I wanted to throw the computer out the window. Good thing Uncle Will wouldn't expect me to rise early. He probably wouldn't be out of bed before noon either.

Then I thought of my "fated mate." I thought of the lustful sneer on Kendrick's face the one and only time I'd seen him, and all of the nasty things I'd heard regarding his temperament. I could deal with the sleepiness if it meant an *out* from a lifetime with him.

I clicked around with whatever combination of words I could think of to find the website.

And got a hit right when I was about to call it quits.

"It can't be..." I muttered, leaning closer and blinking blurry eyes to read the text.

Probably not. The longer I looked at the page, the more it seemed like a joke. A silly thing, similar to the Harry Potter sorting hat quiz online. Probably fiction and a waste of my time.

But I clicked anyway, the way I had every other site before this one.

The Fae Academy for Halflings. Along with an address in Massachusetts.

A light came on inside of me.

Another click gave me a full page containing a brief history of the place including pictures of the old castle. It rose three stories high with turrets in an antiquated style one rarely saw anymore. Old stone and mortar with quintessential English ivy suffocating parts of the walls. Old wavy glass reflected light from the sun burning overhead when the pictures were taken.

It seems like a nice place, I thought, leaning closer still. A place where I could *escape*. If it was real.

In that respect, it didn't matter what the school looked like. It only mattered if they accepted me.

The castle housing the academy was located on fifty acres set well back from the road. It made for more privacy, certainly, and if there were many Fae located in the same place, then they more than likely had magic to protect them from prying eyes.

Though my eyes burned, I read through the process of enrollment and graduation, including how to earn permanent residency.

And then I clicked the button to enroll. Now or never.

The questions seemed ridiculous at first, like pictures of treasure chests and a space for me to answer which one I would choose and why. There were questions asking about Fae weaknesses and strengths with options where none of them appeared to line up with usual lore. An example:

Faebane—deadly poison, delicious tea, or party favor.
Which should I choose?

Those questions were most likely intended to weed out the real submissions from the fake ones. Except I was half Fae and I *still* didn't know the answer.

Anxiety roiled beneath my ribs. Maybe I should put this

off until I could get some sleep. Wait until I had a clearer head—

Kendrick Grimaldi.

Yeah, nope. No time to waste.

Besides the strange multiple-choice questions, the rest of the application read like an online quiz and I finished it easily. There was a space for me to fill in my information toward the end of the enrollment, along with a blank space for me to write about why I wanted to go to the academy.

I paused, biting my thumbnail. I couldn't tell the truth or they would never accept me.

They won't accept you anyway. They will never let some nobody in.

The voice inside my head would not stop with the negative self-talk, no matter how hard I tried to silence it. Despite the screaming, the constant subconscious repetition I would not be good enough and I'd be forced to marry a monster, I filled out the rest of the form. I should have waited to finish until I had a clearer head.

I did it anyway.

What was the harm? Either they accepted me or they didn't. Either they provided the out I desperately needed…or not.

"What are you doing still up?"

I jumped at the voice and swung around to see my uncle's large frame filling the doorway. Scrambling to close my laptop before he could see the screen, I turned to face him and gathered a simple if tired smile onto my face. "I couldn't sleep," I told him through a yawn I didn't have to fake. "Thought I would play around on the internet for a while to try and relax."

"Maybe it's a good thing you're awake. I'd like to talk to you. I want to apologize for earlier," he continued, butter-smooth and surprisingly not drunk.

Then he lost his balance a bit stepping forward over the threshold. Okay, maybe not sloppy drunk but definitely tipsy.

I curled my lip. "You do?"

"Of course." He sounded surprised. "You're my niece, and you know how much I care about you. You *do* know, don't you?"

William walked to the bed and took a seat facing me, nearly missing the edge and grappling to right his balance before he slid to the floor.

"I'm not so sure anymore. The latest bombshell you dropped on me raised a few questions." My spine stiffened with his nearness. At the stench of liquor on his breath.

His brows narrowed but he didn't say anything for the longest time. "I should have spoken to you beforehand, it's true. I thought you would be happy with the news. A match is a good thing, especially for a half-shifter like you. We've kept your true heritage under wraps for long enough. It's time for you to get your happy ending."

A low, incredulous laugh. "I should be happy to be used as a pawn for pack relations? You must not know me well, Uncle Will, if you think a marriage would make me happy. This is *terrible* news."

"Why would you say it's terrible news? You don't trust me to want the best for you? This is the best thing we could ask for," Will insisted.

"For you, maybe. But Kendrick Grimaldi is a beast." Didn't Uncle Will understand what lurked beneath the man's surface? It wasn't a kind heart.

He shot to his feet and lost his balance before settling back down and righting himself, like invisible hands clapping him on the arms to keep him from falling over.

"A man who is doing what he needs to do for the welfare of his subjects is not a beast," Will ground out, becoming frustrated with me. "You should know. Some would say you should be grateful for me finding you and taking you in once your father died. Offering you the chance to live comfortably."

"I should be grateful you acted like *family*?" I questioned.

He wanted to speak more on the subject. I could see it in his eyes, in the way his shoulders tensed and he leaned forward with his elbows on his knees. Instead, he came out with "I hope I didn't ruin your birthday party. Although I suppose now your birthday is over, and I've lost the opportunity to make it up to you on the day of. I'm truly sorry, Tavi."

"I know you are." I played along with the apology and abrupt turn of conversation, because both reeked of a maneuver.

Uncle Will wanted to keep me willing and compliant, a bargaining chip with the Grimaldi pack. An apology was the first step toward smoothing the way and keeping me biddable if not happy.

I inclined my head so he didn't see the way my lips narrowed. The way everything inside of me went cold at this play he'd made. "I accept your apology. Thank you. And I *am* grateful for everything you've done for me."

I thought about the admissions process I'd just gone through, about the Fae Academy for Halflings. Come what may, Uncle Will and I were stuck with each other until I could figure out an exit strategy.

I might as well play along.

"You and Kendrick will be happy," Will said too softly. "And once you get to know him, you'll see it isn't a mistake and it isn't a power play. But if you try to fight me again, if you purposely blow this match, then certain things will have to change and not necessarily for the better."

His words dropped like stones in my gut. I opened my

mouth to argue further, then nodded my head. "I understand. Just give me some time to adjust to the idea, okay?"

We ended the night with a loose hug and a request on his part for me to stop fiddling around on the computer and get to bed. I obliged.

A week passed and Friday loomed large. Although I checked my email twenty times a day, I still hadn't heard anything from the academy. Did I expect to?

Maybe. *Yes*.

I knew it was a long shot to be accepted, but I still held out hope. Elfwaite had assured me they accept anyone with Fae blood who applied and the true culling came later in the semester. That didn't seem to be the case for me. Or perhaps I'd gotten a little impatient.

Still, no one had reached out to me to test my blood. And after another four days of waiting without an answer, I began to panic.

It meant I needed to have a Plan B in place. And more than likely a C, D, and E. I tried to push the niggling bite of panic aside, but the low-level anxiety stayed with me, every hour of every day. I needed to talk to Elfwaite again, so I donned my jogging clothes and prepared to leave.

But just as I reached the stair landing, Uncle Will pushed through the front door with his briefcase in hand, kicking the door closed and using his free hand to loosen his tie. "Where are you heading?" he asked when he saw me.

I continued down the stairs. "I'm going for a run in the park. The same thing I do every afternoon when I'm not working for you," I said lightly.

"Not today, you're not." He watched me, scrutinized my every move, saw the flare of my nostrils at his words. "Go back upstairs and change out of those shorts. I need you to put on a dress."

My stomach sank. "Why?"

He sighed. "Please don't question me today, Tavi. Do *not* question me. I've had a long afternoon of meetings and this tension in my neck is threatening to morph into a hell of a headache."

"Uncle Will, tell me what's going on," I insisted.

"Cook!" Will called out instead. Pointedly ignoring me. "Cook, where are you?"

He dropped the briefcase on the entryway console and then looked up at me. At the concern clearly written across my face.

"Tavi, the dress." He snapped his fingers. "Now. We have very important guests arriving in an hour and I need you to look your best. Kendrick Grimaldi is coming for dinner and he can't wait to officially meet you."

Did my stomach merely sink before? Now it spiraled into a bottomless abyss.

4

Lungs aching, I took the stairs two at a time and slammed the door to my room behind me. I leaned against the wall, trying to breathe, trying to get my heart to quiet against the cold pit opening up in my belly. Nothing seemed to help. The space around me blurred and my mind spun in circles.

I kicked at the wall and bit back a scream of pain when my toes collided the wrong way.

Kendrick Grimaldi would be here in an hour. An hour until I had the rest of my freedom yanked from me. And I was expected to get dressed, to do my hair and makeup, or else risk punishment? *Severe* punishment, if the look on Uncle Will's face had been any indication.

My chest hurt. *Is this what a panic attack feels like?* Like a rabid animal clawing through muscle and bone to reach the heart?

I should run. I should pack a bag and climb out my window, down the portcullis and out onto the street. My running shoes were laced. It would be easy—

Kendrick couldn't possibly cart me off tonight. Could he?

I was ninety percent sure of it. Uncle Will had muttered something about the two of them needing to discuss business, or so I thought I'd heard when I was fleeing upstairs. Business about the match, no doubt, working out the details. The reminder did nothing to soothe my racing heart because there was still ten percent of uncertainty to consider.

I steeled myself for a fight. I had no choice tonight. I'd play the part to the best of my ability, get through this, and make sure the two of us were never alone together. I would do whatever I had to do to keep up appearances while I made my escape plan.

As much as I loathed the idea of being in the same room as a criminal, I shed my jogging clothes in favor of a sheer silk dress. One of the nicest pieces I owned and once loved and would never look at the same after tonight.

An hour later, I stood on the stairway again, only this time everything had changed. Now it felt like I stood in front of the executioner. Rich auburn hair curled around my face and trailed down the middle of my back. I'd accentuated the odd tilt of my green eyes with black liner, cheeks tinged a light peach, and lips left bare for emphasis.

Our guests were already here. Voices sounded from the dining room and although my steps were heavy, although every inch I closed between me and them felt like I lost a bit of my soul, I pushed open the door. And three sets of eyes turned in my direction. They were predators in every sense of the word, ready to pounce on me. I was all too aware of the attention as I stepped into the room.

The men were lounging around the table with empty plates in front of them, sipping from our best stemware edged with real gold—staggering wealth both sets of alphas were accustomed to. There were several prepared dishes scattered around the table and a plethora of scents and spices lingering in the air.

If this were a different day, a different dinner, then I would be starving and ready to dive into the array of platters Cook had prepared. As it was, my head was unnervingly light.

Uncle Will's seat was at the head of the table and he stood when I approached. He was the picture of propriety. And although he was my alpha, he was not the most powerful man here tonight. Clearly.

"Ah, there she is. My niece Tavi, gentlemen. Please take a seat, my dear. Say hello to our guests." He pointed toward the empty chair next to a dark-haired boy...no, *man*.

Kendrick Grimaldi was much older than I and had the air of privilege and superiority that spoke to his status of alpha. But the deep lines around his sunken eyes hinted at a wolf who'd seen too much. Bloodshed must weigh hard on him. Bad for the body.

Was his soul any different?

The world halted around me and I fought against the stillness, oddly off balance. My throat ached and I heard my pulse echoing in my ears.

Uncle Will stared at me eagerly, his arm still held out toward the empty chair. I tried to force a smile and found myself unwilling. My face simply refused to cooperate.

I'm expected to speak, I thought hastily, the slow walk toward the table pure torture. Sitting down, I could feel Kendrick's attention focused on me like the pricking of a dozen cold needles against my skin. I couldn't look at him. Couldn't face him. I wanted to flee.

"Well, Tavi? Say something," Uncle Will urged with a slight chuckle. Only I recognized the annoyance behind his words.

My gaze flicked to Kendrick again. As though this were a normal dinner party. As though the man next to me were any other guest, on any other day of the week, and not the linchpin ready to catapult me into a new reality of nightmares.

I forced myself to say the words to him. "It's a pleasure to officially meet you, Mr. Grimaldi."

"Kendrick, please," he responded.

I barely heard him. And barely registered the introduction of Kendrick's advisor, seated across from me. It was considered bad manners to forgo introductions even though they were being made between rivals who already knew each other well.

Kendrick Grimaldi didn't appear to need an advisor, or a guard to watch his back. His arms and shoulders, larger than normal, were grossly muscled and I noticed the scars on his hands. He had a strong, square jaw, his nose slightly misshapen and narrow as though it had been broken in multiple places and never quite healed correctly. His lower lip held more fullness than the top as though it had been made for nibbles. The lines around his mouth and eyes did nothing to detract from his good looks.

A glint caught my eye and I noted the earring in his right lobe, dark hair waving around it and nearly obscuring the shine. I could see where other wolves would find him attractive. He was a bad boy wet dream.

Or he might have been, if it weren't for the fated mate crap. He did nothing for me.

I felt nothing for him beyond the cold clamp of fear. There was no draw to him, no magnetic pull making me want to scoot my chair closer. If anything, I wanted to go in the opposite direction.

Cook pushed through the door from the kitchen, arms laden with more trays and followed by two helpers equally laden. Uncle Will had really gone all out for this. I wondered how I might have missed the prep, the hustle and bustle inherent with a dinner of this magnitude. Had I been so blind?

"You're more beautiful than I remember."

The sound of Kendrick's voice jerked me out of my head. I kept my face blank and willed my heart to steady as I asked, "Excuse me?"

"Your dress looks amazing. The cut flatters your body. You are truly beautiful. Young and in your prime, filled with life." His gaze dropped to my neckline and the bit of cleavage showing.

I resisted the urge to place my napkin over the area, clenching my hands into fists. "Thank you."

"I'm excited to get to know you and see how things proceed," Kendrick stated, flashing a smile to my uncle, who had more than likely been keeping an ear in our direction. To make sure I didn't stick my foot in my mouth. He and Kendrick's advisor, whose name I'd heard and immediately forgotten, watched me too closely to be casual.

"Things proceed with *what*?" I asked, sincerely trying, and mainly failing, to keep the nastiness out of my tone. Although I knew what he meant.

"Between us. I never expected to be graced with a fated mate. It seems as though the universe is blessing me. Blessing us. Fated mates are rare. I'm grateful." He moved closer, the movement smooth. This was a lethal predator. A man blooded with power.

I wanted to believe what he said, truly I did. It would have gone easier for me, I was sure. But there was something insincere about his tone. And his emotions never reached his eyes.

I also could not return the statement. "It was a shock to me," I said honestly as I settled my napkin on my lap. "I didn't expect the news. Not at my birthday party. Eighteen is so young to consider marriage." I mentioned it hoping my young age might be a deterrent. No such luck.

"It couldn't have come at a better time." Kendrick placed his hand over my own and squeezed. The heat from his palm was noticeable.

I tried hard not to flinch at his touch. "Why?"

"Let's just say everything is coming together, babe," he said with practiced smoothness.

Babe, already. Talking to me and touching me like he owned me within minutes of meeting.

Cook placed slices of rare filet mignon on my plate along with a serving of *haricots vert*, piling both high. I sent her a pleading look. *Get me out of here*. She ignored me.

I began to push the food around on my plate, an excuse for breaking the physical contact. Actually, I wanted nothing more than to bury my steak knife in Kendrick's thigh. Or his hand, to keep him from touching me again.

"Wow, you really are spectacular, Tavi," he was saying. Shaking his head like he couldn't believe his luck.

"How did you know?" I burst out, dropping my cutlery with a clang. Unwilling to touch my food as my stomach was giving queasy heaves of protest.

"How did I know *what*? That you are spectacular?" he clarified with a wink.

"That we are fated mates. The news had to come from somewhere, or someone." I was grasping at straws and did not care. Uncle Will and Kendrick's advisor were engaged in their own small talk. They would provide no answer. "My uncle told me it was the pack elders who decided the match. Did you speak with them?"

Kendrick grabbed hold of my hand and raised it to his chest, pressing it against the fabric of his shirt so I felt the steady beat of his heart. "I knew the first time I saw you. I felt it in my heart, like a thread drawing us together. The pack elders confirmed the match with their scryers. It's meant to be."

I didn't believe a word of it. The insincerity in his impassioned statement sent shivers down my spine.

Everyone turned to stare at me as I broke contact with Kendrick, pushing away from the table. "I'm sorry, I need a minute."

"Tavi, is everything all right?" Uncle William asked.

"Of course. Just give me a moment," I stated and rushed for the nearest powder room.

It wasn't until I was closing the door behind me that I could draw a breath, in and out. Every part of me ached and I realized then I'd been holding tension in my body where it didn't belong.

A few deep inhalations helped to slow my heart. I stared at myself in the mirror. Auburn curls framed my face; delicate emerald-green eyes looked shadowed like I'd taken a couple of punches to the face. Stress, if I had to guess, though it wasn't a shock. Instead of looking confident and in control, I looked hunted. Ready to bolt.

It wasn't the image I wanted to project, the image of quiet confidence and assurance. I threw a pointed look at my reflection and accompanied it with a wagging finger.

Get a grip on yourself, I told my reflection sternly. *You can get through this. It's one dinner. Make it through dinner and we can figure the rest out later.*

I didn't believe myself, though. I didn't expect to.

The few moments of peace awarded to me disintegrated the moment I opened the door to see Kendrick leaning against the opposite wall, waiting for me.

"What are you doing out here?" The question was out before I thought better of it.

His smile turned into a leer. "You ran off."

Close, he was too close.

"I hardly call going to the bathroom *running off*," I said with sweet venom. Then tugged at the hemline of my dress to cover more skin. "You didn't need to follow me. I have been doing this alone for a long time."

When I moved to get past him, he shifted, blocking the way. I finally realized the full breadth of his shoulders. The imposing set of his body and the way his muscles were for more than just show. This was the wolf who had won the alpha status of his pack by sheer and brutal force.

"Excuse me, I need to pass," I said softly. Hating how my voice trembled.

"I wanted a moment alone with you without your uncle and my *advisor* breathing down my neck." The way he said the word made me think the title was nothing more than honorary. Kept around due to tradition and nothing more.

"I'm sure there will be plenty of time for us to be alone in the future, *if* this match goes through." There was enough dismissal in the tone I took a small bit of satisfaction in saying it to him. But the thought of being alone with Kendrick had my head spinning and my mouth going dry in the worst way.

He stepped closer. My breath caught and, nostrils wide, I sensed his musk. Instead of the scent turning me on, I wanted to run far and fast. "What if I don't want to wait?" he asked.

A laugh bordering on hysteria burst out of me. "Then I'd say you're out of luck." A show of false bravado, and one he saw straight through if the heat in his gaze was any indication. "You have no choice."

I tried to step under his arm and lost my footing when he shifted again, sweeping me back against the wall and caging me with his body. Heat prickled on my skin, and my chest ached.

"Tavi…" he breathed. "You really are spectacular. I wasn't

lying. Beautiful in a way few can match. Your skin..." He dropped his face lower.

"Let me go." It came out as a whisper, damn it. Not as the demand I'd intended. I hoped he didn't think I was playing coy with him.

"Don't you feel it?" Kendrick leaned forward, drawing the scent of me into his lungs. He trailed his finger down the side of my face and neck. Further south until it rested on my collar bone. "This connection between us? Fated mates."

No.

Every part of me rose in protest to his nearness. This wasn't how I should feel. Was it? His fingertips skimmed up my arm and goose bumps rose in their wake.

"Let me go, Kendrick." I didn't care about being reduced to begging. "Please."

A growl rumbled deep in his throat. "I can't wait until you're mine to do what I want with." Apparently, all attempts to sweetly woo me were gone.

I wasn't fast enough to move, wasn't fast enough to duck away before his mouth was on my neck, the sharp sting of his canines scraping along my skin. And the hand on my arm shifted to grab my breast and squeezed painfully.

No, no!

"Get off of me!" I tried to push him away and failed.

"Don't you feel it?" he repeated.

I lifted a knee to nail him in the groin. He realized the movement and jerked his hips to the side to avoid it. Fast, he was too fast for me. The cage of his arms shrank around me.

"You'll go when *I* say you can go."

My wolf recognized the demand in his voice, the power commanding the rest of his pack to do his bidding. Cold fear drenched my spine and his grip tightened on my breast. I had no words, no strength to escape.

A throat cleared and when I looked up, Cook stood in the

hallway, her salt-and-pepper brows drawn down in a deep V. "Is there anything I can get for you, Master Grimaldi?" she asked in her old Irish croak.

He took a step back, and though it was little in terms of distance it meant everything to me, his hold broken enough I could breathe again.

"If I need anything, I'll call for you," he snapped at Cook.

But it was an out. It was enough of a distraction. I swept his arm aside and step away.

I made my apologies to my uncle, claiming a stomachache, and before Kendrick had a chance to refute the claim—he was a few steps behind me—I escaped upstairs to the relative safety and comfort of my room. Then locked the door behind me.

But the lock on my door felt like a joke after experiencing Kendrick firsthand.

It wasn't a lie. My stomach did hurt, with piercing pains, and I swore I still felt the searing imprint from Kendrick groping me, his teeth and fingers on my skin like a brand. My breast still ached where he'd grabbed me, treated me like I was insignificant beyond what physical pleasure I could bring to him. Like the lowly female I was.

I shouldn't feel this way with my *fated mate*. I knew in my bones there was something wrong. With him, with me, it didn't matter. Everything about our connection felt out of place, like I'd been forced to squeeze into a shirt two sizes too small for me and made of briars. Tonight's encounter had been an abomination.

I leaned forward on a sob, eyes stinging but no tears coming out. In my bathroom, I scrubbed off the makeup and chucked the dress in the corner. Making sure the door remained locked, I curled up on my bed. I could hear the echoes of barking laughter followed by a sharp growl or two. Whatever the men were discussing, I didn't want to know.

My phone provided a good distraction from my thoughts. Dawn had sent me a funny note, and sometime during dinner Jason had texted. Nothing more than a few confusing emojis but enough to let me know he'd been thinking about me. Perhaps wishing for sweet kisses before my engagement was made official.

Somehow, the idea no longer held appeal.

Then I checked my email. And saw I had a new message.

The Fae Academy for Halflings had invited me to orientation next Tuesday.

5

I'd been accepted. *I'd been accepted!* The academy hadn't forgotten about me, and my answers on the enrollment questionnaire had apparently been enough to secure me a place at orientation.

I slept fitfully, kept awake by dreams of being chased. Chased by someone…to somewhere…I didn't know. None of it made sense and seemed more like nightmares.

Wide awake before dawn, I stared at the ceiling for the longest time, trying to compose myself and failing. I buried my face in my pillow and pulled the blankets higher. I'd need to enjoy every moment I had with my bed. Because soon enough I'd be out of here for good.

My body vibrated. Excitement filled me at the change in the game I had only hoped would come.

After last night, I knew there would be no persuading my uncle to find some loophole in the whole fated mate agreement, to dissolve whatever magical bond people thought had formed between me and Kendrick. To spare me. I didn't even bother telling him about my reservations, or any misgivings I had based on Kendrick's behavior. Uncle

Will would think me a liar. He'd think it just another trick to get out of the engagement.

It left the Fae Academy as my only choice. Tuesday couldn't get here soon enough.

Later, after spending my day interning at the law firm, I dashed through the park, heart racing, with the moon high overhead. With no one around to question me, I let my wolf shine through. Let her sniff the air and inhale the night. My eyes glowed a deep amber and I ran. I ran through the underbrush and the shadows and became part of them without changing entirely.

It might be my last time showing this part of myself so freely.

I'd gotten my invitation. I'd been accepted into the academy, or at least far enough I'd be attending orientation. It was better than nothing, and more than I could have hoped for.

Yet still so far from the finish line.

"Elfwaite?" I called out, slowing as I approached the area she claimed as her own. "Are you there?"

Glancing around, I saw I was alone. My senses remained on high alert, where they'd stayed since the encounter with Kendrick. I refused to be taken by surprise again.

The pixie popped her head out from a whorl no larger than an acorn in the trunk of a nearby tree. "Tavi! You finally came to see me. It took you long enough."

I held out my hand to her and Elfwaite darted forward, resting on my open palm. We smiled at each other. "I know it's been a while. I haven't had the opportunity to get away," I said.

Since the disaster at last night's dinner, Uncle Will had decided he wanted to keep a close eye on me today. He'd tried to make it seem as though the extra attention was nothing. We both knew better.

Elfwaite's eyes went wide. "Something happened to you." I watched her eyes darken, black taking over the white as she saw me without seeing. "It's fresh. An emotional wound you would rather hide. Talk to me."

I told her about last night. I told her about Kendrick cornering me outside of the powder room and how I'd tried to fight him off and could not. There were no scratches on my neck to show her. I healed quickly on the outside.

"He'll pay for what he did. Trust me. Did you hear back from the academy?" Elfwaite tucked her wings behind her, those odd upturned eyes catching mine and holding.

My stomach clenched. "I did."

"And what's wrong?" she blurted out.

The email had seemed like a life preserver. Until I read the fine print. "The orientation email gave me a specific list of acceptable half-breeds. Wolf shifters were *not* there."

My blood had gone cold upon closer reading of the orientation email, warring with the excitement I'd felt from receiving it in the first place. I really should have known better. My kind would never be accepted by the Fae. Just as the Fae were seen as substandard by weres. The two breeds did not mix.

Except for me. Except for my parents, who'd decided to flout the longstanding and unwritten rules of their two kin, and look where it got them.

Elfwaite looked me over from head to toe. "You can't let this stop you, Tavi. You need to keep moving forward. You need to fight."

I didn't want to smile, and I tried not to, but a hint of a grin tugged at my lips. No one had a better outlook on life than Elfwaite. "You know I love you."

She winked at me, her skin a deep periwinkle in the hush of twilight. "I know. I love you too. And I'm sorry this is causing more stress for you."

"I hate asking you for more…" I began. "But you mentioned someone who might be willing to help me?"

Elfwaite made a sound that might have been a scoff were she human. As it was, with her tiny pixie body, it more resembled a slight shift in the low murmur of the wind. "We're friends, and friends help each other. I know a way around this problem. Or rather, I know someone who can fix it for you. The witch I mentioned to you has the magic to get you through orientation."

I swallowed hard. "She can fix my being half wolf-shifter?"

Elfwaite nodded. "She's a powerful creature of much renown, as long as you are willing to pay the price. It is nothing to scoff at."

A part of me relaxed. Money was no issue. Uncle William did well as a defense attorney. Our comfortable living situation attested to his prowess in court. Although I had little cash of my own besides a bank account set aside for me by my parents before they died, I knew I could get the funds one way or another.

Elfwaite and I finished talking and I jumped up from the ground before she could issue another warning about price. Orientation was in two days. If everything went well, this could well be the last time I saw her for a long time.

We said our goodbyes, Elfwaite assuring me it wouldn't be forever and me shrugging, trying to laugh it off. I'd be foolish to assume one way or another. I didn't know what would happen. But I left a small piece of myself behind with her.

The directions to the witch's house bounced around my head as I ran home, the distance providing a chance to conceive some sense of a plan for the future. And then I did what I needed to do.

Every town has a house—creepy, dark, and sinister—where the neighborhood kids spin tales of mayhem and despair. Where the shell of the home is long past its glory, surrounded by dark woods, and inspires new urban legends about children-eating monsters and scary things going bump in the night.

In reality, the only things going bump along the aged and weathered floorboards are those running on four legs and scrounging for scraps. Spiders and raccoons and opossums and the like.

The "witch's house" at the end of Everly Lane was such a place.

Two stories high and set far back from the road amidst the trees, the roofline sloped and cut through the night sky like a dagger. Crumbled gables and turrets decorated the old Victorian, and empty windows stood in mute witness to the march of progress in the surrounding suburban paradise.

Despite the weeds choking the lawn and the overgrown tree limbs draping down toward the fence, magic lived there. I smelled it coming from the land itself. As though the witch's power had seeped into her property.

It was a hell of a place to go at night. I didn't have a choice.

Sunday after dinner, I'd driven over and parked a good distance away, walking the remaining two blocks to the address Elfwaite had given me, trying not to be seen. The stolen money I'd swiped from Uncle William's office burned a hole in my pocket. He and his drinking buddies had missed their habitual meeting thanks to our dinner with the Grimaldis and it left him in a position to push his schedule back even knowing he had work in the morning.

A quick trip, he assured me on his way out the door, and

then he would be back. I was not to leave the house under strict threat of penalty.

Too bad.

When the road, nothing more than a winding gravel drive cutting through the woods, ended in a patch of trees, I swallowed the rest of my misgivings and continued.

The living shadows reached for me the moment I entered the tree line, and the rest of the world faded away. The families living in their quaint cookie-cutter houses down the block, children tucked tightly into bed after urgings for sweet dreams, none of them would understand why I walked toward the house where no one wanted to go.

But when life backs you into a corner and offers you no chance for escape, when your friends and your family believe the monster in front of you is the best choice for a future, and when you're at the end of your rope, alone and losing your mind, you'd do anything to find a way out. You'd do anything to make those problems disappear.

Then you'd find yourself on the witch's doorstep. Then you'd steal from your uncle. Willing to pay any price.

My pupils narrowed at the change in light. The better to see through the darkness. Even so, I lost track of the sloping roofline of the Victorian through the crowd of tree trunks. The woods were *alive*. They shifted and changed and blocked my view. Strange noises sounded from the darkness. There were no owls here, no night creatures whose calls I knew and recognized. I could almost imagine strange beasts hiding among the limbs. Ready to lash out at any moment.

A strange heaviness fell over me.

I stopped, closing my eyes and drawing in a breath. There was nothing out here to hurt me, I reminded myself. The wolf inside of me, an apex predator, could handle whatever flew or skidded or crept among the trees. Right?

It took a moment to move my legs, to strengthen my spine and push forward.

I tried not to freak out or run, although I wanted to do both. Here, magic ran wild and snapped and bit like a rabid creature ready to pounce.

Had I thought myself immune to it?

Heaving in a breath, I fought through the heavy sensation, like pushing a wall of water aside.

Then something on the breeze drew me. A hint of the power I'd sensed before. My nerves tingled, and it reminded me of the way I felt around Elfwaite. It was cool, calming, serene, like dipping overheated feet into a cool lake.

The old house loomed ahead with liminal light reflecting off of rusted sconces on either side of the door. I climbed the four steps leading up to the landing and paused in front of a massive wooden door. The brass knocker looked to weigh close to twenty pounds and for a moment I wondered how the weather-beaten wood managed to keep it held up.

The slight sense of wrongness had me pausing, curling my hand into a ball and keeping it in the air before knocking.

Was I really doing this? Was I really seeking out a woman I didn't know whose house looked like she lured in strangers to eat?

The memory of Kendrick flashed behind my eyes and the knots in my stomach tightened. *Yes, you bet I am doing this.*

Without any further hesitation, I reached out and let my fist fall.

"Hello? Is anyone home?" I called out.

Then nearly lost my dinner when the door jerked open suddenly and I saw a woman holding a double-barreled shotgun leveled at my face.

6

As I stared down the two pitch-black barrels of the shotgun, shivers coursed down my arms and into my stomach like snakes. My mind raced, snapping into two distinct pieces. One screaming at me to run and the other insisting I tear the threat to shreds.

A very human shriek escaped my throat instead as I dropped to my knees in a crouch. "Elfwaite sent me! Elfwaite sent me!"

The statement aired on repeat until I heard the click of the safety being snapped into place.

"Child, you can't be too careful nowadays. Damn people wanting to steal everything you got, not even waiting until a woman is good and dead to do their picking. Little vultures."

I spared a glance up and saw the barrel of the rifle lower to her side. Still not far enough away for my liking but enough to have me coming out of my crouched position to stare at the witch.

In her late sixties, she had stark gunmetal-gray hair. She stood tall and strong, with an aura of power about her at distinct odds with the blue-and-red flannel button-up shirt and holey jeans. Her feet were bare.

She held up her free hand to beckon me inside, her fingernails yellow. "Don't stand out here knocking your knees together, kid. If the old pixie sent you then you obviously have some things to talk about. Come inside before you wet yourself."

Her syllables clicked and ground together. The moment I stepped over the threshold, the door closing behind us with a decisive click, I noticed the ashtrays scattered around the once-grand foyer. Now it made sense. The woman smoked like a train. She reminded me of Cook, though I was pretty sure the latter's vocal issues had more to do with her screaming at her staff than any addiction.

"Thank you," I managed to get out, conscious of my every awkward movement.

Setting the shotgun aside, the witch bent to pick up a still-lit cigarette from a glass tray and gestured for me to follow behind her. "Come on, kiddo. The full moon is rising and I'm sure we both have better things to do than stand around and stare at each other. Let's get this business over with." She bared her teeth in what I thought was an attempt at a smile.

"I'm sorry to bother you so late," I told her.

"Don't worry. You're just lucky I didn't shoot first and ask questions later."

It wasn't a good business model. Her reply did nothing to soothe me, either.

The further I went into her house, the more I noticed things standing out to me, not the odd way in which the witch moved or the lack of typical witchy accoutrements. There were walls made entirely of canned goods. There were cabinets stocked to the brim with ammunition and more guns than I could keep track of.

"What's all this?" I asked her.

"Barbara. You can call me Barbara," the witch said over her shoulder. "And it's supplies. Are you blind?"

"Supplies for what?"

"For *anything*. You can never be too careful. Bad things are on the horizon and it's better to be prepared than be caught with your pants down around your ankles. You want a beer?"

We'd made it into the kitchen and the decor didn't fare any better in there. Glass jugs of water weighed down the top of the kitchen table. I saw more bullets, more pantry items, and a couple of baskets of laundry in need of folding. Two chairs were pushed beneath the round table, with faded red plush seats cracking at the seams.

I shook my head. "No thanks. I'm only eighteen."

"Old enough to drink in my book, but suit yourself." Barbara grabbed one of the chairs and hauled it out, folding her body down and fixing me with a look. Scrutinizing me through a cloud of exhaled smoke. "You got a name, kiddo?"

I tried not to fiddle with my shirt for something to do. "It's Tavi."

"Tavi." She stretched it out into two long syllables and drew in another inhale. Her eyes narrowed. "I need to know two things from you. How did you get to my house, and how in the hell did you make it past my magical barriers? Now, you got any answers for me?"

I resisted swatting the smoke away from my face, despite how difficult it was to breathe. "I didn't see any barriers," I said, "magical or otherwise."

She just stared at me. Perhaps I hadn't said the right thing. "The *wards*, Tavi, try to keep up. How did you get past my wards?"

The smile wasn't comforting and I tried to stand tall beneath it. Tried to feel confident I had made the right decision in coming here. Elfwaite would never put me in danger, I told myself. "I'm not sure," I answered Barbara honestly. "I didn't know there were barriers. I just followed the magic."

Barbara gestured toward the seat on the opposite end of the table and I cleared away a pile of magazines to sit.

"Followed the magic."

I didn't like the way she repeated me. And I certainly didn't like the way Barbara continued to stare at me as though I were some kind of experimental specimen for her to figure out.

If you only knew.

"Tell me why I should listen to a word you have to say," Barbara barked.

"Elfwaite said you could help me." I grabbed the end of my braid and knew I didn't look like much. I'd worn dark clothes to help me blend in with the darkness, loose jeans and a comfortable gray shirt. The braid slapped at my back when I ran but kept the hair out of my face. I'd thought it was a good move at the time.

"Help you how?" My nerves jangled under her scrutiny, but I plunged ahead.

"My uncle is alpha of the Alderidge pack. At my eighteenth birthday party, he announced I am the fated mate of our rival pack's alpha. I'm not sure how much you know about werewolf hierarchy, but this man…he's a nightmare." My hands fisted on the tabletop. "He revels in abuse and violence and does not hesitate to exert his power over others. I refuse to give myself to him. I've been accepted to a Fae school for halflings, but only if I can mask my shifter side. They can't know who I am."

I told her what had happened at the party, at dinner, the stories I'd heard about Kendrick and how he'd accosted me outside the powder room.

Barbara leaned back in her chair and crossed her arms. "And Elfwaite sent you to me," she said eventually.

"She did."

"God, I've known Elfwaite for a long time." Her laugh came fast and sharp, the cigarette squashed in time with the sound. "She's a real kicker, not like the rest of them."

My shoulders relaxed at the affection I heard in Barbara's voice. No, Elfwaite would not steer me wrong. "She's sweet," I agreed.

"Too damn sweet for her own good sometimes. Unlike the rest of her kin. Pixies can be notorious tricksters along with the rest of the fairies, hobgoblins, and all." Barbara's gaze hardened and she looked me up and down as though deciding whether I was worth the effort or not. "But I *hate* the high Fae. Your kind, judging by the smell. I've been burned by them before. Most are only out for their own good. Why should I help you?"

My heart stuttered and skipped a beat. "Please. I have money." I dug deep into my pocket and drew out the bills I'd snagged from Uncle William's desk. "Whatever amount you want, I can pay you. And I can get more if you need it."

They were crisp hundreds stacked perfectly in order, face up. The way Will preferred and a way demonstrating his control over his world.

Barbara shrugged. "I have no need for money. I have all I want that money can buy, and what I don't have, I can barter for easily enough. Cash isn't going to be enough to sway me to help you. And trust me, girl. If you want something strong enough to fool the Fae, then you are going to need a lot of help. Or else start to get cozy with your *fated mate*. Sometimes nightmares can be the best in the sack."

I didn't care for the way she said "fated mate" and liked her sexual reference even less. "You won't take my money," I said, stomach twisting.

"Damn right I won't. You are going to have to offer something else if you want me to get involved with what you're doing." She drew a circle in the air with her cigarette, indicating the whole of me. "It's going to take a lot. I'm not in the general practice of helping the Fae. Even a *half* one." So, she knew what I was. Oh boy. "Sorry, girl."

Staring down at the scarred table, I sucked on my teeth. "Look," I began, "I don't have much love for the Fae either. You obviously know what I am since you can...*smell* me? You know I'm a halfling. My parents fell in love despite belonging to doomed sides. Then my father, the shifter, was killed by Fae enforcers right in front of me. I was six years old."

I was six and I didn't understand who I was, *what* I was, should not exist in this world or any world. I didn't understand how people would hate me and curse me for simply *being*. It didn't seem fair. But Barbara didn't need to know. I'd wasted enough time feeling sorry for myself and my circumstances.

"My mother was carted off by her own people to be tried and executed for her crime. The crime of loving a werewolf and birthing a child by him. So, the Fae murdered my parents." I rose to my feet, brows drawn together and knees shaking, trying to stand my ground. I looked pointedly at Barbara and the sharp tips of her fingernails tap-tap-tapping at her cigarette. "I need this school. I need to escape because I refuse to be some man's sex toy to further *another* man's power play."

Her right hand twitched as Barbara continued to stare at me. Finally, in the comfortable gloom of her survivalist kitchen, she nodded. "All right," she said slowly. "I'll help you."

"How much?" I asked her.

Barbara clicked her yellowed nails before reaching for a

second pack of cigarettes and removing one to light with the burned embers of her last. She drew in a deep breath as though her cells would die at any minute without nicotine. "It's not monetary value I require. I told you. Price is not necessarily measured in cash."

"Fine," I agreed.

A snap of her fingers conjured a contract from nothing, the paper unfurling and floating in midair. A second snap brought a fountain pen into being. Both slid toward me on an invisible breeze. Something inside of me clenched and dropped. I pretended not to care.

"When the time comes for me to collect payment for your debt, you will know immediately. Your signature at the bottom of this document—a binding magical contract, by the way—states you will repay the debt in whatever method the spellbinder—that's me—demands at a future point in time."

My uncle would drop dead on the spot if he knew I was about to sign a contract without proper representation. Or even reading it first. "I...I'm not sure if I should—"

"It's an unnamed favor," Barbara interrupted with a hint of impatience. "You want your cure-all, don't you?"

The price was not explicitly laid out. This was a terrible idea, and the whole of me felt it. Uncle William would have never allowed one of his clients to go through with this deal. Not without the terms being discussed beforehand.

"Do you want my help or not?" she pressed.

Still I hesitated. Literally promising to do *anything* for this crazy lady meant endless possibilities and none of them good. What would she have me do? Barbara could demand I kill someone for all I knew.

But I also knew the Fae Academy for Halflings waited. And I'd do whatever it took to get out from under my uncle's thumb and save myself from Kendrick Grimaldi.

You'll go when I say you can go.

Before I thought better of it, and with the memory of his voice echoing in my head, I grabbed the pen to sign my name on the contract.

7

Like a poor unfortunate soul standing in front of a sea witch, I signed my life away.

Barbara smiled, the discolored skin around her mouth stretching and revealing wrinkles I hadn't noticed before. "There you go, Tavi. There you go. Good girl. Now, with our contract out of the way..." She trailed off and snapped her fingers a third time, this time sparks flying up from where her skin touched together. The table in front of us disintegrated. In its place rose a giant cauldron the size of a bathtub, forged of black iron and balanced on four legs.

I felt my face drain of color. The liquid inside the cauldron throbbed like blood pulsing through an artery. As though the damn thing had a heartbeat all its own.

Here were the witchy accoutrements I'd thought were lacking before. Here was the crazed and magical woman who had the power to save or destroy me. Maybe she hid those things away for guests? No, based on the look of the rest of the house, Barbara didn't have any guests, only customers who were dumb enough, like me, to agree to her terms. And odds were good she didn't care what they thought of her, anyway.

"Oh, stop shivering," Barbara admonished, and the snap of her voice drew my attention. "You got the scary part over with! You can relax. It's all a cake walk from here on out."

I was a magical being but I'd never had the time or a reason to *use* my magic, since I'd lived most of my life in hiding as a full-blooded werewolf.

Watching Barbara work her power with such ease...the visual drew me forward and repulsed me in equal measures. What kind of magic did she possess? And how did I know she would use it for good?

I didn't. I had no idea what this woman would or would not do, only how she had an apocalyptic fantasy that inclined her to shoot people on sight. Maybe I was one of the lucky ones and she already had a sufficient pile of bones hidden in the backyard. Ingredients for her spells.

Sick.

I placed a hand over my belly and rubbed at the slight ache there.

"You're going to need a little bit of calendula, a little bit of..." Barbara apparently spoke to herself, the cigarette dangling from the corner of her mouth. The ingredients were conjured out of thin air. Barbara grabbed them one at a time and dropped in whatever amount she deemed necessary. "A few tadpoles for flavor. Maybe a little bit of black ash. Red string. A large pinch of wormwort—"

"What is the wormwort for?" I tried to ask, coughing at the belch of smoke expulsed from the boiling mess inside the cauldron. It didn't smell any better than the original concoction smelled. "What else are you putting in there?"

Barbara paused long enough to glare at me. "Hush up and let me work."

"You can't blame me for being curious." I wrapped my

arms across my chest and struggled to keep my now blurry eyes on the potion.

"No, but I can blame you for getting the ingredients wrong because I'm distracted."

Okay, message received and lips zipped.

Finally, she completed the potion. Ten agonizing minutes of watching Barbara conjure random plants and minerals out of nothing and throw them haphazardly into her stew-like concoction. There were things I recognized and more I didn't, and at the end the air smelled like someone had lit a pile of tires on fire using duck fat.

I hope she knows what she's doing. Please let her know what she's doing.

I'd done my best to keep track of the ingredients, to see if this was something I might be able to do on my own or if I'd need to come back to Barbara when I finished this round. The thought had me queasy.

"Almost there," she told me. "Hold your horses a while longer and I'll have it for you."

She closed her eyes and raised both hands in the air like she was praying to the Holy Spirit itself. Twenty-eight glass vials rose from the counter, the black liquid equally divided among them before corks stopped up each one. They settled into a container with slots for each of the glass bottles.

"You can keep the cushioned wooden case. I have plenty of them lying around. Well, somewhere," Barbara stated, blinking. "Consider it part of your payment. It's going to help you with storage, because you do not want to leave these lying around. If anyone else tries to take them it won't be a pretty sight, or maybe your classmates will figure out you have something to hide and report you. You with me so far?"

"Yes, I understand." At least the case had a handle. Good for traveling.

"You'll need to ingest a vial every thirteen days on the dot.

This batch will get you through the probationary first year at the academy as long as nothing happens to the vials." She knew about the academy, too, then. Or else she'd put two and two together.

Her finger snap shook me, and when I glanced up, I no longer saw the cauldron. The kitchen table was back in place. I wasn't sure what shocked me more, how she worked so easily with her powers or how normal everything looked now, as though the spooky concoction equipment had never existed.

"How do you know about the probationary first year?" I couldn't help but ask.

Barbara ignored me. "If you need more vials for any reason, then the price doubles."

The price I had no clue about. I nodded to keep her talking.

"And there are rules. There must always be rules, Tavi Alderidge. You would do well to heed them." I could have sworn her voice deepened. "One: You can come into contact with no saltwater while under the potion's spell or the spell will break. No saltwater baths, no accidental saltwater splashed on your skin, *nothing*. Two: The potion cannot protect you from the light of a full moon. If you go out beneath a full moon, your true nature will be revealed, regardless of the potion being in effect the rest of the time."

The weight of her words echoed through the space and shook something inside of me until it reverberated with a twang. They held my life in each vowel, each consonant.

It was a good thing I was a natural born shifter, even half-blood, because if I had been bitten then the full moon would have held sway over me and the potion certainly would not have worked. Maybe if I had been bitten, I might not be in this position.

"Three: You cannot eat garlic. Garlic will break the

potion's effect and reveal you. Four: Do not under any circumstances touch a quartz crystal of any kind. Quartz is a magical stone which will siphon the spell away from you, revealing your true nature. Five: Don't look at your own reflection in a mirror or let anybody see your reflection in a mirror after sundown—the spell will break and reveal your true nature."

My head spun. "I need to write these down."

"No time. We're done here." Barbara wiped her hands on the front of her pants. "You'll remember the rules or else learn the hard way when you break 'em. I've got nothing more for you. You have what you need and I have what I need."

I hated to ask what it was I'd given her, knowing I wouldn't like the answer. If she even bothered to tell me.

"Good luck with everything, kiddo," she said, her voice returning to normal. She attempted a smile once more. This time wasn't any better than the first. "I'll be seeing you again soon. You can see yourself out."

The smoke spun around us in a cloud I could not wave away. It swirled closer and closer until I could feel the touch of it on my skin, ushering me to the door like a thousand invisible fingers. The case weighed heavily in my hand and I wasn't sure when I'd grabbed it.

Wasn't sure I had in the first place.

"Thank you," I tried to say. "For helping me."

Thank me when you pay up, girl.

Her voice sounded inside my head. Barbara's cackle followed me outside and sent chills down my spine. The door closed behind me and I wondered what kind of deal with the devil I had just made.

I still didn't feel any evidence of a ward as I walked through the forest, gripping the case tightly to my midsection. Nothing to indicate Barbara had any kind of magical protection around her place at all, and I wondered if she'd made the whole thing up to fool me. To trick me into thinking I'd done something special.

There was no one on the street when I got back to my car. I placed the case on the front seat, pausing for a moment to stare at the closed lid, thinking of the vials inside. Filled with black liquid.

Was I really going to have to drink those? My head still spiraled, dizzy, the effects of her smoke keeping me in a thrall through the rest of my drive away from Everly Lane. Away from the house and the witch and the nightmares I knew she inspired. For a good reason.

Another late night for me, I snuck up the stairs with Uncle William's snoring echoing off the walls. Shoot, he'd gotten home ahead of me. Good thing he slept heavily after a drinking spree. It was a point in my favor.

Making sure to move as quietly as possible, I placed the box with the vials under my bed and then shoved clothes in front to hide it from view, then straightened out the dust ruffle.

Tuesday was coming faster than I was ready for. I'd need to pack and be gone before anyone knew.

The information in my welcome email gave me a physical address for the campus. When I typed it into my phone, it showed ten hours north. Massachusetts wasn't too far but still a long drive.

Better for me to be far away when they discovered I was gone.

I couldn't take my own car or Uncle Will would be able to track me. He kept close track of my movements and I wouldn't put it past him to have some sort of GPS device enabled. It also meant the cell phone would have to go.

What to bring and what to leave behind? Pausing, I scratched my head, exhaustion weighing me down until I sank to the floor, legs folding underneath me. My chest ached at the thought of leaving Uncle William. He'd been there for me since my father's death, making sure I lacked for nothing.

Until he sold you out to the Grimaldis, a nasty voice in my head reminded me. *Until he used you to get ahead, without thinking of your feelings.*

I sighed, dropping my chin into my hands. Too much to think about. And Barbara had all but wrung me out with the visit. How long would I need to recover from meeting her? Still…

"I did it," I whispered out loud. Although I wasn't sure why or who I spoke to. Maybe Elfwaite, though she was too far away to hear me. "I did it and I'm on my way out." The word drew a giggle, ending with a snort.

I couldn't think about what Uncle Will would do when he discovered I had run away. Or how the rest of the pack might suffer at the hands of the Grimaldi alpha deprived of his prize.

My breast throbbed in remembrance of his rough handling and I shuddered.

All I had to do was get to the school and keep my head down. Get through the selection process without anyone realizing I was really a werewolf shifter—the Fae's sworn enemy—and make it until graduation.

All I had to do was survive without my fated mate hunting and finding me.

8

While I stared at the Tuesday morning sun rising in the sky, I wanted to puke with the thought of what I had to do next.

I had a plan. My plan would break the heart of the man who'd raised me. Would put distance between me and the only home I'd ever known. But at least I knew what had to be done. Now all I had to do was put my plan into motion.

True to his normal everyday routine, I heard Uncle Will shut the door to his office with a soft snick. "Tavi, I'm off for work." His voice echoed up the staircase with a deep rumble.

"Okay." I poked my head out of my room. "Have a nice day and I'll see you when you get home."

"Are you sure you can't come in to the office for a few hours?" He peered up the staircase at me, apparently trying to determine if my claim of feeling sick was true or not. "I know your internship with us is coming to an end soon but we can still use you. Come on."

He wanted to keep an eye on me, I knew. To make sure I didn't do anything to jeopardize his arrangement.

I shook my head, and it wasn't a stretch to look as

miserable physically as I felt emotionally. There were too many things on my mind to think straight and I hadn't slept for more than a few hours at a time. "Sorry, Uncle Will. This weekend has been a little stressful for me and I can't seem to shake this headache. I'll make it up to you," I said, lying straight to his face. "I'll put in extra hours tomorrow."

He looked as though he wanted to argue further. To *debate* me, one of his favorite pastimes. He sighed and drew his briefcase tighter against his hip, looking dapper in his double-breasted suit coat and crisp black pants. Ready for battle.

"I do wish you felt better, Tav. I know we haven't gotten a chance to speak since our dinner and there are certain things I want to discuss further, when you're back to normal." His eyes darted around without landing, fingers tapping out an erratic rhythm on the leather briefcase. Too many things on *his* mind as well. "Things I believe will ease a little bit of the *tension* I'm sure we all feel with this new dynamic."

Tension? Nah, try disgust, nausea, dread. "I wish I felt better too," I told him, and at least it was the truth. "I'll make it up to you."

The repetition did the trick.

"Sweet girl, I know you will. Come here." Will stepped forward and opened his arms. I went down the steps willingly, leaning my head against his chest and breathing in his familiar expensive scent.

Close enough to how I remembered my father. Tears pricked my eyes. I didn't have many memories of the man outside of a few moments of clarity. Big shoulders, boisterous laugh, and his scent. One he and his brother shared. And now Uncle Will was the only family I had left.

Was I really leaving? Could I do this?

"Take care," I choked out. Holding him a little longer and squeezing tighter. "Have fun at work."

William chuckled. "If I didn't know any better, I'd say this is a goodbye. You must really feel poorly."

I tightened my hold again. "I do."

"Well, get some rest." He ran a hand over my head for a brief second. "Have Cook make you anything you like. Although I know it's cliché, chicken soup really does help. I'll see you when I get home."

"Thank you for everything."

He kissed my hair and walked out the front door like any normal day. Except it wasn't a normal day, not for me, and once I followed through with my plan, things between us would never be the same. If I ever saw my uncle again.

I stared after him for a long time, long after the door closed and I lost the sounds of his car driving down the road. Uncle Will would never forgive me for this. I knew it. The act of betrayal would cut too deeply for him to accept me again if I decided to make amends.

This truly was goodbye.

The walk from the house would take me some time. I'd leave my car here, taking only what I might need for the academy and nothing more.

My bags were packed, the vials secured. I'd stuffed them at the bottom of my wheeled suitcase along with clothes and snacks and memorabilia I couldn't live without. It hurt to leave the laptop at the house, just as it hurt to leave the phone, but both of them were too easy to hack and track. I refused to take the chance and leave a trail.

If I disappeared, I did it for good. A trick I'd learned from Jason had me clearing my internet search history so Uncle Will wouldn't be able to find out about the academy website no matter how hard he tried.

Vanish completely.

Under any other circumstances, running away from the protection of the pack would be foolish. But the time had come. I gathered my things closer, tightened my grip on the suitcase, and breathed in the familiar scents one last time.

No turning back, Tavi.

I took one last look around. I'd come back to this place one day, if I could.

Part of me knew it was just a pipe dream, though. I wouldn't be allowed to come back. The pack would never allow it. The betrayal would cut too deep.

Now. I had to go *now*. I couldn't even say goodbye to Cook and the others—not when I knew they would go straight to my uncle and tell him I was acting squirrelly. He would turn the car around without hesitation. Catch me in the act and punish me. Lock me up, most likely.

I couldn't take the risk.

I dragged my suitcase, purse, and duffel bag downstairs as quietly as I could manage, then moved quickly through the den toward the French doors leading to the backyard.

My eyes stung and I swiped the moisture away, then silently opened one of the double patio doors. This would make less noise than leaving through the front, and with fewer prying eyes to report my movements.

I let the sound of my footsteps and the low hum of the wheeled suitcase drown out any lingering doubts as I took my only shot at freedom.

I didn't dare turn around and look back at the house. Soon I was out of the neighborhood, the tree-lined streets shifting to a modern-day cement jungle. Car traffic increased until I heard nothing outside of the honks and roar of engines. Every step toward the car rental place in the city was too heavy, too swift, carrying me away from whatever torment and misery I was leaving behind me, and toward whatever unknowns lay in front of me.

The man behind the counter at the car rental facility was busy helping another customer when I arrived. One of the good things about living in the northern Virginia suburbs, we had wilderness close and city amenities closer. I waited my turn with little patience, choosing a seat from the near-empty line of chairs and keeping my luggage close to me. The sun had kissed above the horizon, rising steadily. Ten hours of driving and I'd be out of this place forever.

Lowering my head to avoid unwanted attention, I thought about the night before.

I'd used the opportunity to scroll through the school's website and memorize any information I could, hoping it would give me an edge over the rest of the applicants. The way a person would research a company before they went in for a job interview.

There hadn't been much there. A picture of the headmaster whose name I couldn't remember now. He looked young, kind, with dusky light-brown hair and an easy smile, ears pointed, eyes a strange shade of orange. I wasn't sure if regular full-blooded Fae aged the same way humans did. There were no other photos of the rest of the staff. I assumed I would meet them when I arrived at the academy.

I knew *nothing* about Faerie. I had no clue about that part of my heritage.

What the hell am I doing?

Escaping one bad situation and catapulting myself into another, where I had no idea about the major players. I didn't know how to be Fae. Unease swirled and settled beneath my sternum. Maybe my entire plan was nuts. Maybe I should have done what Uncle Will wanted and forced myself to go through with the arrangement with Kendrick.

My fingers clenched until my knuckles ached.

"Excuse me, Miss? You're up."

The car rental guy at the counter tapped a finger in the universal sign to hurry up. Not sure where he had to go or why he was suddenly in such a hurry, but I stood and followed him into a small office with beige blinds. When had the other customer left? I hadn't been paying attention.

"Thanks," I told the guy, but I wasn't sure for what.

"What can I do to help you today?" he asked, holding a hand out for me to sit.

I dragged my luggage behind me and took a seat in front of him. I'd think it obvious why I was here. His hand remained outstretched to shake. I ignored it and said, "I need to rent a car, please."

"What are you looking for?" he enquired as he settled into his seat. "Compact, mid-sized, luxury?"

Whatever will get me from Point A to Point B the fastest. I chewed the inside of my lip. "Compact." It would be smaller, less likely to draw attention.

"Perfect. I need to see your driver's license and I can get the process started for you."

Reaching into my purse, I pulled the slim plastic card from my wallet and slid it across the desk to him. The man inclined his head, staring at the information. Then up to me. Then back to the card. The hairs of his reddish beard bristled.

"You're only eighteen," he said.

"Yes, my birthday was about a week ago." *Smile, Tavi. Keep it casual. Don't let him see you sweat.*

"You're not old enough to rent a car, Miss Alderidge." He said it like the information was obvious. "You have to be twenty-five years old. It's the law."

I stared at him for what felt like a good five minutes. "I'm sorry? What do you mean?"

"Twenty-five," the man said again. "It's standard. Do you have a guardian with you? He glanced around as though I'd hidden an adult somewhere. Maybe inside my suitcase.

"No, there's no one." I thought about the money I'd stolen from Uncle Will burning a hole in my pocket, ready to be spent. "Isn't there anything you can do? Something I can pay? How much will it take?"

The man's gaze hardened and at once he wasn't the bland and helpful service provider but someone suspicious, someone who could potentially stand in my way. "No, honey, there isn't." Then his eyes narrowed. "Are you in trouble? Do you need me to call someone for you?"

Uh oh. *Alert, alert!* "No, thank you. Everything is fine."

I hurried out of the car rental office with the knots in my stomach twisting into new and unfamiliar patterns. There were some things in this world money couldn't buy, apparently. Rental cars among them. It was a new experience for me and one I didn't want to repeat anytime soon. Especially not when people automatically assumed I was in trouble.

I *was* in trouble, but not the kind a human could help me conquer.

How would I make it to the academy by tomorrow without a car?

I absolutely could not go back to the house for *my* car. My uncle would track it as easily as he tracked prey in the woods. It left me stuck, scrambling to reset and to find another way to make this work.

I stopped in the middle of the sidewalk, with the sun high and people walking around me without a second thought. No one questioned the luggage. No one stopped to ask if I needed help. Good.

Luckily, I had money in my pocket. Money might not have been able to buy much with the rental car guy, but it could certainly get me a junker. A junker with enough *go* to travel ten hours, at least.

I could make it work.

It would take me a good twenty minutes to walk to the nearest place, if I remembered, but no worries. If it got me out of the city, then what choice did I have? I couldn't risk the bus; the stops all had cameras and there were too many people to remember my face.

I hated this place. Hated cities *period*. I preferred the fields and the wild places where I could let myself be free without fear of repercussion. Instead now I had to put on a face. I had to pretend to be anything other than what I was.

Who was I kidding? I'd been this way my entire life. There had never been a moment where I felt the utter freedom to be safe with both of my sides.

Maybe there had been a time once, before my parents died. But those six years were a blank.

On to a new adventure, I tried to tell myself as I walked. If I could get to the academy, if I could make it through the required years and carve out a place for myself in Faerie, then maybe, just maybe, I could find freedom.

And Kendrick Grimaldi would never be able to find me.

I moved as fast as I could down the sidewalk. Arms aching and legs sore from hustling, I finally stood in front of the used car lot I remembered seeing on previous trips downtown. The owner had obviously made efforts to draw in the crowd with bright and vulgar banners proclaiming the fabulous deals he had to offer. The building, a squat concrete box with barred windows, looked like someone had picked up a tiny prison and plopped it down in the middle of the city block, with walls stained orange by rainwater dripping through the metal gutters.

But I was here, and the more time I wasted, the more time it gave someone at the house to notice I was not in my room.

I marched through the open gates, wheeling my suitcase behind me, duffel bag bouncing, glancing around at the car choices as I passed them. On the left I saw a red Lexus. Something I might have gotten if I'd had my pick of the lot. Even the tires gleamed, everything polished to a sheen. But a car like that would stand out at the academy. It would stand out *anywhere*.

"Well, hello there, little one. You have good taste. The Lexus is a premium piece of machinery, less than thirty thousand miles on her."

A large brown-skinned man dressed in an expensive suit approached me, his smile firmly in place and voice filled with automatic courtesy.

I forced a similar expression on my face. It would make our conversation go much easier. "The Lexus is nice," I agreed, shifting to relieve the pressure of my duffel bag digging into my shoulder. "But I'm looking for something a little more understated."

In one swift glance, the man judged me, the cut of my clothes and the brand of my purse. I could practically see dollar signs dancing behind his eyes.

"Aw, honey, you would look perfect behind the wheel of the Lexus. Think about how your friends will feel when they see you drive up to school in this beauty." His hand came out, smoothly maneuvering me toward the car.

"What's the oldest vehicle you have on the lot that still runs?" I asked him. "Something that's going to blend in."

The question surprised the man, clearly. He blinked as the wheels in his head turned and cogs clicked together. "In all good conscience, Big Dan can't let you drive out of here in anything *beneath* you, Miss…"

I avoided giving him my name, stepping around him and eyeing the line of cars behind the Lexus. There had to be something here. Something nondescript and cheap.

It took less than five minutes of Big Dan trailing me, continuing with his spiel, to find the Toyota with a bumper held on by a hope and a prayer. I detected hints of dull areas where someone had used duct tape as a quick fix and it had worn away at the paint beneath.

Big Dan, or someone who worked for him, had tried to clean the car as well as they could but there were areas where the paint had been roughed and scratched. Even a good cleaning couldn't disguise the wear. Peering inside, I saw a cracked dashboard showing a hint of yellow foam padding beneath.

I wanted it.

"How much for this one?" I purposely ignored the price written in marker across the windshield. If there was anything William had taught me, it was the importance of haggling. The final price wouldn't be what was scribbled on the glass and we both knew it. I could get him down a bit lower. He expected the back and forth.

Big Dan walked over and leaned a massive hip against the hood, staring me down with the typical adult I-know-better-than-you smile with a hint of smugness at the edge of his lips. "Honey, this car…it's not for someone like you," he said.

He still thought he could talk me into the Lexus.

"I think it's *exactly* for me. How much?" I repeated, drawing my brows together. No one would suspect I'd be driving this kind of car. It was the perfect disguise. "What's the best you can do for it?"

"Sweetheart, there are better cars on the lot. I wouldn't feel comfortable letting you drive off in the Toyota. Someone like you deserves better."

"What's the best you can do?" I asked again.

He finally saw I meant business. "Come into my office, little one, and we can talk."

There were only so many cutesy pet names I could tolerate on a normal day. I'd heard them all at my internship with William's firm. People, men in particular, thought they could sweet talk me with honeyed nicknames, nicknames with no bearing on who I was as a person, and it would help me to get my duties done faster. Or get me to do a special favor for them.

Big Dan didn't know me from the next person on the street, and he didn't know where I came from, which meant he could *sweetie* and *honey* and *baby* me until he turned blue in the face, but I wasn't leaving without the Toyota.

There were some things money couldn't buy, true. This wasn't one of those times, I told myself, because I knew what I wanted.

Big Dan didn't know what had hit him by the time I walked out. I left the small office cluttered with file cabinets two thousand dollars lighter, having managed to talk Big Dan down another five hundred off his asking price. It hadn't taken much more than a few well-placed battings of the eyelashes along with tactics I'd picked up during my internship. And maybe a little magic.

Played.

Good, I thought. This was nothing but practice for the academy. I needed to be on my toes there.

A quick stop at a wireless phone store provided me a cheap and untraceable cell I'd use in place of the one I left behind. Who would I call? No one, I knew, but it felt familiar in my hand. And I could use the GPS system on the drive.

This was it.

The first step in the journey to my freedom. Throwing my luggage in the backseat, I finally slid behind the steering wheel and placed my hands on the cracked dashboard. The car smelled of burned microwave food and pine-scented air freshener, the seats cracked and stained. I didn't care. It was my ticket out of here. Beautiful because it meant a shot at escape.

I thought about the stuff I'd tossed in the rear seat: everything important to me, including the empty picture frames from on top of my dresser. I thought about the money I'd taken from my skinflint uncle and hoped, if he ever noticed it was gone, maybe he could forgive me for taking it.

Forgive me for a lot of things.

Once he realized *I* was gone...no, he couldn't get past the betrayal. What I'd done could damage relations between the Alderidge and Grimaldi packs for the foreseeable future. It would impact everyone in the packs from the alpha to the lowest omega.

I shook my head to clear it, tightening my grip on the steering wheel. Running away would be letting my pack down. For what he'd deal with, I was sorry.

Not sorry enough to stay.

The road spread out in front of me. Once I made it out of the city, I made good time. The burner phone, at least, came equipped with GPS and the mechanical voice guided me closer to the academy with each mile.

Closer to my future. Closer to my escape. And once I was out of the city past the early morning traffic, something eased inside of me, a tension I hadn't been aware of. I thought of the vials in the backseat behind me. The vials to keep my shifter nature at bay. The rest would be up to me.

Hours passed. I grabbed fast food for lunch, with extra for dinner, and listened to the radio to pass the time. I decided to find a place to stop for the night. I hadn't seen any road signs for a motel in a while but there should be some ahead. I'd stop at the next one I found. With autumn around the corner, the days were getting shorter, and already it was dark and I was tired.

I tapped on the steering wheel in time with the song on the radio. One step at a time, another mile closer to the academy.

In my head I was already there and figuring out my next step. But fatigue rode me hard, eyes blurring, shoulders tight.

I needed to stop and get some sleep so I could rest up before orientation tomorrow morning.

Close, so close.

The car shook and sputtered, throwing me forward against the dashboard until the seatbelt bit into my neck. My wrist jolted painfully. Smoke curled from beneath the hood and the car wheezed like an old man with COPD.

"No, no! Come on, don't do this to me. Not now."

I managed to yank the wheel and bring the old girl over to the side of the road seconds before its final death call.

Black smoke belching, and the clock marking midnight, the car died a terrible death.

9

The immediate clench of fear in my gut at being stranded began to fade slightly the more time passed. Maybe Big Dan had been right about the car. I was stuck miles away from civilization in a broken-down heap.

The next thought was how I'd made a bad mistake in picking the worst car on the lot when I should have settled for something middle of the road for a little more money.

"Come on, baby. I know you can do this." I spoke softly to the car, cajoling the way one would with a child or a scared animal.

I turned the key in the ignition repeatedly, listening to the slowly fading hum of the starter. This couldn't be happening.

"You have to be kidding me!"

Fumbling to find the release, I popped the hood and stepped out of the car. The night was silent. Heavy. The weight of the silence bore down on me and I stared out into the darkness creeping closer and closer. I was in the middle of nowhere, rural Massachusetts, tall trees blocking my views of the sky.

"Breathe, Tavi, breathe," I told myself.

Hands fisting my hair into knots, I tried to follow my own advice and failed miserably, my lungs aching. I was still too far away from the school to walk and I definitely didn't feel comfortable walking at this hour. Not when I wanted to keep my shifter side a secret—and it left me in a vulnerable position.

I opened the hood although I had no clue what I was doing. Smoke lay in a low blanket over most of the mechanics and I fanned it away on a cough, trying to see.

Not knowing what I was looking for, I couldn't find the source of the problem and ended up choking on the smoke.

"This is fixable." I spoke to myself to break up the cloying darkness pressing closer. I couldn't take the quiet much longer. "No big deal. I'll call a tow truck and get a lift to the nearest garage. I've got money, no problem, I can get the car fixed and maybe catch a ride to the school tomorrow."

A tentative plan in place felt better than the underlying layer of helplessness I wanted to succumb to. But when I unlocked my phone and checked for bars, my heart sunk. A total dead zone. No wonder the GPS hadn't been working.

A cold sweat broke out over my skin. I couldn't even call 911 if I wanted to.

An owl hooted from somewhere in the woods and I nearly jumped out of my skin, diving back into the car. I closed the door behind me, making sure to engage the lock.

Minutes crept by. Only a single car passed me on the road and they didn't stop. I wasn't sure whether it made me happy or anxious.

More minutes. Then an hour. And another.

Teeth clenched, I shook out my hands to try and relieve some tension. "It's okay, it's okay, it's okay." I twisted the key in the ignition again, on the off chance the engine had rested enough to work this time.

Nope, no such luck.

It felt better to have the overhead light on. Then again, with the light, everything outside could see *me* and I couldn't see a thing in return. The battery would only last for so long.

"I'm losing my marbles." I let out a low laugh, letting my head hit the rest behind me. If this was a test, then I was foolish and had failed miserably. I'd wanted so badly to escape my situation I'd backed myself into this corner, the night outside a dark veil snapping with all manner of bad things.

I swallowed hard. Whatever shred of hope I'd been clinging to, whatever foolish optimism about this plan actually working began to shrivel.

This changed nothing, I tried to tell myself, tucking away my fear. I still needed to escape Kendrick. This was nothing but a tiny bump in the road.

Why did I have trouble believing in myself?

A pair of headlights cut through the blackness, slowing when they saw me, although I almost missed them with the overhead light on. I flipped the light off, torn once again between wanting the help and not wanting a stranger to come up and find me in a compromised position.

I didn't want to let the wolf out. I couldn't, or else I'd draw any nearby werewolves to me with my scent.

The vehicle ended up pulling over behind the Toyota. I stilled, hoping it was a police car of some sort. And not a serial killer looking for his next victim.

Maybe I'd overestimated my abilities to handle things on my own.

"Hey, are you okay?"

I cracked the window just enough to hear the stranger but not enough for him to stick his arm inside. I didn't see much beyond a flash of blond hair and tanned skin. It was enough for me to know to keep my guard high. "Not really," I told the stranger. "The car won't start and I don't have any cell service."

The guy ducked down until we were at eye level. I stared at him for the longest time, willing my jaw to get back in its usual place after it dropped, my heart thudding once, twice. The guy was *gorgeous*. Had I somehow broken down in an alternate dimension? My luck wasn't good enough for this kind of thing to happen. Men who looked like him only existed in fairy tales.

My suspicion rose.

He wasn't conventionally handsome, I realized the more I stared at him, not like the kind of guys who graced magazine covers. His nose was a tiny bit too long and his face too narrow for him to fit into any box. But he had intense green eyes and shiny golden hair, ruffled around his face with the night breeze. My age or thereabouts. Some innate female instinct told me he would be a good kisser, and when he looked at me, that's all I thought about.

The suspicion rose higher to choke me. A *seductive* serial killer would be just my luck.

The guy had asked me a question, and I shook my head, not hearing him. "What?"

"I asked where you're headed," he repeated.

I kept the window up although it offered little protection if Mr. Gorgeous wanted to punch his way through it. He had the muscle to do it. "I wanted to get to a motel. I think there's one just down the road but the old girl decided to give out on me. She just won't start."

"How long have you been out here?"

Should I tell him the truth? "Long enough," I answered vaguely.

"Well, let me give you a lift," the guy offered. He glanced ahead at the dark road leading forward. "I'm headed there anyway. Might as well help a damsel in distress."

"I'm no man's damsel." The *in distress* part, on the other hand...

I knew better than to get into a random person's car. If I had to wolf out and eat him, then I could, but it was a last resort for a no-win situation. Even if he was handsome as sin. Even if part of me did draw toward him wanting to be touched.

I trusted my instincts and I didn't get a bad feeling from him so...good thing? That in itself gave me pause.

"Look, you can wait here for someone else if you want. I doubt you'll get a better offer than this, and I can promise you you'll arrive at your motel in the same state I found you." He held his hands out in front of him to show me his sincerity. "I'm not gong to hurt you. I promise."

I debated it for approximately four seconds before agreeing. I didn't want to sit on the side of the road any longer. "Um, sure," I said. "Thank you. I appreciate the help."

"Are you moving?" He pointed to the luggage in the back.

I shrugged. "Maybe. Going far enough from home I needed to pack my bags." Yeah, sorry guy. You might be good-looking but I wasn't going to tell you everything.

I stepped out of the car and stood next to him. He looked younger up close, his face unlined and putting him much closer to my age—or at least what I could see of his face in the darkness looked young. He stood about eight inches taller, the gap between us enough he had to look down at me.

Then his face broke into a smile. My brain turned to mush.

Hubba hubba.

"You look like you're school-age," he said in an echo of my inner sentiment. "Are you taking classes somewhere? An *academy*, perhaps?"

My head snapped up, chest tightening as alarm bells

clanged. There was no way he could possibly know. "What do you mean?"

His eyes didn't leave my face. "It was an honest question."

At least he didn't try to call me any pet names. Score one for the handsome stranger.

His nose, cheeks, and brow were sculpted and sharp, jaw strong and lips plump. The dark green shirt he wore was plain and tight enough to stretch across a broad chest, echoing the color of his eyes. The light gold of his hair reflected the moonlight and through the strands I saw the delicate point of his arched ears.

Oh my.

He didn't bother to hide them from me. My heart beat so fast I thought I would lose my dinner. "You're Fae." Yes, it made sense. No human looked supernaturally beautiful or could draw me to him so easily.

I tried not to consider what this meant. And definitely tried not to look too hard at him.

The gold-haired boy cracked another smile, wider this time. "I wondered when you'd figure it out. You're Fae, too. I noticed the moment you opened the window, sensing a little zip of magic when I looked at you. Which makes my question about the academy a little easier to handle, right? Makes me seem a little less like a jerk?"

I inched closer to the car, letting the metal of the door cool my suddenly overheated skin. He'd sensed the Fae in me immediately. What did it mean for me? Would he be able to sense the shifter part easily, too? I'd need to be careful going forward. But the motel was close. I could make it through a short ride.

"My name is Tavi," I supplied, holding out a hand for him to take.

"Michael. But you can call me Mike." He took my hand in

a firm shake that thankfully did not move worlds. Although it held potential. "Let's get your things out of the car and deliver you to the motel. It's not safe for you out here."

I huffed a laugh. "I like to think I can take care of myself."

His strange green eyes pinned me in place as if he could detect every move I made, every muscle in my body tense and primed to fight. "Of course you can, but it doesn't mean I can't offer to help you," he said with another flash of teeth. "Especially considering I'm heading to the academy, too."

"You are?" I blinked at him, trying to put two and two together and coming up short. I blamed it on the lack of sleep and too many days of worry.

"It's my first semester," Mike stated easily as he gestured for me to follow him. "Please don't think less of me when I admit I'm a little nervous about it. I've never been to a school like this before. It's going to be a new experience."

He was heading to the Halflings Academy as well. Which meant he was my…my competition. With spaces limited, a girl had to look out for herself.

"I'm nervous too," I told him.

"But are you as nervous as I am?"

"Probably more so." I watched him move to the backseat, lug my suitcase and duffel bag out of the Toyota and drag everything to his own vehicle parked several feet behind. He had more than enough room for both of our stuff.

"Oh, doubtful," he said with a laugh. I could tell he wanted to put me at ease and appreciated the kindness. I only hoped it wouldn't turn around to bite me in the ass.

"You don't seem to have a lot packed," I commented.

Mike swung around to stare at his own luggage, mouth quirked. "Well, dudes don't have quite as much as girls. Plus, I travel light. I find it's easier for me to pick up and leave if I don't have too many things weighing me down. You know?"

He turned back to me and my cheeks heated even as I let out a tight breath. "It makes sense." I was in the same boat, yet I'd managed to bring almost double what Mike had.

He finished adding my luggage to his own and slid behind the wheel. I took the passenger seat, noting the spotless interior, the clean dashboard, and the tiny bag of herbs hanging from the rearview mirror. I drew in a breath and caught the scent of lavender and rosemary then clicked my seatbelt into place.

It must be a Fae thing. I had a lot to learn.

"Hey, I'm not going to bite. You don't have to worry so much." Mike flashed me a grin with white teeth gleaming in a way that almost suggested otherwise. Or maybe it was just my imagination but my insides prickled, and not in a bad way.

"I appreciate your stopping to help me," I said as he pulled the car away from the side of the road.

"No problem. Once we get settled in, I can help you call someone to take care of your car, although I don't think anyone is going to bother it. It's old enough to dissuade any would-be thief."

I waved the comment away. "Don't even worry about it. I'm not. There are other things for me to focus on than your old car."

Mike had been respectful enough of me and my boundaries to lead me to believe he was a nice person. Still, I had to be careful and watch every step.

"You know, I'm thinking...you don't need to stay at a motel. The academy will let us in tonight if you want."

I swallowed. "Tonight?" I thought I'd have enough time to settle myself, to figure things out before getting to the school in the morning.

This put me in a tenuous mental position.

"Yup, no need to stop," he said with a quick glance in my

direction. "Besides, then you won't have to pay for a taxi to get you there in the morning. We can get there in less than an hour, if you're ready."

No. I didn't feel one *bit* ready. I forced a grin anyway.

"Okay, fine. Bring it on."

10

I'd made a mistake. I'd gambled and ended up in a car with a serial killer.

My thoughts circled down a dark drain until my anxiety spiked. Binge-watching too many true crime documentaries made me leery of Mike to the point where I kept one hand on the door ready to jump for the first ten miles of our trip. Especially considering I'd just agreed to let him drive us the whole way instead of dropping me off.

An hour in the car with Mike… I glanced over at him. *Please don't kill me.*

There were some handsome serial killers out there, though.

He drove the rest of the way to the campus with light conversation and banter between us. I didn't realize how close I'd truly been to the school when my car decided to break down.

"Are you a member of one of the courts?" I asked him cautiously. I knew about the courts, at least. Faerie was divided into Seelie and Unseelie, one considered dark and the other light. Then I remembered what Elfwaite had told me about shades of gray and wondered again where Mike fit into the picture.

He shook his head until strands of gold obscured the side of his face. "No, I'm not a member of any court. My family is older than the courts, older than most of the High Lords and Ladies of Faerie. We try to stay neutral." Then he stopped as though unwilling to say more.

I chuckled to break up the tension. "And here I thought my family was something because my uncle is a lawyer."

It wasn't exactly giving anything away, but it was enough to keep the conversation rolling.

"Hey, being a lawyer *is* a big deal," Mike answered with gravity.

"I guess it doesn't extend to children though, does it?" I joked. "Or any kind of niece or nephew."

He glanced over, studying me as much as he could without taking his attention from the road. "I don't know. You seem like something to me."

Oh, my word, was I flirting with a murderer? I highly doubted my initial impression of Mike was accurate, but still…

Lingering mortification over what I'd said took hold of me and I pressed a hand to my chest. "Well, good," I replied, trying to ignore my embarrassment. "Nice of you to say."

At least Mike appeared amused. "You'd *have* to be something to get the invite to the academy. Never forget."

"Gotcha. I'll try not to." Another glance in his direction. I couldn't stop looking at him. "Are you looking forward to starting?"

He mumbled some noncommittal response though laughter still danced on his face.

"Ah, the truth comes out! You aren't excited to start at all. You were right about the nerves." I started to laugh, the habitual snort airing at the end until I slapped a hand over my mouth to stop it.

He shrugged and shot me a devilish smile. "It's school, isn't it? If I told you I was excited for school, you'd think me either a liar or an asshole."

I bit the inside of my cheek and wondered at the twists and turns the night had taken. We passed the time with conversation flowing from subject to subject without delay.

At last, Mike jerked his head toward the windshield. "Here we are."

It still didn't hit home, not really, not even as we drove up to the ancient metal gates with the academy logo welded into the wrought iron, a swirling design I couldn't quite understand although I saw it clearly, even in the dark.

"We have reached our final destination," Mike stated with cheerful ease. "The Fae Academy for Halflings and our new home, if we can make it through the probationary period."

"It doesn't look like they're expecting anyone to come in at this hour." I stared at the gates and felt my insides shift. Too bad I had no clue whether it was good or bad. "Are you sure we're allowed to be here?"

Great wide tree trunks kept the majority of the place from view. Stars were bright overhead and I thought I saw the rising turrets of the castle through the night. Fifty acres, though…plenty of room to hide the magical occupants.

"Most new students don't generally arrive past midnight, unless you're *us*. I guess we are crazy after all." Mike pulled to a stop and flipped up the parking brake to keep the car in place. When I lifted my brow in silent inquiry, he continued with, "Don't worry though, there should always be someone up. I'll try the intercom. There has to be a night guard on duty who can let us inside."

The realization hit me like a wave at the beach when my back was turned. Mike slid out of the driver's seat and I remembered I hadn't taken my potion yet to hide my wolf shifter nature, and here we stood at the doorstep of the campus.

Dammit.

Thank goodness he hadn't seen me in direct light. Maybe I should be grateful the conversation kept him distracted, otherwise his magic might have sensed something off about me.

I had to hurry.

"I'm just going to grab something out of my bag," I called out to Mike, stopping short on the other side of the car.

"Yeah, go ahead. I'm still trying to figure out how to get the gate to open. Do you think the whole campus is protected by magic? It wasn't part of my reading. They've got to have wards in place. Right?"

I had no clue, and ignored this line of questioning.

The case was buried in my large case under the rest of my things. Hands shaking, I pulled at the zipper and tossed my clothes to the side, sparing a look over my shoulder to make sure Mike's attention remained on the gate.

Hurry.

I had to move fast before he saw me.

I had the lid open, vial in hand, box locked within seconds before I popped the cork. Ducking, I chugged the entire contents in a single gulp. The potion slid down my throat like mud. It stung my tongue, stomach heaving and threatening to toss its contents, gagging.

It was absolutely disgusting. Worse than the most horrible combination of ingredients my mind could conjure. Maybe Barbara *had* poisoned me.

But it worked immediately, turning my skin molten and making my eyes water. A wrench of pain jolted through my entire body. Dear God, what had I gotten myself into? My gorge rose and I swallowed hard to keep my insides where they belonged.

I am not going to lose it.

My vision went blurry.

"Hey, Tavi, you okay?"

I am not going to lose it.

I was vaguely aware of Mike circling back around the car to check on me when I didn't answer him. Wheezing, I tried to wave and get him to walk away, my limbs no longer belonging to me. They were attached, sure, but outside of my control.

"Dizzy spell," I managed to get out. *Please don't puke.* "Go on without me. I need a minute."

His hands were on my back too close to where my skin rippled. "I'm not going to leave you alone. Are you sure you're all right? Try to breathe. You're okay."

The concern in his voice almost made me lose it for real. Of course, the guy had to be a total knight in shining armor when I needed him to just walk away and not look back.

Cool fingers moved on the back of my neck and Mike helped me to stand upright. The world swam in front of me like I viewed it through the reflection of a funhouse mirror. The back of his hand brushed my forehead.

"Not a dizzy spell," Mike said. "You feel feverish. You're burning up!"

"I'm fine." The insistence came out weak. He was too close to me. Surely, he'd see the way my skin had loosened and morphed. He'd notice something was wrong and report me to the council. I was just the crazy chick he'd picked up on the side of the road.

Shrugging him off, I tried to reach in the backseat and grab my duffel bag and purse. The wheeled luggage I'd have to grab later. If later came for me. I might not survive ingesting the sludge Barbara had made for me.

I slammed the door and winced at the sound, too loud and echoing when it shouldn't have. Stumbled until I hit the gate.

"You're not going anywhere, I'm sorry." Mike wrapped his arm around my waist and helped me into the front seat. "Let's get inside and find a parking spot. Hold on."

I didn't want his help. I didn't want him scrutinizing me, caring about me, especially not when I had to fool him and everyone else to be here. Pressing a hand against my stomach to steady it, I closed my eyes as the car moved forward.

"Almost there, Tavi. Hold on."

I didn't *deserve* his help. Maybe that's what bothered me more than anything. This guy had stopped to help a stranger when he didn't have to, and now he was going above and beyond. For me. For a liar.

Definitely not a serial killer.

The gates opened for us without further delay. Mike pressed the gas and zipped up the curling macadam drive into the darkness of the trees. I thought I saw the driveway branching off into two directions but he continued straight. Soon the forest opened up and the whole of the castle loomed ahead of us. I couldn't see much. Everything shifted and blurred. I groaned, leaning forward before my stomach lost everything.

He parked near the front doors, helping me out of the car and into the front hall, the doors opening automatically to allow us entry. Like magic. The sound of them closing behind us echoed through the large space, with cathedral ceilings soaring toward a peak and a great golden chandelier shedding light. The rest of the entry hall stood empty save for a few folding tables and chairs.

"Hello?" Mike called out. "Anyone home? We need some help!"

I leaned into him when my strength failed. He tightened his hold on me. "It's too early in the morning—"

Heels clicked along the tile floor and a voice cried out, "What's going on? What's all the commotion about?"

I couldn't see the speaker. My eyes were swollen and at once it was hard to breathe, the pain never-ending. I heard Mike ask for a nurse, his grip on my waist tightening further. A wave of agony shook me and I jerked against him. Panting.

The idea of someone scrutinizing me before the potion took full effect...I couldn't allow the risk.

I tried to tell whoever stood in front of us: I was fine, it was *girl problems* and nothing to worry about. No one believed me. In a heartbeat, Mike and I were led down a side hallway. Once they felt my forehead and the fever raging, there was no room for argument. Every hair on my body stood upright as they flung open the door to a fluorescent-lit room reeking of sterile chemicals.

The infirmary.

"Oh my, what do we have going on? Someone isn't feeling well, is she? We've got some light sweating...nope, *heavy* sweating. I can feel the heat coming off of her skin from here. Yowzah, we've either got the magical influenza or someone is going through early menopause. Just kidding! I'm kidding, of course."

I blinked at the nurse with the sweet voice, her image solidifying into two solid presences instead of five. Another species of Fae, with gangly limbs, pointed ears, and shiny wings protruding from her shoulder blades in a blue only a shade lighter than her skin.

Blue skin?

She clucked her tongue to get Mike's attention. "Keep hold of her, young man. Don't let her sag to the floor. Get her over to the table and help her sit up," the nurse said brusquely.

"I'm not sure what's going on," Mike was saying. His hands moved to my shoulders to steady me. "We pulled up to the gate and she said she felt dizzy. Then she almost knocked her head on the car when she went down. It came out of nowhere."

He helped situate me on the examination table but kept his hands on my knees until I steadied. "I'm fine," I told them both again, my words only slurring slightly.

An improvement!

This time, I meant it. The wave of pain at last ebbed, the effects of the potion beginning to wear off. I drew in a breath and didn't feel needles piercing my lungs, and when I opened my eyes again, the world swam into view after a few breaths.

Mike stood at my side with his arms crossed over his chest and concern coloring his every feature.

The nurse was on his right. Her name tag read *Julie.*

She had a stethoscope in hand, startling amethyst-colored eyes darting over me and flashing in warning. *Warning?* A muscle feathered in her jaw and I regretted letting Mike bring me to her, if only for the scrutiny flickering in her gaze. As though she saw right through me.

"What?" I choked out. What did she see when she looked at me?

Her gaze widened as she stared. My fingers clutched the edge of the table. If I had to make a run for it, I wouldn't get far. Still…

"I just had a weird hot flash and dizzy spell," I insisted. "Everyone overreacted. It's nothing for you to worry about. I'm absolutely fine. See? The fever is already fading."

"It's *not* nothing," Mike said. His golden skin flushed. "You went from fine to sick in seconds. Worrisome."

"I'm not so sure…" Nurse Julie trailed off, bending in front of me. Examining me.

I sucked on my teeth for a moment.

Finally, she chuckled, a soft and gentle sound breaking the tension immediately. "I think it should be girls only for a little bit. If you'll excuse us, young man, I need to speak to my patient alone. You can wait out in the hall until we're done here. Go on, now. Shoo! Shoo!"

She pushed Mike out the door with a cluck of her tongue, flicked the lock behind him, then walked over to the sink and picked up a piece of gauze to run under the faucet. "The teachers here can't keep their noses out of students' business," she told me without looking over her shoulder. "They are inherently invested in the goings-on around campus. It's always best to keep yourself to yourself at all times. Get me?"

Whoever this nurse was, I wasn't sure I could trust her, and the ominous tone of her words had the breath whooshing from my chest.

"I don't need anyone in my business," I muttered.

"Who does? Now let me just check a few things with you and you'll be good to go. Your color is already coming back." She turned around and smiled, holding the gauze up to my forehead to wipe away the rapidly drying beads of sweat. Her wings flickered. "A few more minutes and you should be back to normal, although I recommend getting a little sleep. Okay, a *lot* of sleep. You're up late tonight. Have you been eating?"

I answered her questions to the best of my ability. They were perfunctory, going over my personal habits, my pulse, et cetera. She no longer looked at me with the same discretion she had earlier. No longer appeared as though she saw everything I wanted to hide.

"Okay, Miss Alderidge. Off with you now. Go check in and get situated in your dorm. You have a big day ahead of you tomorrow and you are going to need your strength. You look fine to me."

The nurse clearly had her own agenda and soon sent me on my way with a warning to drink more fluids.

I expected Mike to be long gone by the time I left the infirmary, ibuprofen in hand and orange juice helping to settle my stomach. He had no reason to wait around for me.

He stood up from a chair in the lobby and flashed me a smile, one I'd almost come to expect on his face. No, stupid. I couldn't expect something from a guy I'd known less than a day.

"You waited," I said in surprise.

"Of course I waited," he replied, blinking. "I couldn't let you walk out alone. Plus, I have your bags."

I stepped up to him, hissing when I expected pain and found none, my potion now in place. "I definitely appreciate it. You've been so kind to me."

"New kids have to stick together, right?" He leaned closer and knocked me lightly on the arm, a gesture of camaraderie. Not hard enough to knock me off my feet in any way.

Why did it make my skin prickle deliciously?

With soft light pouring down from a crystal chandelier overhead, I saw Mike in full light for the first time since meeting, and I wondered how I'd ever thought him merely *unconventionally handsome*. No, his looks went way beyond handsome.

My heart cracked open a bit the longer I stared.

His skin gleamed with a slight bronze sheen, his hair the color of sunshine itself. His eyes were a vibrant green with gold around the iris, like the personification of a summer forest. Young, sure, but devastatingly beautiful and captivating in a way I had never seen before.

I drew toward him not because of his looks alone, but the inherent kindness he'd shown me. The way he'd offered to lend a hand to a stranger. Then I stopped myself when I took a literal step toward him.

His brows, slightly arched, brought out the color of his eyes.

My breath caught in my throat and I slid my hands behind me to keep from reaching out to touch him. This powerful Fae male. I had to remember *that* above all else.

What species was he? Half-human? I'd put human on my admission application if quizzed.

Or maybe half-Fae and half-elf?

His head quirked to the side, adorable to the point where I had to draw in a breath to center myself. "Come on, Tavi. Let's get back to the entry hall and see if they will let us check in before orientation tomorrow. Our kind never sleep! I saw some tables set up where I guess the professors have prepared for early arrivals. We can get signed in, grab our paperwork, and then they'll administer the blood tests."

I started and felt my face go pale. "The blood test."

I'd known it was coming, even as my heart clutched and I followed Mike back the way we'd come. They'd need to make sure the students fell into the acceptable half-breed categories. They couldn't simply take us at our word.

"Are you afraid of needles?" Mike asked over his shoulder. "You can tell me if you are. I won't make fun of you."

Struggling to swallow, I said, "Yes, totally afraid." It made more sense for me to fear the needle rather than fear the result.

"It's nothing for you to worry about. You won't even see the needle, from what I understand. It's a machine analyzing magic in your white and red blood cells. It should only take a few seconds."

"I appreciate your trying to spin this around for me," I told him with a mouth gone dry.

This was it. If the potion didn't work, then I would not be able to hide the truth from anyone, and they would turn on me.

"Come on, don't be scared," Mike teased. He stood beside me with a calm and steady presence. I tried not to lean on him. "It's a little blood test and then we can get settled. No worries. See? There are already people here."

Scared? No, I wouldn't say scared. I was *terrified*. I wondered when I'd grown so bold as to think I could pull this off and get away with it.

Enough time had passed that a line had formed while I was in the nurse's office. I stared around at the crowd, the beautiful men and women who were all like me. Maybe everyone else had the same idea Mike had, to check in early and save themselves the hassle of doing it in the morning.

Yet I stood alone in the crowd.

My turn in line came up faster than I wanted. The woman in front of me maneuvered my finger into the device as I stood statue-still.

The needle shot out and sliced into my skin.

The moment of truth. If they could see the shifter inside of me…then I was done.

11

If the reader registered anything besides human, I could kiss my place here goodbye. *You're a liar. You're a fraud.*

I waited precious moments for the results to come in, my blood pressure rising with each second, almost hearing the clock in my head.

Tick.

Tock.

Liar.

Fraud.

Darkness crowded the edges of my vision as the machine beeped, clicking, analyzing the drop of blood I'd provided.

My teeth bit down on my lip hard enough to leave a bruise.

"Tavi, try to breathe. It's not so bad."

Mike stood behind me grinning. He thought this an irrational phobia, like people who couldn't stand to see a mouse, or didn't want to walk beneath a ladder because of bad luck.

He didn't know this meant the difference between a future of freedom or a matrimonial prison.

The machine squealed out its results.

"Half human, half Fae," the teacher said with a shake of her head. She didn't sound impressed. "Next."

I stood there for a moment in shock. The potion from Barbara...had *worked*? It was impossible.

"Next!"

The teacher repeated the demand and the few people behind me surged forward for their turns. I drew my finger from the machine, my smile secretive and wide. Nothing but half Fae and half sniveling, cowering human. Barbara's disgusting concoction had done its job and hidden my true self.

Thank goodness.

Maybe the old witch knew what she was doing after all.

"See? It wasn't so bad," Mike continued with a chuckle as we walked toward the next closest table. "You got yourself worked up for no reason. There's nothing to worry about."

For him, sure. I hadn't paid attention to his results. I cradled my hand to my chest and watched the pinprick heal seconds later. "Not bad, you were right. I'm not even sure why I worried."

"I told you, you wouldn't see the needle."

"I'll never doubt you again," I cooed, which drew another laugh from Mike.

"Oh, I'm sure eventually I'll do something stupid to have you doubting me. Never say never, Tavi."

The rest of check-in went by in a blur, whatever other students were there before first light getting their papers and sleeping assignments before the masses. All first-year students were obliged to sleep in separate dormitories with other members of their specific breed and gender.

I'd been allocated a bed number and sent on my way with directions to my new home.

Everyone stayed in different wings of the castle, I saw now. How big was this place, really?

"Hey, wait for me," Mike said from over my shoulder, trotting to catch up.

I was immensely glad for his presence. It made the process a little less lonely to have a friendly face close. "I'm not sure what I'm doing." I shook my head. "It's all happening too quickly. Do you have any idea where I'm supposed to go?"

"Let's see where you're staying." Mike craned his head to glance at the papers I'd been given. Wow, he smelled good. Better than any boy I'd ever met, a combination of sandalwood and sea salt. "Ah. You're in Tamerlain Hall. I think I know where to go. I can walk you there if you still want the company."

Feeling much better, the weight lifted off my shoulders, I knocked against him playfully. "If I didn't know any better, I'd say you've been here before. *You know where to go.* Are you sure you're a first-year student?"

He held two fingers straight up in front of him as we walked. "My honor as a Scout, although I've never been in the Scouts. I *did* study the school's website before I came."

"Ha! Me too. It doesn't seem to be helping much."

I tried to shuffle through my armful of orientation papers and dropped several in the process. On our way we passed by several students, species I'd never seen before, some tall and more human-like than fairy, while others were very clearly pixie or elf or *other*. I tried to avoid staring at them. Good practice for later, because I didn't need the attention either.

"The area is laid out pretty well. We have a map. And it's not like we can get lost. The castle might be huge but at least there's no reason to go outside."

Better for me. Better to avoid the moonlight since I'd taken my first potion vial. It wasn't a full moon *yet* but I'd need to be cautious and find alternate routes for future moon cycles.

"I must be on your map too," I joked with Mike, giving him a long look. "Because you keep finding me no matter where I wander."

"You do tend to stand out. Not many people with this shade of hair. Makes you easy to spot." Mike reached out and tugged on a corner of my braid. I almost sizzled at his nearness. "I'll have to find you tomorrow to get your stuff out of my car."

"What am I going to do until then?"

"Get a little sleep? I plan to pass out immediately. We don't have anything on our schedule until luncheon, plenty of time for a few hours of shut eye. Then orientation in the afternoon." He winked. "Here you are. Tamerlain."

I stopped in front of a giant gray stone arch with a green-painted placard displaying the name of the dormitory in flowing script. "Already?" I'd been enjoying the walk and the company.

"Already. Have a good night, Tavi. I'll see you soon. Try to get some sleep." He inclined his head in goodbye.

"Thanks, Mike."

I watched him leave for his own dormitory on the next floor, if I had to guess. I still didn't know what kind of half-breed he was—why hadn't I paid attention to his test results?—and he didn't seem to be forthcoming with the information. I set my lips in a line. One of these days, I'd get to the bottom of it.

But I had a friend. I hugged the knowledge close to me, warmth spreading through my chest. I could use a friend in this place.

A gust of wind shook the eaves of the castle and echoed down the drafty hallways. Shivering, I pushed through into the dorm. Sleep, yes. Definitely next on the list of priorities.

The doors to Tamerlain Hall opened into a small common room with couches and a large fireplace housing roaring flames filling the space with warmth. Easing open a second door to the left, I walked into a square room bedecked in hues of red and orange and gold, lined with oak shelves like a library. Similar to being surrounded by an autumn wood. There was no hint of the dreary castle here. A low ceiling made the space cozy and intimate.

Each shelf, I now saw, was an alcove of bunk beds, giving the illusion of each girl having their own private space.

A long table sat beneath a window to the right of the long room, covered in books and writing utensils.

I squinted down at the paper in my hand and noted my assigned bunk number. So many, there were so many girls here. All half Fae and half human. My bed was the top bunk above a sleeping blond. Trying to be quiet, I crawled up the ladder and flopped down on soft sheets with my purse and papers and duffel next to me. The moment I went horizontal, the full weight of my exhaustion hit me. I yawned.

At least I had a change of clothes with me. Good enough to get me through a few hours of sleep without feeling like the living dead. And looking like it, too.

I tucked the bag near my head to keep my personal possessions close. I'd have to figure out where to store my things once the sun rose. When the room wasn't dark.

Crawling beneath the covers, I drew them up to my chin wearing everything except my shoes. I was here. *I'd made it.* My heart seemed to calm at last.

And at once I realized how incredibly alone I truly was. I still had my phone in my pocket, and when I glanced at the lit screen, I saw I had full bars for service. But who would I text? I had not only walked away from Uncle William, I'd walked away from every aspect of pack life, including my friends. Everything and everyone I'd ever known.

Flash back to any normal day at home with Uncle Will and I'd be asleep now with the alarm set to wake me for my internship at the law firm. If I were home, I'd have a hot breakfast waiting for me, a smiling Cook telling me how she'd made my favorite waffles. I'd savor the pre-dawn moments listening to the chatter of birds outside my window.

Instead, this bedroom was far from silent, the beds filled to capacity, and a part of me missed the quiet hush.

I slept fitfully for the few hours before the rest of the girls woke with the sun. Soon the sounds of movement and whispered conversation were too great to ignore and I peeled my eyes open against a layer of grit and sleep.

Someone had thrown the curtains open and let the morning light filter inside. Someone I instantly wanted to strangle before I thought better of it.

I didn't want to climb down. Not yet. I didn't want to leave the solitude of my bed, and had to mentally slap myself to move. The girls were talking, laughing, as though they had already made friends and divided into groups.

How was it possible?

I sucked up any lingering fears and doubts, rising and stretching my arms above my head.

"About time you got up. What, do you think you can just sleep in while the rest of us are getting ready? There are places to be."

Excuse me?

I frowned, craning my neck over the side of the bed to see the same blond girl from the bottom bunk. She stood in our alcove, with three other girls beside her that looked more like clones than separate beings. They were all tall, thin, with curves in the right places and near-identical heart-shaped faces. Even if I didn't know anything about Fae, I would suspect something otherworldly about the three of them.

Despite their similarities, it was easy to pick out my bunkmate from the rest of the pack, the obvious leader. Stronger, more charismatic. The others fell in behind her as she stepped forward to address me with a sneer.

"You think you can sneak in during the night and sleep the day away, newbie? Are you too good to meet with the rest of us?"

"I'm sorry," I blurted out, shifting to take hold of the ladder, forcing my fingers to wake before the rest of me. "I didn't mean to disturb you. I thought I was quiet."

"If you think a rampaging bull is quiet," the girl retorted.

"I didn't think anyone would hear me coming in so early—"

She looked me over from head to toe and found me lacking. If the look on her face wasn't obvious to this fact, she opened her mouth and said with a scoff, "*This* is how you plan to impress the professors?" she asked with a titter. "Seriously?"

I glanced down at my rumpled jeans and black t-shirt, glanced over to the worn sneakers I'd kicked aside before getting into bed. I hadn't had time to shower and had simply left my hair in the braids from the day before.

In contrast, my bunkmate had styled her blond locks to perfection, not a hair out of place. When did she have the time? Here was the ethereal beauty the Fae were known for, evident in the uptilt of her sky-blue eyes and perfect pink lips. She wore a dress the color of spring crocuses designed to hug her eye-popping curves.

"Do you really think you belong here?" she asked.

I might have kept apologizing were it not for the snort of derisive laughter she gave me. Oh no. She'd taken things too far. I crossed my arms. "I belong here as well as anyone else."

Who are you to say any different?

The girl seemed poised to spit on me, her sharp eyes

narrowing. "You'll never be one of us, new girl. No matter how hard you try."

If she wanted me to have a new nickname, she might have at least come up with something a little more original.

"Why would I want to?" I said, trying to calm my racing heart. I navigated the ladder and finally stood facing her. Noting I had several inches of height on her. "Why would anyone want to be part of your little group of *meanions*?"

The four of them shared a long look, my bunkmate barking out another laugh. "You don't have what it takes to hack it at the academy."

"You don't even know me."

"I don't need to know you. I've seen your kind before."

My blood went cold. "My kind?"

"Yes. Your kind," she stated, pushing her hair over her shoulder, "where your human outweighs your Fae. You might as well give up now."

I refused to let her get under my skin. I refused to give in to the taunts designed to knock me off my game. But as the four of them continued to scrutinize me, I shrank a little beneath their gazes and wondered. If the students here were like these girls, then I had a long road ahead of me.

And I wasn't sure I could handle the pressure without shattering.

12

I'd let them get to me without making an effort to defend myself, and although I tried to remind myself their reactions had nothing to do with me *personally*, it still stung. I tried not to actually run away from the awful foursome, following the rest of the mass exodus out of the dormitory and toward the auditorium.

There were so many girls like me. There had to be at least twenty-five others in my dorm alone, not counting the number in the boys' dorms. I'd have competition to stay here. More competition than I'd bargained for.

All part of the game, I reasoned, tugging my t-shirt lower. I was still wearing the same sweat-soaked clothing from my drive yesterday. At least I'd managed to put my shoes on. But I didn't have time to waste on worry or self-consciousness. The assembly would start soon enough and orientation after.

Mike had said we didn't have anything to do until after luncheon. But it seems he hadn't gotten his times right. The introductory welcome was scheduled for nine.

I didn't need my map to know where we were headed. The rest of the girls led the way, chatting easily with each other on the walk to the auditorium. We moved down a grand staircase toward the main floor of the castle and turned left. Soon the hallway widened, opening up into a large room with great acoustics. The seats were done in red velvet similar to what you might see in an old opera house. I noted some of the same details in the plaster designs covering the walls and ceiling.

Wow. I'd thought the place grand from the photos on the website but it was nothing compared to what I saw in person. Rubbing the rest of the sleep from my eyes, I took it all in.

So many students, all so different. All here for the same reason I was. Well, probably not the *exact* same reason, but we had the same end goals in mind. To make it through to senior year and earn our place in Faerie.

I managed to find a seat in the assembly along with my dormmates, watching the rest of the students pour in before the welcome began.

At nine on the dot, the headmaster, a man I recognized from his picture on the website, strode across the stage and took his place behind a podium. Lean and fair, he possessed classic Fae features including pointed ears breaking through his hair. His eyes were like two lumps of burning coal.

"Welcome, new students," he began, his voice magically amplified to reach every seat in the auditorium. "Welcome to the Fae Academy for Halflings. Congratulations on making it through the application process. On behalf of the staff, I want to say we are very proud of you all and happy to have you here with us. As I'm sure you're aware, I'm Headmaster Leaves."

The assembly responded with perfunctory applause. I leaned forward, needing to catch every word. Exhaustion rode hard on me but I had a feeling this was important.

Headmaster Leaves continued. "No, the Academy does

offer scholarships to all our new students, to allow you an environment to compete at the highest level. If you make it through to graduation, you will be expected to participate in a work study, your duties providing for others the way we have provided for you, serving in whatever capacity the Elder Council feels you are able. If you fail out, then you simply leave. End of story."

Wow, that was a great opportunity, to be honest. No other college would offer the same scholarships to regular kids.

"As you all should know, your first year here at the academy is probationary based on your performance. You will be scrutinized on your participation in class as well as your interactions with your classmates and professors. Your every move will be noted and recorded by staff and compiled as part of your overall scores. Every student who comes through our doors begins with one thousand points. Teachers and staff can subtract points for any infraction, large or small. Written grades and test grades add points to this number. Any student who dips below five hundred is automatically expelled."

Expelled.

The word echoed in my head.

I swallowed over the lump suddenly growing in my throat. One thousand points might seem like a lot, but if we had to watch our steps here, *literally*, then the number could drop easily. Did they have a written manifesto on etiquette and expectations? Something I should memorize? I'd have to find out.

"This is a cutthroat system for a reason," Headmaster Leaves continued to explain, and the smile on his face was anything but reassuring, "and that is because only the best of the best are accepted into Faerie. We want to make sure you show your best. Nothing less will be tolerated."

I'm a fraud.

I was starting out on this path hiding my true nature. I was already doomed to fail.

I'm a liar.

But I was already as good as dead to everyone back home. They would have discovered my absence by now. I had nothing to return to if I couldn't hack it here.

Headmaster Leaves went on with the welcome information, going over class structure and what would be expected from us during our time at the school. My mind went blank listening to the rest of the assembly.

Afterward, everyone was shuffled out of the auditorium and back toward the hall I'd only glimpsed the night before. The tables from our earlier check-in had been reassembled and piled high with syllabi and other supplies for classes. This in addition to the literature I'd already received.

Guess my blood test did the trick and ensured my place. For the present, at least. No one had spoken about payment, which led me to wonder if we'd be expected to work to stay or what. Hopefully this wasn't another "payment at the end for an unspecified price" type of deal.

By the time I walked out of the hall, I had a second folder full of paperwork handed out to me by teachers and a massive headache brewing behind my eyes. I tried to ask about breakfast to see if I'd missed it, received no answer, and continued down the hallway pushed along by the crowd, without an exit in sight.

I'd been assigned an upperclassman mentor meant to help me acclimate and would be meeting her shortly. Great. Another pair of eyes ready to examine me, someone else to find me wanting. Acid reflux threatened to eat away at me and if I didn't get something to eat soon, I was going to faint.

"Can someone tell me where to find the cafeteria?" I called out.

No answer.

If I hadn't taken the potion then my nose would have led me there easily. As it was, my senses were dulled and I wasn't sure how to react. I had left my map in the room.

"The cafeteria is on the floor below us. Pretty easy to find. My map must be working because here you are again," a voice said from behind me.

Mike popped from out of nowhere with an identical folder in his arms and an easy grin at the sight of me. It was an effort to keep the surprise from showing on my face. Or to keep my fingers from my hair when I wanted to fidget. Ugh, I looked utterly gross next to him.

How did he manage to look so dang handsome after only a few hours of sleep? No one could say the same about me. I'd caught my reflection in a window, eyes tired and puffy and skin slack and dull from stress. The few wisps of dark auburn hair escaping my braid were lackluster but at least they weren't greasy.

And yeah, no makeup.

The shadow inside of me hadn't lightened with a few hours of sleep. If anything, it had grown. I couldn't let Mike see it.

"You're going to spoil me if you keep showing up when I need help," I told him, smiling, digging my nails into my palms as he stopped at my side. *Get it together, Tavi.*

"How did you sleep?" he asked, stepping closer to avoid the rest of the crowd knocking against him. "I got a few decent hours in myself. One thing I can say about the school, the mattresses are top-notch."

I stared at the ground without really seeing. "I didn't sleep well. It seems I'm having some major delays acclimating."

"Hey, don't beat yourself up about it. Sometimes it takes a while. Is your head feeling better?"

"Barely." I tapped against my temple. "Headache. My

stomach is growling, too." But I didn't want to keep complaining in front of him. He'd already seen me at my worst. Any more and he might decide it wasn't worth being my friend.

"You just need a little something to eat and then you'll feel better. I snuck in a chocolate bar and it's the only reason why I'm standing here right now." Mike glanced around us at the rest of the students as though someone would overhear and come attacking for a piece.

I scoffed, mouth rounded. "And you didn't think to share? I love chocolate."

He shook his head. "Sorry. I can be greedy with my sweets. It's nothing personal, Tavi, let me assure you."

"I understand." I forced a shrug as we walked. "If the roles had been reversed then I wouldn't want to share with you, either."

"You wouldn't share your chocolate with me? Then why am I even here?"

Yeah, I didn't know either. "Your guess is as good as mine," I teased in return.

Mike let his head drop back on his neck, raising his face to the sunlit window and letting the sunshine bathe him. Honest to goodness, it did something to him, brought a radiance to his skin I could never hope to match. It was... magic. "Look, I think I have a few free minutes this afternoon. Why don't you meet me back here to get the rest of your things?" He winked.

Oh. Oh my. "Sounds good. I—"

A male student stepped between us and Mike cleared his throat at the intrusion. "Hey Tavi, allow me to introduce my closest friend, Roman Bantam. Roman, this is Tavi Alderidge. We met last night when I gave her a ride to the school."

It was kind of Mike not to mention the circumstances of said ride.

I forced a grin. "Hi Roman, it's nice to meet you," I said, staring at him. Why hadn't I at least *tried* to shower? I looked like I'd just run a marathon in Sahara-level heat, and here was another handsome Fae boy probably thinking *where did Mike find this one?*

It made me wonder if Mike had a habit of finding the lost and distressed.

But Roman's handshake was strong, his palm warm, and his face was open, easy. Pleasant. "How's it going?" he asked.

This drop-dead half-Fae was the polar opposite of Mike. Roman stood a few inches taller with less muscle, a leaner frame, and darker hair. Chestnut-colored eyes sparked with a kind of inherent intelligence.

I tugged a bit at my t-shirt, wishing I'd insisted on getting my luggage from Mike earlier. Wishing I'd had time to throw a little makeup on my face or do a few other things differently. But then I would have missed the assembly.

"It's a big change from what I'm used to," I answered Roman, making sure to keep my answer vague. "I think I'm going to like it here once I get used to all the people."

Another lie.

He blew out a breath, pushing dark hair away from his eyes. Yes, a perfect contrast to Mike's lightness, I saw, like two different sides of the same coin. "I can understand. I'm not used to being around crowds either and it's a little intimidating. Hey, at least we're here together."

"How long have you two known each other?" I asked.

"Years," Mike supplied. "We were friends before applying to the academy. It was our luck to get in together."

The conversation continued as we made our way down the hall toward the cafeteria. Roman seemed like a personable guy, his jokes charming, his manner easy. It might be the exhaustion, or it might be a sense I hadn't realized I had, but he almost seemed insincere in his charm. I shrugged off the observation. I was used to guys like him in the pack, fully familiar with the behavior. They wanted to make a good impression with the ladies even if it meant laying the charm on thick.

"Anyway, we've gotta get going. Full day." Mike tapped his folder. "I'll meet you here around three to go get your luggage, okay? Go eat, Tavi!"

We said our goodbyes and I watched Mike walk away, leaving me at the entrance to the cafeteria. I'd gotten lucky; that was my only thought. Having someone like him in my corner, while less than ideal in some ways, meant I wasn't really alone here. His devastatingly handsome looks didn't hurt but they sure did leave a girl wondering where and how she fit in.

"Oh my God. Were you *seriously* just talking to Michael Thornwood? You have to be kidding me."

The melodic tone took me by surprise and my breath caught a bit. I turned around quick enough to feel lightheaded, staring at the caramel-skinned upperclassman who'd spoken. "I'm sorry. Who are you?"

Okay, it came out a littler harsher than I wanted. Food just bumped up to priority number one.

The older girl didn't seem to take offense at the statement. She kept her attention focused on Mike and Roman's retreating backsides with a cluck of her tongue. "I'm the person freaking out about you talking to *the* Michael Thornwood," she said. "Do you have any idea who he is?"

"Apparently I have no clue who anyone is at this point. My car broke down on the side of the road last night and Mike stopped to give me a ride." Why was I telling her these things? "I'm not sure what the big deal is."

Finally, Mike disappeared in the crowd and I lost sight of him. The girl let loose a sigh at his disappearance. "Pure gorgeousness." She'd been watching Mike as well, her mouth rounded in an O of surprise. "Goodness, just when I thought I'd seen everything. Tavi Alderidge, you are one lucky girl. A hell of a lucky girl. You *are* Tavi Alderidge, right? I had your picture in my files but I left them on my desk. Jeez, I'm sorry. Melia Haversham." The girl made the introduction as more of an afterthought, too wrapped up in Mike's presence to remember her manners.

I could understand.

Shrugging, I reached out to shake her hand. "Are you my mentor?"

"Girl, *yes*. I've been assigned to you for the duration of your stay at the academy. Well, until I graduate, of course." Then she broke off on another sigh. "I still can't believe you rode here with Michael. *No big deal*, you say. Yeah, it's a big deal because *he's* a big deal. Oh damn, we're going to be late. Okay, let's hurry. I've got something to show you first."

She pulled me away from the cafeteria doors and I cast a glance over my shoulder filled with wistful desire. No snacks for me.

If Melia was flabbergasted at my interaction with Mike, I felt the same way trying to follow her in conversation. She didn't make it easy as she led me back the way I came.

"Come on, come on. You're going to want to see this, Tavi. Can I call you Tavi? Is it short for anything? Like, would you prefer I call you by your full name?"

"Tavi is my full name," I told her.

She hurried me up the staircase and along a small hallway off the main entryway. The space opened up into a grand ballroom with oil portraits hung on three of the walls. The fourth wall was cut through with floor to ceiling sliding glass doors leading out onto a pretty garden patio. Beyond the patio was extensive greenspace perfect for games and lounging in the summer.

"Look." Melia gestured dramatically to an oil painting

dominating the wall to my left, hung centered over a marble fireplace. "Now you'll see why I'm acting a little cuckoo for Cocoa Puffs."

I stepped closer, rubbing my eyes to clear them. The painting showed a handsome gray-haired gentleman in regal navy-and-red clothes with his arm around the shoulder of a smiling woman sitting on a velvet chair before him. To the woman's right, a young man stood, one hand curved around the lapel of his suit jacket. A man who looked suspiciously like Mike.

I shook my head. "I don't understand. Why are you showing me this? Who are these people?"

Melia laughed, the sound rich and honeyed. "Oh Tavi, you are sweet. You don't know a thing about Faerie, do you? That's King Tywin and Queen Laina with their son Michael. Michael Thornwood, the *crown prince* of Faerie."

13

Mike had lied to me about his identity. Everything I thought I knew fell away, and I was left holding the shattered remnants of everything we'd started to build...

"No," I told Melia with a shake of my head, brows drawn together in disbelief. "No, you can't be right. If Mike is the prince of Faerie..." *Dear God!* "...then he's *full* Fae. Why would he be here?"

I stared at the painting for what felt like hours, my head continuing to shake and causing the ache between my ears to deepen.

Melia shrugged, the movement emphasizing her delicate shoulders clad in a white button-up shirt leading down to a dark skirt. School uniform? I'd need to ask her where I could get one. When I came down from the delirium cloud I currently rode.

She was a few inches taller than me with the delicate build I now expected from the Fae. Despite her slender frame, Melia looked as though she could handle her own in a fight. I didn't expect there to be one.

"I wish I knew," she replied with equal disbelief. "I'd heard a whisper he was coming, and the rumor mill said it had something to do with King Ty wanting him to understand more about their people in the mortal realm. Or something like that. But you know how rumors are. You hear dozens of statements and only one is correct. Or maybe none."

"I don't understand."

I floundered to keep up with this new piece of information, my gaze riveted on the painted rendition of Mike. The same Mike who'd carried me into the nurse's office hours earlier and waited for me outside the door. The same guy who'd offered me a ride when I'd been broken down on the side of the road. The same one who'd helped me find my dorm last night.

"I don't either, but at least we can be confused together." Melia flashed me a smile showing very white teeth. "And now you know who he really is and how crazy it seems to see you guys are buddy-buddy."

My chest hollowed out and I merely said, "Yes, I do."

The one friend I'd been grateful to have turned out to not only be a liar, but a royal liar. Someone I could absolutely, positively, under no circumstances let into my life on the off chance he'd find out my secret.

"Come on," she said, hustling me out of the room. "We have a lot to get through today. Time to begin your tour, new friend!"

The more time I spent with Melia, the more I saw how her inside matched her beautiful outside. Her eyes were a vibrant golden-brown lit with an inner fire. Her hair fell in a heavy curled fall of rich brown and dark bronze, the ends brushing around her narrow waist to offset the caramel of her skin.

She moved with ease and grace as though she didn't notice how, when she crossed a room, people stopped to stare at her. A year or two older than me if I had to guess, yet decades ahead when it came to poise.

And she was kind. The kindness took me by surprise.

"You really are going to like it here, I can tell," she told me on our tour as we walked side by side along a third-floor corridor "You aren't one of those first-years who thinks they can make it through probation *just* because you're half Fae. There are so many kids like that, it's honestly shocking. They think they're tough shit until they figure out this isn't a game of favoritism and their so-called natural powers are shared by, like, literally *everyone*."

Classes weren't slated to start until tomorrow morning to give students more time to acclimate. Fine by me. For some reason I felt like I needed more time than most, despite being so excited to be here.

"How can anyone think that?" I wanted to know. "Being half Fae doesn't guarantee you'll be good at your classes. We're all in the same boat."

She gave a little sigh. "I wish I knew. There are just so many who think they are better than everyone else when really, once you come through those gates, the staff lay it out as an equal playing field. We all start at zero once we walk through those doors. Or one thousand, with their point system, and from there the only thing moving you forward is you. Not your magic, and not Mommy and Daddy's money. Take me, for instance. I'm a fourth-year but I had to earn my spot with my claws."

She flexed her fingers for emphasis though the tiny roar she gave made me laugh.

"You don't really have claws," I burst out.

Melia laughed again. "No, girl, I don't, I'm using claws as a metaphor. I got through with my wits." She tapped the side of her head. "I happen to be a natural-born nerd for all things book related."

On the tour, I found out every main hallway throughout the main castle was decorated with golden-framed mirrors. Those I would have to avoid like the plague. Or start walking around wearing a full-body covering like a ghost.

Great, I can't walk anywhere or I will break the potion's spell.

I had to be on guard no matter where I went, clearly.

"You are going to love this. Ready?" Melia stopped outside of the library, pressing her hand against the wall to draw my attention. "You see this? The plaster fairy on the sconce here?"

I nodded.

"There are a bunch of them around the school. Look for them, they're all over the halls and they mark the secret passages most students know nothing about." She dropped her voice to make sure no one else heard her. "You are going to flip. They're super easy to navigate. It's a simple word, the spell to open the door, and once you're inside you say it again to seal the passage from the inside. Then boom! You go wherever you want without anyone the wiser."

Melia closed her eyes, muttering the word *"elaphrium,"* and I watched the wall slowly melt into nothingness. Empty blackness met us, though I had the distinct impression of space accompanied by the damp scent of mold.

"Are first-years *allowed* to use these passages?" I asked, leaning closer to inspect the doorway. *This could definitely come in handy…*

"Girl, no one is supposed to know about them. Now *you* do, and you must use this knowledge only in case of emergency." Her voice dropped into *serious* territory. "Or if you need to get away for a little alone time. Just keep it to yourself. I'm not really supposed to know either. My mentor told me years ago on the down low and now I pass the secret on to you." She clapped a hand on my shoulder. "I'm proud of you already."

I learned two things about Melia then. One, we were going to get along just fine. And two, she had a quirkiness about her that made her unpopular with Fae halflings like my bunkmate, the blondie, despite her good looks.

People not only stared at her because she was pretty but because she didn't give a crap what anyone thought of her and it brought out a lot of jealousy and disdain. She kept her chin raised and the conversation animated in a way putting me instantly at ease. I'd lucked out getting her as my mentor.

She dropped me off at the last part of my orientation for Tuesday, the homeroom meeting. This was a class I'd go to once a week to cover the history of Faerie and meet one on one with the professor assigned to check on my progress.

"You're going to be fine," Melia stated, miming drawing in a deep breath and releasing after a few seconds. Did she see my nerves already? "Nothing to worry about, okay? You have a good head and a keen eye. Don't let anyone tell you different. Anything you need to know, you ask me. If you feel out of place or anything, or if you just need a pick-me-up pep talk, I'm here."

I didn't have to force a smile this time, pausing outside of the carved wood door to my homeroom. "Are you sure you can't stay a little longer?" I asked her.

She rolled her eyes before saying, "Tavi, you managed to make friends with the most influential Fae in the land before you even arrived. I'd say you have everything you need."

It hurt to say goodbye to her, even knowing I'd see her again soon. Melia was definitely the best part of this experience by far.

Then my mind flashed to Mike and the wink he'd sent me earlier. Okay, *one* of the best parts.

"Are you going to stand around and loiter all day or are you going to take a seat, Miss?"

The teacher's voice snapped me out of my head and I

stared at him, tall and slender and gorgeous. I should have expected as much from the staff. They were all full Fae and their kind of bloodline came with perks like perfect hair, a killer body, and a cold smile to match the ice of his eyes and white hair.

My gaze fell on the first row of students who all turned to stare at me, their faces familiar. My bunkmate and her goonies.

Dammit, no.

"Hurry up, hurry up," the teacher urged me with a wave of his hand. "Everyone else is already in their seats and you are wasting our time."

"I'm sorry," I muttered under my breath. There was a single empty chair left in the back and I grabbed it without further hesitation.

My stomach sank as the professor glared daggers at me.

"Well, since we are all here, *finally*, perhaps we can begin with an introduction," he stated.

Throughout the course of the lesson, I learned the man—Professor Hoarfrost—had a very strict hold on his classroom. There were certain things he would and would not tolerate without exception. The students around me lost points for breathing too hard, for raising their hand to answer a question and getting it wrong, and once for losing their pen on the floor and having to retrieve it.

Beneath his scrutiny my mouth went dry and would stay dry for the rest of the class.

Hoarfrost tapped a finger against the blackboard behind him and a map of the area burst into life, white lines appearing from the endless black until a clear picture formed. "Can anyone tell me what year this academy was established in the mortal realm as a separate yet equal entity to Faerie?" he asked.

I raised my hand when his attention fell on me. I knew

the answer to this one; the year was clearly posted on the website. Thank goodness.

Then the pretty blond raised her hand and Hoarfrost nodded his head, ignoring me completely. "Yes, Persephone Glaski?"

Her correct answer earned her an extra fifty points. Fifty points and praise for nothing other than repeating common knowledge available to anyone who could read.

"Very good." His smile warmed by a bit. A second rap on the board had the picture changing. "And who can tell me when we received our charter to pay for our scholarship students?"

All of us, right? Weren't we all scholarship students?

Again, my blond bunkmate raised her hand, higher than the rest of us who knew the answer, and again Hoarfrost picked her to answer.

My stomach soured. He was clearly playing favorites. I had no doubt about it. But I had to keep my mouth shut if I wanted to stay here, safe and far away from Kendrick.

The thought certainly brought my attention back to the situation at hand.

When Persephone Glaski turned around to proudly smirk at me for her third round of extra points, I said nothing, mentally zipping my mouth shut. I kept my face blank.

Persephone was nothing but another pawn, no one I needed to worry myself over. I intended to win. Yes, I'd win.

These were the opening salvos of the battle that would either make or break me.

14

Michael Thornwood, the Crown Prince of Faerie, waited for me outside the cafeteria at three on the dot, and I wasn't sure if I should smile at him or drop into a curtsey.

Oh God, what had I gotten myself into now?

Sunlight shone on the golden strands of his hair, hanging below his ears. His green eyes fixed on mine immediately with a singular focus twisting my stomach into warm knots. Any more time with him and I'd start to crush—if I hadn't stepped into crush territory already. Which wasn't a good idea. In fact, it was a very *bad* idea.

"Hey there, Tavi." He raised a hand in greeting. "You're early."

Early? "No, apparently I'm late, since you're already here," I teased. "Homeroom went well for you?"

Did the rest of our professors know why the prince was here?

He shrugged, unconcerned and amazingly put-together in his dark blue jeans and red v-neck t-shirt. "My orientation ended early and I had a little time to spare. I guess it went well. It was boring."

I didn't know what to say to him, honestly. I hadn't exactly been sure back when he was regular old Mike, but now? Talking to a prince, for cryin' out loud?

"Let's go get your suitcase," he said. "It's a nice day outside and I'm sure we could both use a walk and fresh air."

"It's not much. I can get it myself if you point me in the direction of the car." We fell into step beside each other. Maybe I should have stayed a step behind him. Were people looking at us?

Oh, *definitely*.

I struggled not to wrap my arms around my chest against their attention. I really needed to shower.

"Nonsense, I'm happy to help," Mike said with a chuckle and a twist of his lips. "And I'm not giving you the keys to my car. I've seen what you do to your vehicles. Can't risk you steering *my* poor girl into a ditch."

I couldn't help but laugh in return. "It wasn't my fault! I bought the worst car on the lot for this trip. I was in a hurry to get here." Then I shut my mouth. I didn't need to give too much away. But he didn't press me about Big Dan, and I was grateful.

We chatted lightly as Mike led the way to the school's parking lot. I didn't remember much of the walk. My attention was focused on Mike and how closely we walked together, our arms knocking occasionally. Was I supposed to stay a certain number of steps behind him? Was I supposed to address him in any kind of certain way? *Your Highness* felt stuffy after everything he'd helped me through.

He was *still* helping me.

Mike clicked the keys to open up the back door to the car and then proceeded to drag my suitcase out. "This is large enough to fit a body in," he grunted. "What did you put in here?"

I watched the way he moved, the way his muscles bunched and flexed beneath tanned skin. The red shirt brought out the startling color of his eyes and put me in mind of spring grasses yet again.

More than a small part of me warmed this time.

Prince Michael Thornwood of Faerie.

No, bad idea, I told the warmth, urging it to disappear and quickly. I didn't need any other complications, let alone entertaining dirty thoughts about someone like Michael. Someone who was way out of my league on a good day and was in a bad position to rat me out if my secret ever came to light.

"Yeah, I know it's heavy," I said at last, purposely turning my gaze to the ground and my dirty sneakers. The most comfortable pair I owned. "I may have brought too many things."

"You packed everything," he teased. "Let me guess. You chose some of your favorite rocks from your garden so you wouldn't get homesick."

"No rocks, but everything of importance, because there's nothing to go back to."

Dammit!

Open mouth, insert foot.

Mike stopped and stared at me, leaning heavily on the top of the suitcase. "Tavi, I'm sorry."

I scrambled to smooth over my last statement. "It's not a big deal, don't worry about it." I'd already said too much. "Let's just say I'm going to make sure I do the best I can to stay at the academy. This place..." I turned to look at the castle looming through the trees. "This is my future. I have no reason to go home."

And no one would accept me back if I couldn't hack it here.

His smile widened. "I'd think nothing less of you." He kept the suitcase in hand as we walked back up the hill toward the castle, and he didn't press the issue.

I appreciated that, too. No prying into my past. I did the same for him even when I was dying to know about his presence at the school. He pulled the suitcase along the winding cement path through the trees until the castle loomed before us.

We chatted about the school's expectations and the point system. We chatted about the weather and what would be done about my car, presumably still on the side of the road. But we didn't talk about our pasts, and I was pleased Mike left the subject alone.

Everyone else had already gone to dinner by the time we walked into the dorm. Another meal missed. Looking over at Mike, somehow I wasn't upset about it, no matter how my stomach grumbled for me to fill it.

He hauled the suitcase up to my bunk when I didn't know what to do with it. "You're going to have a hard time later," he warned. "Unless you take everything out. Pretty sure the drawers on the left are yours. The one set into the wall there, you see?"

I followed where he pointed and nodded. "I'd rather have everything up where I can sort through it in my own time than leave it on the floor. Besides, I'm not sure the girl beneath me would like coming back to see a giant suitcase next to her bed." He continued to watch me and I picked at my shirt, refusing to meet his gaze. "What's the matter?"

"I'm not sure. You seem different."

"I'm still just me," I replied easily. "Besides, this is the first time you've really looked at me in direct sunlight. Otherwise it's been dark." I held my hands out at my side, head quirked and single eyebrow raised, model pose. Wondering if he liked what he saw and why it would matter so much to me that he did.

"I guess you're right." Then he shook his head when the realization struck him. "Oh. Oh, man, I see. I get it now."

"What?" I asked anxiously.

His gaze went direct even as his mouth smoothed into a tense line. "I get why you're looking at me like that. Someone told you. About me. Who I really am."

The knots in my gut smoothed. I'd almost thought he'd figured *me* out. "I'm sorry, Your Highness. My mentor did. She...ah, she showed me your portrait on the wall in the great hall." I flashed him a sheepish grin.

Mike flinched at the title and glanced left and right over his shoulder before taking a step closer until I felt caged between him and the ladder to my bunk. Leaning toward me until I ached to close the distance. "Tavi, I'm still just me, too. I'm the guy who gave you a ride last night when you needed help. Nothing has changed," he insisted. My chest hollowed out when he groaned. "Everyone always gets weird when they find out who I am. Maybe can it on the *Highness* stuff."

I pulled my finger across my lips, mimicking a zipper, then snorted for good measure.

I couldn't tell him I wasn't being odd about him being a prince, although it had certainly crossed my mind more than once. But if we remained friends, and he found out I was really a shifter, then it could spell ruin for me. I would never get into Faerie. He would be obliged to tell his parents and they would hand me right over to my uncle. Or worse, Kendrick.

Not only the thought of being returned to my so-called fated mate, but the look on Mike's face right now, at this moment. Both tore me apart. The pain of heartbreak I saw casting a shadow on his features. My heart clenched in response and all thoughts of Kendrick disappeared.

"Hey, you aren't *my* prince. I grew up human." Or close enough. I playfully tapped him on the shoulder to get him to move back. "I just thought maybe you were too cool to be my friend. Although we might have a problem if you expect me to curtsey every time we see each other. I'd trip over my own feet."

His smile returned slowly, and it lit something inside of me. "Maybe you're too cool to be *my* friend. Did you ever think of it in those terms?"

I looked around the empty room, thinking about how we were missing out on dinner and I didn't even mind. "Me? Cool? You have me mistaken for someone else. Although just maybe we can be too cool as friends together."

Mike held out a hand. "Shake on it."

We did, and that was that.

A week later, rough hands shook me awake. I tried to burrow down into my pillow until those same hands, most assuredly not a part of my dream, yanked at my hair and I jumped up with a scream.

"Keep it down, newbie. Jeez. It's not like we *hurt* you."

I knew the voice. It wasn't a dream, more like a nightmare. The nightmare of my reality.

"What do you want, Persephone?" I grumbled.

"I want you to wake up," she said snidely.

When I cracked open my eyes, Persephone and two of her goons were there staring at me over the edge of the bunk like little gremlins. Their eyes practically glowed in the dark.

They'd dressed in black and had their hair in long ponytails down their backs.

"A bunch of us are going outside to play Capture the Scroll. Do you want to come play?" she asked.

Glancing over toward the wall, I saw the batter of rain against the front window.

"It's raining."

"Don't you think we know?"

I shifted and dragged my blanket closer. "I'm sorry. I don't want to get out of bed for some stupid game of yours."

"Tavi, get real. You're the *outsider* here. I know, you know, everyone who has met you knows you don't belong." She shared a smile with her friends. "But winning a game of Capture the Scroll can go a long way toward changing your image."

Like I'd believe she wanted to help me. She'd rather toss me out the window than work toward "changing my image."

"I don't even know how to play," I hedged.

She leaned forward further, smile widening. "Exactly. We grew up playing Fae games and you did not. It's about time you learn a thing or two. We're giving you the opportunity to learn. And you *seriously* want to lie there and blow us off? How lazy can you get?" This to the other girls, who agreed with her with a low snicker.

I also *seriously* didn't want to get out of bed because I needed my sleep. Rain, plus a game I didn't know how to play, plus Persephone more than likely plotting to make me look like an idiot? It sounded awful. No thanks.

"One game," I finally agreed, against my better judgment. "And then I'm out of there."

Persephone nodded. "Of course. One game."

I caught the second look she shared with her friends. This one full of promise to make my night a living hell.

Barbara had warned me to stay out of direct moonlight.

Or was it the full moon? *Gah*, I knew I should have written these things down. It wouldn't have been a problem at all if I'd stayed in my bunk, which remained in the shadows most nights. With the rain pouring down outside, which meant no moon, I could manage one game with relative ease. But I had to make sure I followed the rules of the potion no matter how Persephone taunted me. My safety came before the acceptance of my peers.

But with the rain…

"Fine." I pushed out of my bunk, crawling down the ladder with care and grabbing a sweatshirt from a nearby peg. The rest of the girls waited for me to dress, to lace my sneakers, before gesturing for me to follow them outside.

I raised my face to the sky, letting the water sluice down my cheeks. My hair sopped up the moisture and hung in heavy red strands. I drew in a deep breath and held it inside my lungs.

I should have been sleeping, the logical part of me growled, upset at being woken up for some stupid game. I should have been conserving my energy in preparation for classes tomorrow. Instead, I trailed behind Persephone and her *meanions* toward the center lawn of green I'd only glimpsed in the daylight. It stretched away from the circular drive and extended toward the border of forest trees keeping us hidden from the outside world.

"What are the rules to this game?" I asked, striving to be overheard above the relentless rain.

"You've heard of Capture the Flag, haven't you? It's along the same lines, except more dangerous because we can use magic," one of her friends snapped. She glanced over her shoulder at me and her one look held enough disdain to fill a crater on the moon.

"I've played it before. It's just been a long time." I tried not to affect the same kind of tone. These were the people I needed to compete against for my place here. I didn't want to stoop to their level.

Although maybe tonight they'd see what I could really do *without* magic.

"Try to keep up with us, will you?" Persephone called back to me. "There are the boys."

And when we reached the center green, I saw Mike waiting there with Roman at his side, along with a group of other half-Fae from the boys' dorm.

His eyes found mine without hesitation, his hair a beacon in the gloom. "Hey, Tavi. I didn't think you'd be joining us tonight." He inclined his head in greeting.

Persephone moved to his opposite side, sliding her hands along Mike's shoulders in a proprietary move. "I finally managed to get her out of bed, in case you were wondering why we're late. This should prove to be a fun game, don't you think?"

I didn't like the way my blood boiled while watching the two of them together. I didn't like the way part of me, a *large* part of me, wanted to stride over and punch Persephone right in the face. I knew how to make it hurt.

Rather than give in to my violent desire, I forced a smile on my face. "So, let's get the game started already."

Moonlight was something to fear for the first time in my life. Luckily, clouds covered the sky and kept the moon from sight. But the weather could change at any moment. I'd have to make this quick despite the rain.

Roman walked over and gave me a short rundown on the rules and soon we were split into two teams. I found myself beside Mike, balancing on the balls of my feet, ready to capture the scroll wherever it landed.

One of the boys next to him clenched it in his hand, his lips pursed in preparation for the spell to send the magically-protected parchment airborne.

"You're going to do fine," Mike told me. He blinked against the rain. "Follow my lead."

"I think I can handle it," I replied swiftly, and kept my eyes focused on the paper.

"I don't want you to think you have to win just because Persephone is super competitive. She can be a little crazy sometimes."

I didn't like the way he spoke about her. "I didn't realize the two of you were such good friends."

"She runs in the same circles as my parents and some of their friends. I wouldn't say we're close, exactly—"

"Tavi," Persephone snapped. She'd affected a similar posture, her feet apart and balanced, her arms loose at her sides. "Focus."

Oh yeah, she didn't like me talking to Mike. *Good.* Her irritation added another level to this game.

They didn't expect my reflexes. I took satisfaction in their surprise. When the scroll shot off into the air, I bolted after it, my shifter nature reacting without hesitation despite the spell keeping it contained. I rebounded off one of the trees, twisting my body midair and reaching out to grab the scroll before it even hit the ground.

"Foul!" one of Persephone's goons called out.

I clenched my fist around the scroll and dropped down to a crouch. "It's not a foul," I argued.

Mike came up behind me and clapped a hand down on the top of my head. "Good job! You're a natural."

This time, my smile was easy. "Damn right."

"Throw it again," Persephone demanded, fixing the boy who'd uttered the spell with a look designed to peel the flesh from his bones. "And this time, let's make sure we have it in play for more than five seconds."

We continued with the game, and now my dodging became real as the moon peeked out between the clouds here and there between the raindrops. There were a few near-misses where I had to twist away seconds before I landed in a shaft of light. Like a damn vampire instead of a creature who'd once run free beneath the same light.

I missed the pull of the moon. Felt entirely too human.

Still, time and again I captured the scroll before Persephone or anyone else had an opportunity to grab it. Soon the last bit of sleep left me and my movements became sharper. Faster. It became a game I played with myself. To see how fast I could move, to see how adroitly I could play, how I could show the rest of these girls who they were really dealing with.

I raised my arm to the sky with the scroll in hand yet again.

This time, *this* win, Mike came over and grabbed me around the waist. "You're doing a great job! What did I tell you?" he crowed to the others as he twirled me in a circle. "How did you get so good?"

"Natural talent."

I was breathless. I was floating and flying in his arms and I never wanted the moment to end. We tumbled to the ground beside each other and the dampness sank into my clothing. My arms flung out to my side, fingertips grazing against something as I stared at Mike, at his smile.

Whatever my outflung hand had found felt familiar. What... A shoe?

I broke his hold on me and pushed up on my elbows to grab the shoe, staring for the longest time. I glanced down at my own feet to see if I'd accidentally knocked my own sneakers off during the game. Mine were still there, and so were Mike's, as well as the rest of the group.

"Whose is this?" I asked, holding it up. "Someone lose a shoe?"

Mike shifted to stare at the shoe, and then to take the

same inventory I'd taken. Nope, not one of ours. I was about to toss it away when something else caught my eye, flopping back onto the wet grass as I slowly raised my other arm and pointed straight up.

Lodged in the tree above us was a body. Dead, from the looks of it.

15

I didn't remember which of the girls screamed. Might even have been me.

I didn't remember anyone going to fetch Headmaster Leaves, bringing him out along with some of the other professors. I didn't remember being instructed not to touch anything, although that wouldn't have been my first inclination, I was sure.

I also didn't remember being shuffled back to the dorm along with the rest of the girls and changing out of my drenched clothing, unable to stop shivering, the whole of me filled with the heavy lead weight of dread. The rest of the night was a blur until the sun rose, the headmaster making sure the rest of the class kept a healthy distance from us until we could be questioned by the authorities.

The rain had stopped finally. I realized when I followed the rest of the girls into the auditorium for the second time in as many weeks to speak to the headmaster, who demanded an explanation though I knew the detectives who were still on the scene hadn't found much beyond the identity of the body.

The boy we'd found in the tree last night turned out to be the top candidate for the first-year class, or so rumor had it. From the tone of his voice, even Headmaster Leaves had expected the deceased boy to be the top of our class by the first elimination, with a clear path to earning his place not only at the academy but in Faerie.

Those dreams were stolen from him and yet no one could figure out a motive. It was a waste of life. A waste of talent.

I didn't understand why either, and it scared me.

Wasn't it supposed to be safe here? Wasn't this place my escape from my one true danger in this world: the ceremonial binding to a man who would torment me for his own amusement?

I tried not to think about those things as I sat down next to Melia in the cafeteria afterward. She saw them on my face anyway.

"You look like you've seen better days," she said at once, raising her gaze and chewing as she stared at me. "Did you get any sleep last night?"

"Not much," I admitted. Rubbing the side of my head, I went on to say, "I'm the one who first saw the guy, Mel. Sweet dreams aren't exactly on the menu tonight."

"Yeah, I understand, but you're going to have a hard time getting through your classes if you don't sleep." She watched me shuffle in my seat, uneasy.

I scratched my head. "I'm sorry. I'm a little bit preoccupied with things lately."

"No one blames you."

I glanced up at the familiar voice. Mike and Roman stood there for a moment before settling into the empty seats across from us.

"It was a wild night," Roman agreed. "The police came to our dorm room and went through Loudon's things. Took most of them away as evidence."

"You...you..." Melia snapped her jaw open and shut. They'd never sat with us before. It left her visibly surprised and tongue-tied for the first time since I'd met her.

"A dead student," I mused, my hands still clenched on my lunch tray. "I'm not sure *wild night* really covers things. Try insane. Ridiculous. Scary."

"It came as a shock to everyone," Roman said. "Poor Loudon. He was a really great person."

"Does anyone know what really happened? I mean, have they examined the body?"

Mike shook his head. "I haven't heard anything yet, but I'm sure the staff is trying to keep things hush-hush. My guard detail has been extra cautious while the cops are here."

I started. "The cops are still here? Why?" And also...Mike had a guard detail?

"To continue their investigation, I'd imagine," Roman answered as though I should have expected the answer.

"I...I kind of thought the Fae would take care of matters themselves," I admitted.

"And normally they would, but the kid was half-human, and policy dictates the human authorities must be involved in the proceedings."

I looked at Mike. "You said your guard detail has been extra cautious?" I hadn't even noticed his guards. Wasn't I supposed to be on high alert? Apparently, my observational skills were pretty crummy.

"Yes. They want me to leave here and return home until the matter is settled, but..." Mike paused and spared a glance at his friend. "Classes are going on like normal and I don't want to leave. If the academy is going forward with business as usual, then I'm staying. End of discussion."

"What do your parents have to say about the incident, Your Hi—M-Mike?" Melia asked. She'd finally found her voice.

Mike shrugged and grabbed a piece of bacon. "They haven't said anything yet. I'm not sure if they're just waiting for more info from the police or if they're trying to formulate a public statement for the benefit of the school and I'm simply not privy to it yet."

He took a bite and ripped the bacon in half.

"Don't worry about it," Roman answered easily. Somehow, he'd become the voice of reason. "I'm sure it was an isolated incident. We were the unlucky ones who found him, but with the security at the school, I'm sure this isn't going to happen again."

I finished my eggs and moved on to my hash browns, dipping them in ketchup one by one. "I can't help but worry," I told them all between bites. "This kind of thing isn't supposed to happen. The academy is supposed to be a safe place."

Mike reached across the table and placed his hand on top of mine for a brief moment, giving me a light pat. "No one is going to hurt you, Tavi."

I jerked my hand away. "You can never be too careful."

I'd saved the best for last, taking a bite of my biscuit and gravy, watching Mike and Roman talking to Melia about our game of Capture the Scroll last night and taking her through it from start to finish.

And felt suddenly like a bucket of ice-cold water had been thrown over me.

There was no water, not really. But there was cold. The cold bit down deep to the marrow of my bones and I stared at my hands, the skin rippling before my vision went blurry. I grabbed on to the side of the table when it felt like an earthquake shook me, unable to keep from groaning.

"Hey, girl. Are you okay? You look a little pale."

I glanced up to see Melia rising, crossing around to crouch at my side to bring her to my eye level.

Clearing my throat, I tried to think of a reason why my potion spell had apparently broken. I felt my shifter senses returning, vision finally clear and sharp, sense of smell rising to the point where I could focus on the sweet-smelling sweat on Mike's forehead.

"Is there garlic in this?" I pointed to the gravy then hissed as a rush of cold had my fingers shaking. It was the only explanation I could find. Sure enough, the more I tuned in to the scents, the more I could make out the tang of garlic.

Melia reached out to steady me when I tipped to the side, my balance off. "I'm not sure. Why? Are you a vampire?" she joked, though I could hear the concern in her tone.

The rest of them laughed while the whole of me filled with dread. Did they see me for myself? Was there anything different, now that I'd been exposed?

"I have to go."

I bolted out of the chair, leaving my tray behind and fighting to clear a path out of the cafeteria.

It didn't matter what anyone thought. All that mattered was reaching the dorm and getting a new vial of potion. I kept one hand raised to my face as though to shield it as I ran. One vial behind already, I thought, pushing through the door to my dorm out of breath.

At least the room was empty.

I fumbled up the ladder and thrust my pillow to the side, flipping the latch on the box and grabbing the second vial. Chugging it down. The concoction again tasted absolutely disgusting but it worked immediately. There were no crazy side effects this time. I didn't fall to my knees on the edge of death's door. My head swam a bit and I watched my skin crawl as though an army of ants were making their way from wrist to elbow.

Disgusting.

But it worked.

I felt an invisible blanket of haze and heat fall over me, a dulling of my shifter senses until my inner wolf sank down with a low growl.

Damn garlic.

Who put garlic in sausage gravy, anyway? I hadn't been thinking about the possibility. I hadn't been thinking about anything besides the body we'd found. I was going to have to be much more careful in the future.

My first class of the afternoon began at one, giving me enough time to compose myself before I sat at what had become my usual desk. I struggled to focus and make a good impression when I couldn't seem to get my brain on the right track.

A dead half-Fae boy.

A contender for top of the class.

No apparent motive. No real leads.

I couldn't make sense of the text in front of me. The teacher's voice had become a blur of syllables and none of them were clear. Part of me wondered if things like this happened often and the school just pushed it under the rug… or if my being here had something to do with his death.

No, it couldn't possibly have anything to do with me. I didn't even know the boy. No one here knew about my wolf side. The potion made sure of it. Besides, if they did, they would come after me, not anyone else.

A knock on the door interrupted the lecturing professor and she stopped, magic fluttering around her fingertips. "May I help you, Ma'am?"

I didn't recognize the woman at the door, although her face was vaguely familiar to me. "I need to see Miss Alderidge, Mr. Meuller, and Miss Elspeth, please."

I stood slowly along with two others and we shared a look. They'd been outside with me last night playing Capture the Scroll when we found the student in the tree. My heart dropped to the bottom of my feet. The headmaster had spoken to all of us. Now it was the police's turn.

The three of us followed the office assistant over to a private room just off the headmaster's quarters. I recognized his title on the nameplate outside the door. We were told to sit, trying not to stare at each other as we were urged into the office one by one by a man with a shiny pewter badge pinned to his jacket lapel.

The human inspector the school had called in. It made sense, I told myself, for him to talk to us as well. He was doing his job and trying to get a sense of what had happened last night. It didn't lessen my terror.

I tried to wait my turn while my insides churned and the rest of me felt hot and itchy. The two others were called in first, their interviews lasting less than fifteen minutes total before they walked out past me with pale faces and gazes averted. Soon I waited alone.

And couldn't help but overhear the low murmur of voices coming from the other room.

"I refuse to allow a werewolf into my school. Tell the force to send someone else."

My spine went iron-straight and I nearly fell out of my chair at the words.

A werewolf. Had they somehow figured out my secret?

Had Nurse Julie really seen something weeks ago when she'd scrutinized me with the knowing look in her eyes?

Oh no…

"I might be a werewolf but I work for the human world. Do you want humans to know about your magic school by revealing my true nature to them and asking someone else to take the case?

Because I'm the best on the task force and the only one truly equipped to deal with your little problem here."

My eyes widened as I figured it out at last. They weren't talking about me. Whoever Headmaster Leaves argued with, they still hadn't found me out. I glanced left and right, making sure there was no one else in the room with me. Then crept forward and pressed my ear against the door to hear better.

"I'm simply not comfortable letting someone like you handle the case. You'll pardon me if I have a little hesitation to move forward with this investigation," the headmaster stated. I heard his fingers drum against the desktop as he sighed.

Fabric rustled. "If neither of us says a word, then your kind and my kind remain hidden. Safely. But you have to let me do my job without question. You can't follow along behind me or sit in on my interviews. You certainly cannot speak to my superiors at the station about having me removed."

"Without question?" Headmaster Leaves squawked. "You're asking a lot, Wilson."

Someone growled, the sound ending on a groan. "I'm asking for the *minimum* you would afford a detective of any other kind. Stay out of my way and I'll find your killer. End of story. Do you understand?"

The headmaster didn't like the other man's closing statement, if his indignant sputter was an indication of his feelings.

The door swung open and I scrambled back, nearly making it to the chair in time before Leaves and the detective strode forward. The *werewolf* detective, I told myself, schooling my face into a semblance of nonchalance even as my heart raced. Headmaster Leaves didn't even look at me on his way out the door, his teeth clenched and a muscle twitching in his jaw. Apparently, he'd been booted from his office for this.

"Miss Alderidge?" the detective barked out, staring down at me and not liking what he saw.

Were my cheeks flushed? I swallowed hard and nodded.

With a sniff he gestured for me to follow him. "Come."

I paused for the briefest moment.

"Well, come on!"

I jumped at the sound of his voice and poured on the speed, closing the door behind me.

Lean and sinewy, the detective moved with the supernatural grace inherent to shifters, a kind of predatory slowness coupled with a surety and confidence matched by no other species.

Clearly the detective had worked hard to cultivate a thuggish appearance. I could understand how the headmaster would underestimate him even if the man weren't a werewolf. Still, beneath the loose cut of the jacket I noticed muscle and definition. Not a handsome man, but the detective defined masculinity from his black hair to his scuffed boots.

God, I hoped he sucked at his job.

He gestured for me to take a seat and I did so with as much poise as I could muster. Not much, as it turned out. I almost fell off the edge of the seat when I missed it by an inch.

"Miss Alderidge, are you feeling all right?" His nostrils flared. "Your heart is nearly beating right out of your chest and I can sense your perspiration."

I tried not to tug at the white button-up shirt I wore beneath my school blazer. "I'm fine."

"And you're the one who found the body?" he barked. When I stared at him, the werewolf chuckled. "I apologize for diving right in. You're my last interview of the day. I'm

Detective Douglas Wilson, by the way, lead investigator on this case."

I wanted to tell him it was nice to meet him but I couldn't manage to force the words out. "How can I help you?" I asked instead.

"I want you to take me through everything from last night. We've heard from some of the others about the game you were playing." He glanced down to consult a piece of paper in front of him. "A game of Capture the Scroll? From what I understand, your reflexes were better than your peers expected them to be. That is the singular consistent statement to all their versions of events."

The rest of the blood drained from my head. "Yes, sir. I'm sorry to tell you they underestimate me in a number of ways. I'm not well liked."

"Why, Miss Alderidge?"

I shrugged, uncomfortable with his attention. "I'm new. People who have already found their group of friends don't usually take kindly to newcomers. Especially those who are half-human." I tried not to stress the last word too much.

Detective Wilson continued to stare at me with his shoulders tense and his face giving nothing away. "I find it a little hard to believe. Your entire incoming class is made up of new students who surely do not all know each other. Why should *you* be singled out?"

I shrugged again. *Calm those shoulders!* "Your guess is as good as mine," I told him.

He wouldn't even blink and a wave of terror crashed down on me. Was Detective Wilson able to smell me even under the effects of the potion? I had no way of knowing. The room was suddenly too small, too hot, the walls closing in around us.

"Why don't you tell me everything. Take me through the evening as you remember it." He grabbed a pen from his jacket pocket, setting the tip against a fresh sheet of paper. "Spare no detail."

I walked him through my memories of last night, answering whatever questions he had no matter how strange they seemed. The clock ticked on and I noticed thirty minutes had passed. I'd missed the rest of my class.

He kept me longer than he'd kept the others.

"I think we're done for the day," Wilson stated finally, leaning back in the chair after another ten minutes of questioning.

"Okay. Thank you?"

Was it the appropriate thing to say in this kind of situation?

"If you remember anything else…call me immediately." He slapped his business card down between us before standing. Cracking his neck with a single twist of his head. "You're free to go. *For now.*"

16

I lived on a diet of nerves and chewed fingernails, waiting for the first elimination of the semester to arrive.

A month of classes at the Halflings Academy passed alarmingly fast, bringing us closer to the elimination where the school culled the weak links, and I prayed I wasn't one of them. The first year, as I found out, focused mostly on book work and history until fall break would bring the first cull, followed by a shift in emphasis to spell work and magic.

Magic... The thought excited me.

Unfortunately, I'd never been good at book work. I had a terrible memory and a bad track record with taking tests. Uncle Will had lamented my unfortunate memory many evenings during my internship with his firm, where most of his coworkers had taken to leaving sticky notes of reminders for me to find. *Everywhere.*

I'd once found a note on the inside of the women's bathroom stall reminding me to order ink for the office printer.

If I couldn't remember to order ink then how could I be

expected to pass a test on Faerie history and lore? It was all new to me.

Notes wouldn't help me here. I spent every waking moment of those first four weeks studying, deep in the books and doing my best to memorize everything, and maintaining a constant low level of anxiety. At least my hair wasn't falling out. Yet.

Fall break would be the first real test to see if I belonged, I thought, biting my nails yet again, surrounded by books.

If I failed now, I had nowhere to go. Nowhere else to turn. So far, luck had been on my side. I hadn't sensed an inkling of Kendrick Grimaldi or any other member of either pack. There were no more killings, and though Persephone remained an annoyance I found if I stuck to the library when I studied, I rarely saw her.

It became my personal sanctuary.

I also hadn't heard from Detective Wilson since my interview, nor seen him sniffing around the castle. His business card burned a hole in my pocket all the way back to the dorm and I ended up sticking it into the box with the rest of my potions. It sat there, a reminder, when I opened the lid every thirteen days.

Talk about the dead student in the tree eventually died down and became old news, Loudon's identity known but the murder unsolved. The police hadn't found a shred of evidence leading to a culprit. Soon the speculations were only a low simmer as the rest of my class stuck their noses to the books and got down to work.

We all wanted a place here.

Everyone felt the same kind of pressure I did, the pressure to make the cut and move on to our second semester. Outside, the trees began to change color from emerald green—the same color as Mike's eyes—to dappled shades of red and orange and yellow with the approaching autumn.

Then we were two weeks into October.

The only real problem I'd run into was the food. The damn food—I'd found out the hard way—I couldn't eat because the academy chef loved garlic the way some people loved chocolate, and the more time passed the more garlic he added to every single dish. I ended up having a salad and fruit most days because I couldn't take the chance anything else contained his precious garlic.

The big day arrived, and I spent more time than I wanted hyperventilating in a panic. I muttered a curse, struggling to take deep breaths thanks to our laundry service overly starching academy uniforms, the seams and creases too crisp to make for easy movement. The fabric scratched at me. Everywhere.

"Don't be nervous," Melia soothed, walking beside me on the way to the auditorium where first-years would be tested.

"How can I not be nervous?" I asked breathlessly. "This is the make or break moment. I'm going to pass out. I can't breathe."

She blew a raspberry designed to lighten the mood. "You don't have to think about it in those terms. This isn't your make or break moment."

"Don't I?" I said with a fake laugh, attempting to moisten my dry mouth. "You're safe. You're already almost out of here and on your way toward earning a spot in Faerie."

"But I remember being in your position," she replied. "I remember being so crazy out of my mind, I wanted to rip my hair out. In fact, I did. I ended up with a tiny nickel-sized bald spot above my right ear. And you know what?"

"What?"

"It didn't help me pass my exams. It took forever for the hair to grow back and I had myself going crazy for no reason." Melia stopped and grabbed me by the shoulders to make her point. "Just concentrate on *you*. Forget everyone else, forget about the competition aspect of the process. That's what the professors want you to focus on. They want you worried about everyone else so they have you stressing and they can weed out the weak. Focus on you and your literature because it's the only way to get through it. Keep your mind sharp and your wits about you."

I pressed against my roiling stomach. "You tell me this now? Exams are literally five minutes away."

"Then get in there and kick a little butt, baby girl. You got this!" She sent me on my way with a playful swat on the rear and a smile. It did nothing to settle my nerves but I appreciated her enthusiasm.

Melia believed in me. I couldn't let her down.

The oddity of the situation struck me as I took a seat, a quill popping out of the air in front of me along with a bottle of black ink. Months earlier I'd planned on finishing up school with the rest of my class, regular shifters like I'd pretended to be. With my friends Dawn and Jason, and together we'd make our plans for the future. College choices. Majors. Normal things.

Now look at me.

The rest of the auditorium went quiet and the silence had mass. It had depth and substance. At one point I remember looking out across the space and trying to find Mike's familiar head. I wondered how he felt about the tests, and if he did poorly, would his parents force the school to keep him here or would he have to be cut like any other person?

But those thoughts wouldn't help me pass. They didn't help me in the least.

I didn't remember anything about taking the test. The entire three-hour time limit passed in a blur and I wasn't sure if I answered all the questions or passed out at my seat in a sure flunk.

A week later, the headmaster called an assembly to announce the students who had been cut. I didn't have any nails left on my hands at this point. I'd chewed them all down to the quick while Melia laughed at me and questioned my eating habits, telling me I'd gotten too skinny from my special diet. Ha ha.

I didn't remember the assembly, either. Not until it was over and I stood outside the door with the marks sheet in my hand.

I was in the top 25 for the whole class.

Top 25.

Me.

Me?

The next thing I knew, Melia had me by the shoulders yet again, drawing me into a dance of epic proportions that had the others around us grimacing and moving out of the way before we stepped on them.

"Didn't I tell you? You had nothing to worry about!" she squealed.

"What's going on?" I said in a daze.

"Girl, you did so well! All your worry for nothing. You only have to stay in the top 100 to be safe, and look at you! You're in the *top 25*. You beat my first-year scores by a long mile." Melia paused, pushing a crazy curl of hair away from her eyes. "What did I get? I think I was in the top 60 or something. Nothing to write home about, not like yours. I knew you were going to do great things."

"I'm not sure how this happened," I murmured, allowing her to move my limbs in a loose dance until my heart lodged in my throat.

"Let's go get celebratory ice cream!" Melia insisted. "You deserve it."

"Wait a minute. Ice cream? We're not allowed off campus."

"Have I taught you *nothing* so far? Those secret passages, Tavi! One of them leads directly into the kitchen where we can pillage the lunch lady's personal stash of sweet treats. I do it all the time. They have no clue."

Melia linked her arm through mine and led me away, the paper hanging limp in my hand.

Top 25...

It had to be some kind of trick.

No one went home for fall break as I had expected they would. I already had excuses prepared as to why I chose to stay in the dorm instead of visiting my family. There was no one I wanted to see, anyway. Except for Elfwaite. I would have loved to see the pixie and let her know what a crazy twist my life had taken because of her.

"My score was in the top ten," Persephone gloated later that evening in the dorm. Blond hair fell in long waves down to the small of her back and she ran her brush along the length. "Number 7. Can you believe it?"

"You are beautiful and smart," one of her friends said in a simpering tone.

I had a book open in my lap. I'd had to adjust to not using a mirror, and since coming to the school, I'd stopped wearing makeup. It did knock my confidence down a bit but not so much to have me worry what someone like Persephone thought of me.

"Good for you," I whispered under my breath.

She didn't hear me. She didn't need to.

Persephone held her hand mirror aloft, staring at herself and watching each brush of her hair with her lips pursed in a perfect pout. "It was never a question of me making it through to next semester," she continued. "I always knew I would do well. I just didn't know I would do *that* well. But then again, my parents expect perfection from me."

"You're always so good with tests," another of her friends gushed.

What a sorry pack of sycophants.

"It's a question of intelligence. Intelligence and class, both of which I possess in abundance. Not to mention my good looks." Persephone stared at herself in the mirror. In her reflection she caught sight of me, her eyes narrowing. "But I suppose not everyone can make those same claims."

Yeah, dig at me again.

"I got top 25. It's nothing to turn your nose up at," I replied. And knew immediately. I shouldn't have given in to her power games. She'd made the remark on purpose, of course, and I fell into her trap.

Something about Persephone's voice just rubbed me the wrong way and made me want to fight back.

"You might have gotten through with your grades," she began, brushing her hair until the strands gleamed, "but nothing is going to help you with your hairdo. I mean, look at you, Tavi. Do you always take such *pride* in looking like you crawled out of a gutter? Your hair is like a rat's nest. Come on, look at yourself. Maybe you'll see why we all laugh at you."

She flashed the mirror in my direction. I glanced over, eyes locking on the glass because I hadn't been thinking.

I felt my spell shatter.

The same cold washed over me like taking a dunk in a river in winter, my skin rippling and my stomach bending over backwards to make me sick. Oh, *no!*

Persephone was giggling. "What's the matter, Tavi? You can't stand seeing your own reflection? Do you think it's going to turn you to stone? Maybe we should start calling you Medusa!"

I heard her as through a wall of cement, clawing for the box of potions before anyone noticed something was really wrong with me. My skin itched, squirming, shifting as the spell dissipated to reveal my wolf.

A swell of anger ripped through me and the she-wolf part of me snapped her teeth from inside my head, my dual nature reacting to Persephone's aggravating cackle. *We could rip out her throat, if we want. She'd be nothing but a snack between our teeth.* The wolf had been suppressed for too long and would love a chance to attack.

The lid flipped. Ugh, no. I'd only just drank my latest dose the night before. It was too soon, too soon. No choice.

My fingers scrambled over the empty spots, those empty spots for the vials I'd already drank and disposed of.

I chugged the potion with a cough.

I was down to the last of my bottles, all because I'd been careless.

17

I found myself struggling to catch up to the rest of the class, scrambling to stand on the ice because I knew if I slipped, I was *out*. Just when I thought I had the hang of things, the class load shifted entirely for the first half of the new semester.

Labs started as soon as fall break ended. Each class I had now dealt with a different type of magic, with hands-on work being the emphasis of this portion of the semester. Quite a difference from the study I'd grown accustomed to.

Thank God. I wasn't sure how much longer I could have dealt with the book work. My eyes were practically bleeding.

That was probably the way the staff wanted things to work. Their watchful gazes were everywhere, constantly, waiting for us to mess up, waiting for an excuse to take our points away.

I tried to look at things a little differently after my last talk with Melia, shifting focus to remind myself about how the professors didn't want us to succeed. They wanted us to be strong. They wanted the best people to move on to the next level, and the next level, with a spot in Faerie being the ultimate goal.

Paranoid, I peeled an orange for breakfast, not trusting anything else the chef made, the garlic demon. I'd never used magic before. I knew *nothing* about magic. Could I even do this?

Barbara had told me I'd broken through her wards, something I didn't remember doing. Was it magic?

Melia sat down next to me, her plate filled and a grin on her face. "Are you excited to start your practical studies?" she asked me.

I tried to nod and nearly choked on my orange. "Sure," I said with a groan. "Hey Meli, does magic come naturally to everyone? What I mean to say is, I've never had much of a chance to practice it. Does every half-breed have a kind of natural proficiency when it comes to magic?"

"Well…" Melia trailed off, her gaze distant. "For some people I suppose it comes more naturally than to others. I'm not sure about the same level for every half-breed. I think sometimes it depends on your own talents, and for others it takes hard work. I've never seen anyone completely fail at this portion of their curriculum." She paused, then gestured with her fork. "I take it back. My second year, I saw a first-year boy completely fail to produce any kind of magic. They got rid of him really quickly. But I think he was half-Fae, half-troll or something. Maybe his two parentages canceled each other out."

"I wonder how it will work for me," I muttered, popping another orange segment into my mouth.

"You've never used magic?"

"Not once."

"I wouldn't worry too much. You'll get your chance to practice. And practice and practice and practice. You'll end up using so much magic you'll dream about it at night," she told me.

In the afternoon I sat down at a long table for my first Divination class.

Things didn't feel right at the academy today. Maybe it was my imagination but the air was filled with pressure despite the empty halls, so many students given the boot and sent home after the first culling. I'd gotten used to the low-lying energy of all those Fae singing in my veins as I navigated the strange world of academia, but I couldn't shake the sense that there were things going on here I still didn't understand.

An undercurrent I could not put my finger on.

"Attention, students! Please, eyes up here. Pay attention." The professor snapped her fingers to get all eyes on her. She stood taller than most of the boys in the class, her back ramrod-straight and hair falling in a gleaming trail of slick fire down her back. She'd emphasized her almond eyes with black liner bringing out the curved shape, her pupils mere slits like a cat's eye.

This wasn't the flighty hippy I'd expected when I heard the word *divination*. I expected the classic wild-haired, gaudily dressed gypsy who spoke in a high whisper and communed with spirits.

Not hard-ass Professor Marsh with her porn-star stiletto heels.

"Students, take your places, sit your rears down on the cushions, and take out your tarot cards." Marsh tapped the desk in front of her with her own deck. "These are brand new, gifted to you by me. Touched by no other hands than your own so they get a feel for your energy and yours alone. Make sure to keep it that way."

I found a spot down the table from Mike and Roman, shooting them both a smile and thankful for the familiar faces. Seeing Mike soothed my heart. It was a reminder. There were still bright spots in the world, and my yearning to do well here, my yearning for freedom, did not have to push me over the edge of stress.

"Are you ready for this?" Mike asked me out of the corner of his mouth.

Had he saved a seat for me, knowing we'd have this class together? I liked to think so.

I sat down cross-legged on the red velvet cushion at his side, letting my bag drop with a clunk. "No," I answered easily. "I don't think I have any magic."

"*Every* Fae has magic," he insisted with a chuckle. "You just have to know how to harness the power."

So *he* said. I wasn't sure I believed him.

It became painfully evident in our first few weeks of Divination: I had no natural talent and couldn't divine to save my life. Yet despite my shortcomings, I actually liked the class. I appreciated the way Marsh took her students in hand and didn't tolerate any bullshit. She also didn't play favorites.

Thank goodness. I'd had more than enough of Hoarfrost, even though I only saw him once a week. Still, she gave me a weird feeling whenever she stared at me. I couldn't explain it, but she felt familiar to me, like a friend I'd fallen out of contact with.

Almost like...like *pack*.

Ridiculous, because shifters were not allowed at the school, much less allowed to teach.

She didn't lecture me about the terrible way I read tea leaves, or how my tarot cards always flew out of my hands and onto the floor. She didn't lecture when I spent more time staring at Mike than I did on my studies. More points in her favor.

Later, my footsteps echoed through the dorm room,

painfully empty since a bunch of my fellow female half-humans had been sent home after the first test.

The first purge had not been good to my kind.

Somehow, I'd managed to make it through, and part of me still couldn't believe it. Like my body refused to relax because it had become so used to living in a constant state of anxiety. My muscles were tense and my back ached from keeping it straight.

I'd no sooner drawn my covers over my head than a screech filled the room. I bolted upright, heart ready to leap out of my throat. A red light descended from the ceiling. A strange alarm.

"Fire!"

The call came from my left and though I didn't smell smoke, I got the hell out of there. The rest of my dorm mates scrambled out of the room and I followed, keeping a blanket over my head as we walked outside. I didn't need to risk breaking my spell. A full moon and no clouds meant a death sentence if I let even a single shaft of moonlight touch my skin.

Students milled on the back lawn staring up at one of the tower rooms and the trailing smoke curling from one of the windows.

"There you are! I've been looking for you."

I moved toward Melia's familiar voice in a daze. "What's going on?"

"I'm not sure. Fire alarm, I think. I was having the best dream about a guy named John in my scroll-making class…" Melia clutched at her pajamas. "Look at you, with your blanket. Good idea! Scoot over and let me in." She grabbed the corner of the blanket and tugged it open to step in beside me. "It's a little chilly tonight, isn't it?"

I barely had time to react. "Wait, what are you doing?"

"I'm chilly and you're the smarty-pants with the blanket.

See? There's enough room for both of us. Good thinking, girl."

We stood together under the blanket, the heat of her body seeping into me. I was too surprised to think about the implications of the movement. But I felt the moonlight on me when she tugged the blanket the wrong way. The same thing I'd tried desperately to avoid by using the blanket in the first place.

Dammit, Meli.

It wasn't her fault. She didn't know. But as the cold feeling of my spell breaking washed me with shards of ice, I gritted my teeth. Three bottles wasted. *Wasted*. For no good reason. I kept my head ducked down to avoid people staring at me, hoping they would be too concerned with the smoke to look around.

"Do you think someone pulled the alarm on purpose, after they set the fire? Or do you think it was an accident?" Melia asked, staring around at the rest of the students gathering on the lawn.

She stood close enough to notice how I tensed. But she said nothing. The shifter in me rose immediately in response to the full moon overhead. My eyesight sharpened, the nightscape coming to life in startling clarity. Nostrils flaring, I drew in her scent, a combination of cinnamon and honeysuckle belonging uniquely to Melia.

Then my focus moved to the woods. What I wouldn't give to let my wolf have her freedom, to feel the way my bones shifted and my muscles sang, running on all fours—

"Tavi? Are you listening to me?"

I tried to tune in and push the wave of feeling aside, still huddling under the blanket. "Who would be awake at this hour? Does this kind of thing happen often?"

Melia shook her head. "No, not really. The upperclassmen know better than to mess with those kinds of things. If they got caught, their points would be gonzo and it would mean automatic expulsion. No one is willing to risk it when they're so close to graduation next semester. You know?"

Keep her talking, I told myself. Keep her distracted before she realized how my scent changed. How the small hairs on the back of my neck rose and my energy signature shifted into something other than human.

Would she be able to know if she looked at me?

It took another twenty minutes before the students were allowed to return to the building. A police car swung up the circular drive and parked in front of the Castle entrance. I didn't pay it much mind, needing to get back inside. I kept the blanket over my head while I said goodnight to Melia, launching myself through the doors to my dorm and climbing the ladder like a spider monkey.

Another vial down, I thought with disgust. What was wrong with me? I needed to be more vigilant. I shouldn't have put myself in this position.

I was smarter, wasn't I?

Yeah, I'm not so sure.

My internal monologue sounded sassy and I didn't appreciate the judgment.

"Oh my God, did you hear that the cops are here?"

The whispered statement echoed back to me and I shook my head, not wanting to eavesdrop.

"Wait a minute, someone called the cops?"

"It's bad. I heard they found something."

"What did they find?"

"Another body."

18

Another student dead. Another first-year front runner taken out, with the fire as a cover-up.

It didn't take long for the dead girl's identity to make the rounds. Carmela Luzon, the first-year with the highest points. She'd stolen the number one spot with ease after the last round of testing.

Poor girl.

I hadn't gotten to speak to her much but I remembered her being quiet and shy. She didn't make friends easily, preferring to keep to herself and focus on classes. She certainly didn't have any *enemies*, either.

It would mean another visit from Detective Wilson, surely. Things had been going well for the longest time—

"Did you hear what they're saying about Carmela?"

I glanced up from my oatmeal, chewing and considering Mike and Roman as they sat at our table with matching solemn expressions. Swallowing over the rock in my throat, I said, "I heard a little."

"Don't you think it's weird how both the kids who died were top students?" Roman offered. He shook his head, pushing the macaroni and cheese around his plate. "This is more than a coincidence. I know it."

"Keep your voice down," Melia warned, jerking forward to place her finger over his lips.

It had taken her a few weeks to be comfortable around Mike and Roman, given the former's status and the latter's good looks. Fortunately, she'd settled into a routine fairly quickly because I wasn't sure what we would have done otherwise. Mike was the sweetest person I'd met on campus, somehow still miraculously my friend, and Melia…she might have been my mentor but she'd quickly grown into the person I trusted the most.

I needed the four of us to get along.

"Come on, Mel, you have to admit, this is bad," Roman continued. His gaze hardened suddenly. "You're a fourth-year, you're probably safe, but the rest of us are at risk."

"Of course it's bad," she agreed with a vigorous nod. "Someone is killing off the first-year competition. One top student dead is something, but two is more than a coincidence. It's a pattern." She glanced over to me. "Sorry."

"What? No way," Mike argued. His cheeks flushed.

"What else could it be?" Melia shot back. "I mean, nothing else makes sense. We have already moved on. Why would someone else be offing the kids in your year? And the kids with the highest points? It's more than a coincidence."

"You're insane." Said lightly. But the laughter we four shared was strained around the edges. I agreed Melia's theory was the best of any I'd heard so far.

As if I wasn't worried enough about making it through the probationary period, now I had to consider some nutcase trying to murder me because of my good grades. Luckily, I was in the top 25, far enough away from the number one spot to be safe. Right?

Was it too much to ask for the killer to be Persephone?

Two birds with one stone? Get rid of her *and* keep my class safe?

I stifled those gleeful thoughts as being unworthy. Entertaining, but unworthy.

But no, it just didn't make sense. She had better grades than I did. If anything, she had the potential to be the next victim, especially if the rest of the kids ahead of her continued to drop like flies.

I couldn't worry. Or at least I tried not to. Easier said than done, obviously, because I was a champion worrier and this was a good opportunity to hone my skills.

After classes, I met Mike in the library to study divination together. He knew I was absolutely hopeless with all forms of telling the future and had offered to help, an offer I jumped on without hesitation.

Any chance I had to spend time with him alone was one I'd take.

"Are you ready to figure out the secret path toward reading tarot?" Mike joked the second I let my bag drop. He wiggled his hands in the air woo-woo fashion.

I took off my school jacket and hung it on the back of the chair, the look I gave him pure skepticism. "*Is* there a secret path for tarot?" I asked.

"I have no clue, but we should figure it out because Marsh has been giving you death stares every time you get something wrong. I mean, she's been decent about it but I wouldn't want to get on her bad side."

"Which is all the time," I supplied. "I swear, when I told you I have no clue how to access my own magic, you thought I was lying. I'm totally *not* lying. There's a steep learning curve."

I had the book open in front of me. I wasn't paying attention. I couldn't, not with Mike smiling at me in the certain way he had. Like the world narrowed down until I was the sole recipient of his focus.

Yeah, *hubba hubba* indeed.

"We can figure it out. I know it. What did you think of Melia's theory at breakfast? About the murders?" he asked.

"It's not the worst theory I've heard," I evaded, because I wasn't sure I wanted to tell him my true feelings on the subject: we were all in danger.

He chewed the inside of his lip and shifted to lean on one elbow, dropping his voice down to a whisper. "Come on, you don't need to watch yourself with me. You can tell me what you really think. Are you worried?"

"As worried as anyone, I guess."

"If you keep getting those good grades, you're going to make *me* worry. And worrying about you is one more stress I'm not prepared to handle right now."

I tossed my pencil at him. "Get real. You know it's not possible."

"What? You getting good grades or me worrying about you?" Mike asked with wide eyes.

"Both. I'm going to make sure I earn my place here but I can't claim to be the best in class. Far from it," I replied.

"Okay, Miss Top 25."

"Okay, Mister Top 100."

He pretended to be wounded, clutching a hand against his heart. "Ouch, the hurt!"

"You don't have as much pressure on you as I do," I teased. Although as Uncle Will was fond of saying, many a truth was said in jest. This time I surely told the truth. I wondered if Mike knew.

"You don't want to talk to me about pressure," he said with a shake of his head, causing a lock of gold to fall across his eyes.

I leaned forward with my arms folded on the desk. "Oh

yeah? I'm sure being a prince is a really tough gig." Did he want to trade places with me?

"Let me tell you something, Missy..." Mike glanced over at a couple of students walking by, pausing in his speech until they passed. I still hadn't seen his personal guards anywhere. We'd been studying together a few times a week and those guys always managed to stay hidden. "Being a royal has its ups and downs and I'm not going to sit here and tell you it's rainbows and sunshine all the time. There are definitely some black times. Some moments I would trade if I could."

I appreciated his honesty. "I can understand."

Mike mimicked my posture, his left eyebrow raised. "You never did tell me your story, young lady. Did you think I wouldn't notice you have been avoiding any talk of your home life with me?"

"Because my story isn't a happy one," I retorted quickly. I had to work overtime not to let his nearness get to me. "And we're supposed to be learning the secrets of tarot, not gabbing about my past."

"We've been friends long enough I'm going to start to think you don't trust me with the information. Unless you really want to stay with your mysterious vibe thing." This time his eyebrows waggled.

I chuckled at his needling. "The mysterious vibe thing has kept me alive until now. I'll give you a little history, then, to soothe your wounded ego." Those brows drew down at the statement. "I've already told you I lived with my uncle. He was—is—a defense lawyer in the South. He wanted me to follow a certain path he'd set out for me. It wasn't anything good. I want to be my own person and not be used as a pawn in his power games. I came to the academy to get away from everything."

"Wait a minute." I watched him blink. Blink again. "Your uncle doesn't know you're here?"

"No, he doesn't. And I need to make sure he never does," I insisted, making sure Mike understood the need to keep the information to himself. "Bad things would happen if he knew where I was. I wouldn't want to put anyone in danger if he decided to send people after me."

Mike mimed locking his lips. "Don't worry. I'm not going to tell anyone."

"I really didn't expect to get in," I admitted. I leaned closer still and dropped my voice. "The school provided me with the *out* I needed, the only means to escape a bad situation."

"In the spirit of candor, I should tell you about my own dad," Mike said. Glancing behind him again to make sure there was no one else around before diving in.

"Are you sure your guards aren't going to mind you spilling state secrets?"

"It's common knowledge. Or at least it should be, to anyone who bothers to look beneath the surface. My father is the same way as your uncle. He is only concerned with power and how he can keep it. I've known since I was a baby, my role would one day be to step up as king of the Seelie court. Seems I've never really lived up to my dad's high expectations. He's not happy with me."

"Do you…not want to be king?" I asked after a period of silence.

He raised his gaze to meet mine. "Would you? I'm not sure what I want. I mean, I've never been given a choice. What else would I do? I've trained my whole life for the role. The position of a lifetime. But I don't know if I'd be a good king."

"I truly believe you shouldn't be made to do something you don't want to do. I'm also trying to be supportive, so I'm not sure what to say to you. I'm not sure there is a right thing to say in this situation. If I tell you to step up into your destiny, it makes me a hypocrite."

"We wouldn't want you to be a hypocrite," he said with a grin.

"Then again, I think maybe the best kings aren't kings who are forced into their position, but kings who want to be there, who want to help their people and lead with dignity and strength," I finished. As though my opinion mattered.

Mike reached out to grab a lock of my hair and tug gently, the space between us greatly diminished. "Now I see how you got to the top of the class. You're too smart for your own good."

"Stop it." I swatted him away despite the warming in my cheeks from the contact. I wanted him to touch me. To put his fingers on my skin instead of in my hair.

"I'm serious. Not everyone would have the guts to be so honest with me. You don't know how much I appreciate it, Tavi." He kept hold of my hair.

"You're joking."

"I'm *not* joking."

We leaned in closer still until I could sense the sweetness of his breath. Until I breathed in his exhalations. My gaze dropped to his lips. They drew me forward like a magnet. Another inch and we would be—

Laughter sounded and when I glanced up, Persephone and her cronies were crowding through the shelves of books, arriving in their usual loud attention-craving style despite a sharp *shush* from the librarian. Clomping around like ponies in a parade.

The moment was shattered.

And here I'd thought this my safe space. My bubble of peace burst as Persephone glanced over and saw Mike and me sitting so close together. Her brows narrowed together, mouth smoothing out into a sharp line, but she kept moving to a different table with her girls in tow. Keeping eye contact with me until the last possible moment.

Mike cleared his throat, shifting back in his chair and shaking his head. Our moment was gone. "I guess I should get going. I have a test tomorrow in a different class," he said. "Which means I need to rest and study."

It was an excuse, I thought with a rush of embarrassment. A lame excuse to get out of kissing me. Maybe he didn't think I noticed the way he refused to meet my eyes now.

But I did. And it hurt.

"I guess we didn't get much studying in, did we?" I pointed down to our still-closed books. We hadn't done *any* studying.

"No, I guess not. I'm sorry."

Mike packed the rest of his books in his bag and hurried out of the library without looking back. I blew out a sigh, taking my time in gathering my books and papers. What was I *doing*? Almost kissing the future king! I had a lot of nerve. Especially considering how I couldn't be completely honest with him. He deserved honesty. He'd been nothing but open with me, open and helpful in every possible way when he didn't have to be. A good friend through and through.

"What were you doing alone with Michael Thornwood?"

I jerked up to see Persephone staring at me. By herself, for once. She must have left the rest of her lemmings to fend for themselves. "It's called studying," I told her. "I'm sure you don't need to worry about it but the rest of us do."

Persephone shifted until her thigh cocked against the table to emphasize her full hips, her narrow waist, and the way the buttons of her white shirt strained against her ample bosom. She stared off into the distance with a contemplative smile I knew didn't come naturally to her. "You know, the king has been closed off for years," she said nonchalantly. "No one has seen him. *Super* secretive. And now suddenly his only son has emerged from their remote castle to come to school here."

"What are you trying to say?" I asked nastily. There had to be a point to this story I had missed. Persephone did *nothing* without a reason.

"I think there's something wrong with him. With the monarchy in general. Just my opinion, mind you, but it seems strange. Why would a full-blooded Fae would want to attend a school for halflings? Why would he want to talk to and befriend half-breeds in general, considering the expectations for him? Think about it." Persephone tapped the side of her head.

"I'm not interested in your theories—"

"Just be careful, Tavi," Persephone said as a parting shot. "I think you should stay away."

Stay away from the only boy I wanted? *Never*.

19

Despite my secrets, I knew I would rather lose a piece of myself than give up on my budding feelings for Mike, no matter how crazy it sounded.

Persephone only desired what I had, and would do whatever she could to get it. She definitely wanted Mike all to herself, I told myself the next morning as I brushed my hair without the aid of a mirror. She would do her best to drive a wedge between our friendship, then she could swoop in and steal him.

Persephone wanted it all. She wanted power; she wanted the prestige of royalty. It fit her nature and would be the next crowning achievement in her already blessed life. For some reason, she thought *I* stood in her way and she could clear me out with a few well-placed threats.

I stopped brushing with a sigh, dropping my head against the wall behind me and letting the stone cool my overheated skin. There was no way I could have anything with Mike, if I were being realistic.

Who was I trying to fool? I was half werewolf, hated by the Fae. It didn't matter we went to school together, that we were friends and studied and laughed together. That we'd almost kissed this afternoon. Almost.

Oh, *those lips*.

And look how badly I'd bungled things since I'd been here. I'd have to spend the rest of my life hiding no matter how things turned out.

I couldn't tell Mike the whole truth about me because I'd be kicked out in an instant and thrown right back into Kendrick's slimy grasp, and I would never allow it to happen. Not when I'd come this far already.

My schoolgirl crush on Mike would have to remain a pipe dream. A fantasy I entertained at night and told no one about. Let Persephone have him. I didn't care.

Okay, I *did* care. I cared a lot.

Although she did bring up some good points…

I rapped the side of my head with the brush to clear it of those thoughts. No, she *didn't* bring up good points. She was a jealous rival and nothing else. Whatever was going on in Faerie with the king, I'd worry about it later. After I earned my spot there and found myself under his rule.

Walking into the divination lab the following day, I saw Mike at our usual table. He raised his hand with a warm wave and beckoned me over into my usual seat. As though nothing had happened between us.

Sure, if he wanted to play things this way, I was game. I could pretend nothing happened as well.

"Hey you," he said right off the bat once I slid behind the desk. "What are you doing tonight?"

"The schedule is clear, my friend," I told him with a rushed smile, dropping my bag and reaching inside for the tarot deck.

"Do you want to try studying with me again?"

Hmm, curious. "I thought you had a test and needed to get your beauty sleep?" I joked.

Roman cut in with a snicker, pushing dark hair out of his face. "If this one doesn't get his normal ten hours of sleep then you'll see his real face. Which is not pretty. So yes, he needs his beauty sleep, take it from me."

Mike shut him up with a well-placed elbow to the ribs. "I *do* need to get my rest, and I *do* have a test, but neither of those things mean I don't want to study for this class. I'm still interested in learning the back-door shortcuts to being a great tarot reader. What do you say?"

My inner pep talk from earlier didn't seem to matter. One look at his smile and I melted like butter in an Arizona heat wave. "Sure!" I replied with way too much enthusiasm. *Dial it back a notch, woman.* "I'd love to."

"Let's say our usual table in the library?" Mike clarified. "Seven o'clock? We can study in sprints and see if we can annoy the librarian during our breaks."

"I like the way you think."

Professor Marsh approached the class with a swish of fabric, her pencil skirt emphasizing her slender lower body, and fixed us all with a stare that silenced conversation within seconds. "Everyone!" she called out, her cat-like eyes flashing. "I'm sure you have noticed the covers on your stations today."

In fact, I hadn't. I'd been too busy mooning over Mike. I looked down now and noticed the plush pile of purple velvet and the hard lump beneath it.

"Today we are going to be working with crystal balls. A crystal ball is another tool for the practice of divination," Marsh continued. She lifted her own velvet cover to reveal a clear orb of quartz crystal on a solid gold stand. "Most who stare into the depths of the crystal are able to conjure visions of the future. Now, the key lies in interpreting these visions. Interpretation is where the masters break away from the amateurs, the dabblers. Everyone, raise your cloth and see what the crystal has to show you."

A sliver of apprehension shot through me as I recalled Barbara's warnings. Garlic, moonlight, and…quartz crystal. Well, as long as I didn't actually *touch* it…

I watched Mike for a moment, the cover cloth set aside and his large palms cradling the small softball-sized clear sphere in front of him.

"Have you ever done anything like this before?" I asked him as my nerves began to sing.

"No. But I'm sure there's nothing to it," he said.

"Clear your mind and focus on the future," Marsh instructed, raising her voice over the low murmur of chatter. "Imagine a blank space. Stare into the crystal and picture the blank space expanding. Larger and larger. I said to *clear your mind*, Roman!"

I wasn't sure what the professor had picked up from my friend's head and surely I didn't want to know since it brought a chuckle from him.

Mike bit his lip, the picture of concentration. I snickered at both of them. "I'm curious to see what you conjure," I whispered.

"Ah, so I'm going to be the guinea pig today. You want to follow my lead?"

"Seems like it."

He had all of his focus on the ball, his hands caressing the surface, lines of tension fanning out from his mouth. As I watched, a blurry image began to form inside the crystal ball.

Fascinated, I shifted closer to him. "What is that?"

"It's…it's *Faerie*. It's my home."

The image solidified into stone spires and flags, a massive forest stretching out beyond the castle enclosure. I saw the turrets and the parapets where Fae would march in neat lines. I saw stained glass windows and smoke curling from chimneys.

Smoke curling from *everywhere*, it seemed.

"Mike," I urged, shifting to get a better view, "is the castle *on fire?*"

We moved closer in unison, the image now blurry to the point where we were unable to make out the finer details. But I clearly saw the lick of flame and the burning of embers in multiple places.

Mike broke the connection with the ball and pulled away, his cheeks white and sweat beading along his hairline. The crystal ball turned blank and clear at once.

"Fire?" he repeated. There was so much innocence—and terror—in the single word.

"You know, I'm sure it's nothing," I tried to tell him with a soothing stroke of my hand on his knee. "You told me you were worried last night. I think those worries are front and center in your mind and this is what's coming up. I'm sure it's something easily explained." I felt his muscles bunch.

"Yeah, maybe you're right." His smile was shaky. "You're right, of course."

"Okay, dabblers, move aside. Whatever weak image you conjured from your own nightmares, bro, prepare to be astounded." Roman rubbed his hands together and moved toward his own crystal ball. "Watch the master at work."

The crystal swam with murky images even before his fingertips touched the sphere. A vast evergreen wood sprang into life within the depths, trees gently swaying in a breeze beneath a pulsing full moon. Utterly different from the brief glimpse of Faerie I'd gotten from Mike's divination ball.

My eyes widened at the clarity of the image. Roman's vision was strong. Much stronger than any of our classmates around us. Before anything else could form, he broke the connection, shaking his hands out at his sides like he'd been burned.

I blinked and something inside of me shifted. "What's the matter?"

Roman shook his head. "I'm not sure." He sounded confused. "Something felt wrong."

"What do you think you saw?" Mike pressed.

"It's where I grew up in Faerie. I saw my home, too."

Wait. That…didn't seem right to me. But then again, I'd never been there myself.

"I'm afraid to see what comes next," Roman admitted as he rubbed his chin.

Mike chuckled but the sound was anything but amused. "Any reason why, bud?"

"Because it's dangerous for people to know their futures." He grabbed the velvet cloth and tossed it over the crystal ball. "I might be the master but even I know that. I'm going to have to use my talents elsewhere."

Yeah, I couldn't disagree with him there. A strange sense of foreboding settled on my skin along with the weight of both their gazes when the boys turned to me.

"Your turn, Tavi."

"Maybe you'll do better than the both of us," Mike supplied with a forced grin. "This could be your thing. You never know."

"Somehow I doubt it," I grumbled, turning to face my own ball.

Focusing on the clear depths, I held my hands on either side of the sphere, close but not touching, and tried to concentrate. Tried to blank my mind of anything blocking my vision of the future.

Show me.

But I was afraid. What if it showed me visions of

Kendrick? Then everyone would know what I needed to hide.

My fated mate.

As Roman had said, it was dangerous for people to know their futures. I continued to stare at the ball for the next few minutes with nothing changing, nothing showing. Okay, maybe it wasn't my thing.

I shouldn't have been so happy about it.

"How is it going over here?"

Professor Marsh made it to our table as I continued to squint at the ball. I blinked, glancing up at her and struggling to bring her into focus. "Nothing is happening," I stated. I wasn't surprised.

She cracked a smile. "Don't worry, Miss Alderidge. There are several students in the class who are slow to start with crystal ball gazing. It takes some people years of practice. Continue to keep your mind clear and stop trying so hard. Open the connection by cupping the ball with your hands as you look inside."

She grabbed my hands, moving to place them gently on the ball. I jerked and ripped my hands from her grasp.

"I'm sorry," I said quickly. "I'm allergic to quartz crystal." It was why I hadn't tried to cup the sphere in the first place.

She stared me down. "Sweetheart, there's no such thing as an allergy to quartz crystal. What's the real reason for your hesitation?"

I was out of excuses.

"I'm sorry." I deflated, sinking down into my seat. "I can't do this. Please don't make me do this." If I touched the ball, it would break my spell and reveal me to everyone and I was getting low on vials.

I cast a pleading glance toward Mike. He just looked confused.

"You've barely begun," Marsh stated. And in her tone, I heard a mixture of incredulity and impatience. "Try again."

"I *can't*," I insisted.

"This is going to affect your grade, Miss Alderidge." Marsh's voice hardened further and I had a hard time meeting those piercing cat eyes. They made me squirm. "You do understand. Don't you?"

"I do. But I can't do this," I replied miserably.

"Fine. If you continue to insist you *can't do this*, then replace the velvet cover and sit the rest of the lesson out. Without speaking."

She wasn't happy with me, not in the least. My skin broke out in goose bumps as she walked away. I did as she ordered and tossed the velvet cloth back over the crystal ball.

When I turned back to my friends, Mike still wore a semi-quizzical look but Roman stared at me, his eyes narrowed. He blew out a breath and turned away, like he knew the real reason I hadn't continued.

There was no way he could know that I couldn't touch quartz. Was there?

But a strange sense of his suspicion toward me remained. One I couldn't shake.

20

The suspicion in Roman's eyes tailed me closer than a predator stalking prey, and it took work not to break into a run and escape. I didn't blame him but it added a new element to my distrust.

A normal Fae like Roman would have no way of knowing about witch magic and the rules with it.

Right?

His dubious look was just because I'd been acting weird about the whole crystal ball business, without a good explanation. Nothing else. I didn't understand much about Faerie magic, but I knew it was different from witch magic.

It seemed I had trouble with both, because not only was I hopeless in my favorite class but I'd managed to waste multiple vials of my very precious potion over stupid mistakes.

I walked out of divination class at the sound of the bell and hurried back to my dorm before Mike or Roman could confront me over the incident. They'd have questions I couldn't answer.

There have been too many strange things happening lately. I'd gotten myself locked into a constant state of paranoia and now I worried what my friends thought of me.

"You're going to have to talk to me about this quartz allergy because I'm baffled, honestly," Mike told me later when I sat across from him in the library for our study session. It was the first thing he said to me. Not even a hello. Straight into the questions.

I blinked innocently and fought to keep the heat from rising to my cheeks. "It's the weirdest thing. I break out in a rash and my face swells. Like a bee sting but worse. I wish I knew why, because it's a real pain in the ass. There's certain jewelry I can't wear."

He clearly didn't believe me. "I've never heard of an allergy to quartz."

"What can I say?" I shrugged and tried to sound unbothered. "I'm special."

"Yeah, one way of putting it," Roman stated.

I jolted. I hadn't seen him walk over. "Hey. I didn't realize you'd be studying with us tonight."

Roman sat down with a smirk because he knew, *he knew* he was interrupting the cozy idea I'd had in mind for tonight. "You guys aren't the only ones who need to study. Mike invited me. Figured I could use a quiet place to get some notes written for my transfiguration class."

"Oh yeah, sure, it's fine. Why wouldn't it be?" I hurried to say, tossing my braid over my shoulder like the motion would show how much I *didn't* care.

Did Mike not want to be alone with me anymore?

I really needed to get a grip. I was slowly losing my mind at this school and it showed. Still, I'd been really starting to fall for Mike and hoping our near-kiss the other day meant he liked me as well. Secretly I'd hoped for a repeat tonight.

Roman certainly was a wrench in our cozy dynamic. But he was better than Persephone, so maybe I should start thinking of it as a win.

"Okay, maybe you guys can help me with something before we start," Roman stated. He gathered a book out of the bag he carried over his shoulder and set it on the table between us. Dust rose and if I didn't know any better, I'd say he'd never opened the thing. "I'm having a lot of trouble with my levitation spell."

"You're not in class with us at noon," I replied, wanting clarity.

"No, mine is a little later in the day, at three. Same teacher though, so I figured it wouldn't hurt to ask you for advice. One of us has to have an idea."

"Your levitation game is weak, man," Mike agreed. "I've seen you trying to figure things out in the dorm. I'm not sure one study session is going to help you improve but Tavi and I will do our best."

I liked the way he linked our names together.

"Hey, I'm not ashamed to ask for help. Why do you think I'm here?" Roman wiggled his fingers over the tome like some kind of hoodoo would help him. "I'm not sure if my intonation is off or if my magic is not built for this kind of spell."

"It's a basic spell," I said, adding my two cents. "At least, it's a little easier than some of the other things they're teaching us."

Roman raised a brow. "Well, all right, Miss Know It All. If it's such a basic spell then please show me how it's done. I would like to see the master at work."

At least this one I had in the bag. I was doing well in transfiguration class. Hopefully I'd be able to keep up the momentum tonight with an audience. This might be my opportunity to make up for what had happened earlier today with the crystal ball.

My strength for transfiguration might outweigh my lack of progress in divination.

"Stand back, boys, and prepare to be amazed." I clapped my hands together and rubbed, preparing for the spell. I remembered the words as I'd practiced them over and over in the shower with my bar of soap.

This, at least, I knew how to do. I tried to summon the confidence I'd felt earlier when I lifted my book off the desk in class. Easily, without effort. Maybe I wasn't such a loser with magic after all. Maybe I just needed practice finding my niche.

I closed my eyes and eased out a breath. And when I opened them, when I blew out the breath, Roman's textbook shot ten feet into the air toward the top of the massive book shelves ringing us.

Mike and Roman followed its progress with their eyes.

"Wow," Mike murmured.

Maybe I really was starting to come into my powers. *About time.*

I crooked a finger and the book flew back to me, landing softly on the desk, the pages fluttering open to the center, the dust gone.

"Okay, so maybe you aren't completely hopeless," Roman stated with a small, nearly silent clap.

"For some subjects, yeah, but not this one. Come on, Mike. Your turn now."

Mike followed the same spell, used the same incantation. His book wobbled in front of him but did not rise. A few more minutes of agonized concentration had it moving four inches in front of his face and dropping down just as quickly.

I remembered his crystal ball divination earlier. How the

image had blurred without ever forming into anything solid. I wondered if he was holding himself back to make me feel better. Mike was a full-blood Fae, preparing to rise to the position of king. He should be blowing my work out of the water easily.

"Hey, it was a great try," I told him with an encouraging smile. Part of me softened. If he was holding himself back for my benefit...it made me like him even more.

But it was completely unnecessary.

Mike puffed out a breath and let the spell break. "See?" he told Roman when his book dropped and lay still. "This is why she's in the top 25 while the rest of us struggle to catch up. And why she's going to definitely make it to the next level."

"I'm not doing as well as you think. The score was for the examinations," I clarified. "If you take into account my classwork then I'm only in the top one hundred."

"Top one hundred is still better than me. I'm currently stagnating. And only the top one hundred make it through to the next semester." Mike pointed to his chest. "That's why I need these study sessions. You think we're here for you only? No way. Someone needs to whip me into shape and I think you have the discipline to do it."

"Don't worry. We'll make sure you stay," I fussed. "Although I'm not sure why you're worried about it. You're only here in the interest of goodwill and learning about your people, right?"

"Yeah, sure." His smile went tight. "Still, it seems I don't have nearly the natural aptitude you do. You are going to zip through the rest of the semester and pass on with flying colors. I have no doubt about it."

"I'm glad one of us is doubtless. Because on a normal day I'm not sure why I'm here." I smoothed my skirt because I couldn't handle him looking at me any longer, especially with Roman dividing his attention between us with an all-knowing grin.

"You're here because you work hard and you care about making your dreams come true," Mike said. "Not everyone can claim the same. There are a lot of selfish people around."

"You better be careful because if someone hears you, they will think you don't really care for your classmates."

"Maybe I just have a knack for seeking out quality friends."

And boom, the warm fuzzy feeling again. I was becoming addicted to it.

We finished the study session with Roman improving his levitation spell by leaps and bounds. He'd had some of the text pronunciation off and I wondered why no one had bothered to correct him up to this point.

Not my business. At least we left the library in good spirits.

I sat down to dinner next to Melia, the guys off for a prior engagement neither one of them had bothered to tell me about. Men.

"What's up with them?" She jerked her thumb over her shoulder at their twin retreating forms.

"I don't know. I'm not in the inner circle of trust, apparently. They haven't said anything even though we've been studying for hours." I stared down at my salad and apple, my gorge rising. What I wouldn't give for a big juicy burger dripping with cheese.

"Ooh, you had another afternoon study session with the prince." Melia leaned closer and said in a conspirator's whisper, "Any kind of hanky-panky going on there?"

I picked up a grape and tossed it at her. "Not even funny. Besides, Roman was there too."

Once I finished my lackluster dinner, I headed back to the

dormitory with my spell books. They made for dry company but unfortunately, I hadn't been lying when I told Mike I was worried. I might be in the top 25 overall for now, but there were still a few more hurdles to get through before I could feel safe about my position. There were too many variables for me to worry about.

There was no one around when I pushed through the door, breathing in the familiar scents of the dorm. Lemon wood polish on the floor and the floral scent of lavender and rosemary sprigs hanging from the windowsills.

I let out a sigh of relief. I could not deal with Persephone and the rest of her mean girls right now. I'd gotten lucky in this little piece of alone time.

But my tentative quiet came to an end soon enough. Turning the corner toward my bunk, I stopped short.

The drawers built into the wall where we stored our clothes were thrown open. Only mine. My mattress had been tossed down and feathers and springs littered the floor where someone had taken a knife and slit open the fabric.

I dropped my books and bolted forward. "No!"

My clothes had been rummaged through, my intimate belongings spread around for anyone to see. I climbed the ladder to see if anything had been left. Nothing.

Which meant—

My vials.

I dropped to the floor and flung through the ruined remains of the mattress, searching for the box.

"No, *no*."

My heart began to race and I tasted copper in my mouth. I finally found the box lying on its side amidst a pile of broken glass.

This couldn't be happening. Who would do something like this?

I'd been targeted.

My stomach dropped to the floor. I followed it, slicing my finger open searching for the last two vials and blood dripped down onto the wood. The only *two* vials I had left. They couldn't be broken. If they were, then I'd lost everything.

21

Two vials. All I had left to make it through until winter break and the end of the semester when I could see Barbara again and sign the rest of my soul away on another unnamed favor.

I groaned, dropping my head down in my hands amidst the chaos.

Someone had deliberately destroyed all but two of my potions. Who? And how did they know where to find them?

The idea of going back to my uncle and a life as Kendrick Grimaldi's *bitch* had me so scared I lost my breath. I couldn't draw air into my body.

Why did I have the worst luck with these things? Two vials for a whole month, which would be stretching it. Then I'd have to make the trek back to see the witch and sign the rest of my life away on whatever unnamed favor she'd demand from me.

Before anyone had a chance to come into the dorm and see the mess, I searched for a broom to clean up the broken glass, shuddering at the thought of having to pledge more debt to Barbara the bitch witch.

I didn't have a choice. I was so close to being safe—I couldn't lose my courage now.

It took me a good half hour to clean up the mess and put everything back to rights. I grabbed a new set of sheets from the laundry room, making up the mattress in a way that didn't show the exposed patches where the knife had ripped the fabric open. No way I could explain the damage to the higher-ups.

Besides, no one else needed to be involved in my mess.

I'd do whatever I had to do in order to stay. And no matter who tried to cut me down—whoever had broken into my dorm and tossed my things—would have to deal with me. I wasn't about to lose now, not after having come so far.

Friday, a few days before Thanksgiving, the first-years assembled in the auditorium once again for the second round of purging, although the staff thought to brighten up the culling process by calling it a lottery. A *lottery* made the students think they were winning their place here instead of clawing it out through hard work and natural aptitude.

I wasn't fooled. Neither were the girls around me, although I also wasn't as nervous as I had been the first time around. Book work might not be my forte, and I surely didn't have a natural aptitude for divination, but I'd done well in my other classes. Well enough I wasn't too worried about making it through to next semester.

Okay, sure, I hadn't made any friends besides Melia, and she'd already survived her first semester lottery, which left me on my own. But otherwise, I'd fallen into a comfortable groove and almost forgot about the dead students.

Almost.

The upperclassmen were required to attend the

assembly as a show of moral support but they sat in a separate area of the auditorium. An audience to our mortification if we didn't make it through. Or maybe an example of what we had to look forward to once the lottery ended.

I chose an empty seat near the back row just as Headmaster Leaves cleared his throat, already standing at the podium. The lottery began the same way as every other assembly held at the school, with his magically amplified voice echoing across the space.

"Welcome, students." Insert fake smile here. "Thank you for joining us here today for our first-year lottery! This is our last major purge before winter break, and I know you are all anxious to get through it and hear the results of the rankings. There have been a few updates since fall break and your last examinations, and firstly I want to congratulate those of you who made it through." His phony smile grew wider and fuller. "There have been many unexpected stressors this year and you have handled them with decorum and ease. I am very proud of you all."

He gripped the sides of the podium, pointed ears poking through his artfully slicked-back hair. He looked like a political candidate who needed to win our votes to make it through to the election and he'd do whatever it took to win. I rolled my eyes at his phony enthusiasm.

"The full updated list will be posted outside the door by the end of the assembly today. Of course, I have spoken to our staff and after many agonizing hours, we came to the order and ranking you will soon see. Now on to our top five students! I must say, I have never been prouder of a first-year class. At number five, we have Persephone Glaski. Everyone please give her a round of applause."

I watched Persephone stand from the third row, demurely nodding her head toward her adoring public. She'd risen higher. Expectedly so, if one listened to the way she boasted.

"Number four is our very own Chase Timmons."

We paused for the perfunctory applause and I leaned forward in my seat, anxious to hear the last few names. The ones with the targets potentially painted on their backs should the killer strike again.

"At number three, we have Cain Andrews. At number two, Aurelia Rose. And at number one, a big round of applause to our dark horse, Tavi Alderidge. I'm sure no one expected this twist!" Leaves finished the exclamation with a wink and a laugh.

If I'd been in my right mind, I might have been insulted, but I didn't hear a thing through the roaring in my ears.

Applause broke out around me and I sat frozen, my neighbors clapping me on the shoulder in congratulations.

"What...? How...?"

I remember mouthing the words, but no sound came out. I stared at the stage and the headmaster, his gaze unerringly finding me through the crowd.

Me...number one. *Number one?*

No, absolutely not. It wasn't possible.

At some point Melia found me in the midst of the jabbering crowd, grabbing me in a hug and swinging me around in a circle. "I am so proud of you!" she gushed. "I knew you could do it. How did you manage to turn things around? What kind of secrets are you hiding from me? Girl, yes! You're moving on to the next semester! Those late-night study sessions must be the ticket."

I didn't know what to tell her because I didn't have any secrets. Not those kinds. Not the kinds she wanted to hear.

I should have failed divination after refusing to do the crystal ball lesson. Professor Marsh had made it painfully clear every time I walked into the classroom. She was disappointed in me.

So how the *hell* had I managed to reach the top spot in spite of it?

Someone must have rigged the lottery to show my name first. I didn't know how and I surely didn't know why, but that had to be the case.

Despite Melia's protests, I rushed off after the assembly and sought out my divination teacher. She and I needed to have some words. The door was open and I pushed through it without pausing to knock.

"Hello?" I called out.

"Come on in."

The muffled response came from the back of the room and I shuffled inside. "Professor Marsh, where are you?"

"Tavi, is that you?"

I followed the sound of her voice into a small office I'd never noticed before. Marsh sat behind an oddly neat desk with her fingers flying over the keyboard of a sleek and compact laptop. She glanced up when I entered, those silvery-green eyes without their normal black kohl liner. It didn't make them any less odd.

"Aren't you supposed to be at the assembly?" she asked with the quirk of a brow. Then returned her attention to the screen. "Did you get out early? How did the lottery proceed? I assume you are here because you have some kind of question on your final grade."

I took a seat when my legs felt too shaky to hold me up. My heart threatened to beat right out of my chest and the sound of my pulse echoing in my ears resembled the crashing of ocean waves. "I'm number one," I said, coming right out with it, my words barely above a whisper.

Marsh jerked her head up to stare at me unblinking. "Come again?"

"Number one. On the list." My tongue felt swollen to three times its size. "I somehow managed to get the highest spot of my class and I don't know how. Or why."

"Correct me if I'm wrong," she began slowly, "it seems like something you should be celebrating. Making it through the lottery is a great delight. And occupying the number one slot is an amazing feat. You should be proud of yourself."

"There's no way I can be number one," I insisted. My skin had broken out in a cold sweat. "I didn't finish your crystal ball lesson. You told me it would impact my grade and I was ready to take the risk. There's no way I can be number one after failing the lesson. It's not possible. Especially not when I've been in the middle of the road with all my other classes as well."

Marsh clicked her nails together in thought, lips pursed. "I admit I did give you high marks for the class despite your failing with the crystal ball and making an absolute fool of yourself with your ridiculous excuse." The woman sounded amused but oddly pleased with me.

"Why did you place me so high?" I needed to know because it didn't make sense to me. I saw no reason why Professor Marsh would want to push me through to next semester. I was an average student on my best day. Then I remembered how long she'd stared at me on my first day. How she'd felt like home. Felt like *pack*.

I leaned back in the chair. Did my reaction have something to do with her reasoning?

We hadn't really spoken much since the day when I'd lied about my quartz allergy. Marsh hadn't pushed. But she'd continued to sigh with audible disappointment whenever she came over to chat with our table.

Her fingers paused on the keyboard and she sighed yet again, closing the lid. "You want the truth, Tavi? You're one of the brightest students I have come across in my many years of teaching," she told me. Then scowled at my sound of derision, which of course ended on a snort. "No, don't make light of my statement. You may not believe this about yourself but I'm telling you the truth."

It sounded insincere to me.

"Miss Alderidge, I didn't want you to fail my class because you have some kind of problem with quartz crystal you won't tell me about." Marsh avoided my gaze now, staring out the window instead.

"So, you passed me through because you *like* me?" It didn't sound right when I voiced it out loud.

She shook her head, her straight hair catching the light and illuminating the strands of red. "No, I passed you because I think you have what it takes to go all the way," she corrected. "I rely on my intuition every day of my life. It impacts everything I do. I have a sense you will gain your place in Faerie. It would be wrong to fail you, to go against my own intuition in a way that seems unjustified."

"I didn't think professors were allowed to play favorites."

"You think I'm playing favorites? I'm sorry if you think so. I don't believe in playing favorites, unlike some of the other professors here."

I stored the last bit of information away for later, although it still didn't answer my question. Something smelled fishy about this conversation and I wasn't done getting to the bottom of it. Intuition, eh? It made sense, but it also didn't feel like the whole story.

We finished our chat and I left her office feeling torn. Did I really earn my spot or had Marsh done something to get me the top spot on purpose?

I didn't want the top spot. Not in the least. Not when the last two front runners of my class had been murdered.

22

I shook my head at the name changes posted on the doors to the cafeteria until TAVI ALDERIDGE reached the top slot, literally glowing with magic and marking me as a target. Dread settled beneath my chest in a tight knot no amount of massaging could loosen.

"I can't believe you did it. Is it wrong to take credit? My guidance is what got you this honor, this prestige. You can thank me now, and thank me again later."

I knew Melia was joking as we stood watching the rest of the list change to reflect the new stats, including the deletion of several of my classmates. And there I was, my name shining from the top, and I couldn't be less thrilled.

If anything, I wanted to throw up. But I didn't think anyone would take kindly to me emptying my stomach right there in the hallway.

"You can take the credit if you want," I told Melia with a grin. "I don't mind." She was probably the only reason I stayed sane in this place. She *deserved* the credit.

Melia leaned her head on my shoulder and her curls tickled my nose. She groaned, a happy sound. "I can't tell you how proud I am of you. Seeing your name at the top of this list is my crowning achievement for this year."

I wrapped my arms around her automatically and closed the distance between us. "I couldn't have done it without you. And Mike. You two were and are so supportive of me."

But I kept my suspicions to myself, drew any and all worry into a dark corner of my mind and stashed it away to examine later when I was alone. I didn't want to worry Melia if we were right with our theory about the top students being murdered.

"I'm still shocked you and Michael are friends," she said with more than a little incredulity. "Have I told you lately?

"*We* are friends," I corrected her. "The four of us. I will never forget our heated lunch debates. Maybe one of these days when we aren't stressed, we can get together and do something for fun."

"Yeah, the four of us…lunch debates! I'm shocked about that, too. The Crown Prince of Faerie wants to sit and talk to me at lunch. Me!" Her laugh was disbelieving.

We moved away from the list when more students crowded closer for a second look. I tried to ignore the congratulations I still heard in my wake without seeming ungrateful for the sentiments. But it wasn't right. It didn't feel honest.

"What do you think about Mike and the royal family?" I asked, remembering what Persephone had told me. "I mean your real opinion of them."

"What do I *think*?" Melia repeated. She shrugged the strap of her bag higher on her shoulder. "Well, I like Mike. Never thought I'd meet *him*, girl, let me tell you. But I like him. He's genuine and he seems to have a good head on his shoulders. He's more down to earth than I would have thought after seeing his pictures."

We fell in step together, away from the crowd of students. "Why do I sense a *but* coming on?"

"You are not going to repeat this to anyone. Understand?"

I crossed my heart with my index finger. "Yes. I understand."

She dropped her voice low to prevent being overheard, turning the corner toward the library in order to avoid the main hallways with all the mirrors. She thought it was just a quirk of mine, the way I avoided mirrors. I hadn't told her about the real reason and didn't plan on it.

"Something about the king has never set right with me," she whispered confidentially. "From everything I've heard, he's a bit of a mystery, and I don't like secrets in a leader. He's also been in power for a long time. Longer than any other monarch in the history of Faerie."

"Wow. How old *is* he?" I wanted to know.

"No one seems to have any idea! Our kind are long-lived, of course, but his reign has outlasted all who've come before him. He's managed to squash any kind of rising threat without casualties to his family or court. I don't know, girl…I kind of feel like maybe his long reign has warped his mind. I haven't met him, okay? But I get this odd sensation when I think about him or hear his voice. Something I can't shake telling me to look deeper. Then I get nervous and switch off entirely. I try to change my thoughts around."

I started and tried not to let Melia see my reaction. "If what you say is true, then it's a scary thought."

"I mean, this is just me sharing my opinion with you. It does seem scary. And his wife is almost never seen in public. It's like the king hides her away, ashamed of her or something, I don't know. Now you understand why it really took me by surprise to see Michael here. I think it's great how he's learning about his people and really becoming immersed in the experience. It shows he cares. And that's a good thing, don't get me wrong. But something smells off about the whole situation."

I stared at her, the way lines of intense concentration formed on her brow, the set of her chin. "Why haven't you told me this before?"

"Because it makes me sound like a crazy person!" Her hands went wild around the side of her head. "Would you believe me if we had just met and I came out and told you there was something wrong with the monarchy? Heck no, people don't say those kinds of things. If anyone overheard me, I'd be interrogated. Or worse."

I tried to shrug off the slight chill. This was the second time I'd heard about how things with the royal family weren't quite how they appeared. But it wasn't my place to question it. I had enough to worry about in the present without thinking how the monarchy of Faerie would impact me once I got there. I needed to keep my gaze focused on getting through the Fae Academy. Once I was safe, then and only then could I let my imagination run free.

We stopped outside of the library, the press of students slowing down to a trickle on this end of the castle. Not many people would choose to spend their afternoon among the dusty tomes. No wonder I liked it here.

"This is just a feeling I've had, Tavi," Melia clarified without blinking, her honey-brown eyes round. "And I want to make sure you don't repeat this to anyone."

"Not a chance. My lips are sealed."

But something about her statement struck me as truth, and feelings among the Fae are often a lot more truthful and insightful than commonly accepted facts. If anything, I'd learned to trust my gut more and more since coming to the academy.

Lunch came and Melia and I took up our normal seats across from Mike and Roman.

"Hey there, you," I said immediately, flashing a smile toward Mike.

He responded with a grunt and pushed his fork around his plate.

"Okay, someone is in a bad mood today," Melia joked. She and Roman made eye contact, and he shrugged. "What's the matter with you guys?"

Mike didn't want to answer. He kept his gaze trained on his tray as though it held the secrets of the universe.

I sat down across from him with my plate filled with greens and fruit. Swallowing my distaste at the monotonous salad, I said, "I didn't see you at the assembly today. I looked for you."

Mike didn't want to answer either, and soon Roman had to speak for him. "We were in the back. We came in a little late," he said. "We got caught up elsewhere and came right at the tail end of Leaves' speech about the top five."

I waited for the congratulations I almost expected at this point. These were two of my best friends, after all, and we'd helped each other get this far, boosted each other with our study sessions.

But I recalled a saying about expectations leading to disappointment, and soon the feeling settled on me hard.

"I guess we've all had a rough week," I said. "We are going to need more than a week of vacation when this is done—"

"I can't believe you got the top spot."

I jumped at the harsh sound of Mike's voice. He still wouldn't look at me. "What? Why?"

"It should have been me at the top." His grip tightened on his fork until his knuckles turned white. "I'm not sure how you managed to work up to number one but I don't think it's fair."

I gasped, though it sounded more like a huff. "Mike, it's not fair you're *saying* these things to me," I told him. He raised his gaze to meet mine briefly, long enough for me to take note of the puffiness, the rims of red around his eyes. The way it looked like he hadn't slept for days. Had he been pushing himself too hard? Disappointment warred with guilt. Both cut deeply.

He ran a hand through his hair, his gaze in the distance. "I'm sorry, Tavi. I'm really sorry, but I think you beating me for a spot in the top is ridiculous. I'm not even in the top *ten*."

Jealousy didn't sit well on him. It colored his cheeks and the tops of his ears a blush-pink but turned his knuckles white. I never would have expected such a reaction from him. Sitting here with him day after day, it was easy to forget about his royal status, and how we sat in the middle of the room surrounded by other students doing their best to politely ignore us. As if we weren't even there.

Yet I knew they were listening to every word.

"Jeez, I didn't realize you really thought so little of me you'd be jealous I out-scored you." I pushed away from the table. "I don't have to listen to you rant and rave about the unfairness."

I still didn't feel I'd earned my spot, still felt it was some kind of fluke, but I didn't need to let Mike know. At least not right now. That would only compound the hurtfulness.

Mike grimaced as though this were the most painful conversation he'd had in a while. My heart stirred and I dropped my gaze to the floor so he didn't notice the change. No weakness, I reminded myself, because if he saw weakness it would give him an opening to hurt me more.

"Don't bother leaving, Tavi," he stated, rising at the same time. He left his tray on the table and gestured for Roman to follow him. "I'm the one who should go. I've stayed long enough."

Melia and I watched them walk away, Roman shooting us

a small, sad smile over his shoulder before moving faster to follow his friend out. He didn't offer an apology.

"*Wow.*" Melia stressed the word and drew the vowel out. "I didn't expect him to be bitter about his place in the ranking."

I plopped back down in my chair, still stunned. "Yeah. Neither did I." I took a slow breath, my nostrils flaring, and rubbed my arms. Worries bit at me repeatedly, and no matter how hard I tried to calm down I had no success.

"You didn't deserve him going off on you." Melia placed a hand on my knee and squeezed. "Don't pay any attention to him. He'll come to his senses soon enough."

I stared at the door until well after the boys had gone, wondering if I could have said something, done something to ascertain what was really bothering him. I couldn't get a read off of Mike. I thought maybe he was angry, or even a little guilty, but neither made sense to me. Perhaps he feared disappointing his parents. It seemed plausible, but not enough to justify his emotional outburst. The only thing fitting his reaction—

My stomach froze in a flash of cold. Could Mike have had something to do with the murders of the other two top contenders, and that's why he didn't want me at the top?

No, that…that was absolutely ridiculous.

Utterly. Ridiculous. Wasn't it?

23

Michael Thornwood might be a full Fae, true. His blood didn't make him better than me, and it certainly didn't entitle him to treat me like I didn't matter, like I was a piece of trash.

I knew everyone in the first year was my competition. I didn't need a reminder. Not from him.

He ignored me for the rest of the day. Then the next. Eventually, a week later, I'd had enough. I definitely didn't need him blowing hot and cold with me. We'd been through too much together for him to act in such a petty way.

And yet even with all the bitterness and jealousy smeared across his face, he was still handsome. He still stirred my heart.

Boys! What could you do about them? They were impossible to understand on a good day and even more impossible on a bad one. Mike must be having several bad ones in a row, deciding to take his stress out on me. On the one person who wanted nothing more than to stand beside him as a partner.

Yeah, wishful thinking there.

I stalked to the library after my last class of the day, still fuming a week later from what he'd said to me. Well, fine. If Mike wanted to act like a jerk and ignore me because I'd done better than he had on our tests, then he could *be* a jerk. I was better off without him, especially if he continued to act like an envious asshole.

Studying alone didn't make a difference to me and I definitely didn't want to see Mike right now. Not after his behavior. I slammed my books down hard at my usual table, loud enough to earn a glare from the librarian. She raised a spindly green finger to her lips, wings fluttering behind her.

Sorry, I mouthed to the librarian before I turned my back on her.

Melia's story about the royals had stuck in my head as well, playing on a looped repeat. I couldn't stop thinking about the king's odd behavior, the way no one had seen the queen in public, and Mike's unexpected enrollment at the Halflings Academy despite his full Fae blood.

Did Mike's reaction have something to do with how he'd been raised in the palace surrounded by servants ready to bow to his every whim and desire? Was he just a spoiled brat? He'd been given everything he wanted his entire life.

Jealous much?

I shook my head. It wasn't my problem either way. His reaction belonged to him and deep down probably had nothing to do with me.

Try telling my subconscious.

None of it added up, because I'd seen how sweet Mike was with me and with others in our class. He was a good guy deep down no matter what happened with his father. Or with me in this current situation.

I'd grown up surrounded by wolves. I knew shifter culture inside and out because I'd been hiding among them since my father's murder. Yet what did I really know about the Fae? Enough to fudge my way into this school and enough to pass my exams, apparently, but not enough to make a concise judgment call about one of their kind.

Enough to earn the top spot grade-wise, a snarky voice said inside my head, *and slaughter the competition*.

About the intricacies of Fae culture, I was ignorant. It was a huge piece of me left to shrivel and die and no amount of memorization for tests could take the place of cultural immersion. Uncle Will and I had needed me to tamp down *everything* about my Fae nature in order to fit in with the pack. In order to survive, get them used to my unique scent so they wouldn't ask questions. Weird enough I'd showed up at age six and no one mentioned my parents.

Now, it seemed, the tables had turned.

Instead of studying, as I knew I needed to do to keep my top spot, I grabbed as many books as I could carry about the royal family and the history of Faerie, those I hadn't tapped during the first round of examinations. These books were older, heavier. Like the amount of knowledge inside added to their weight.

I blew the dust off of a few and wondered if I should be handling these without gloves.

After a few hours, my eyes blurred and burned to the point where it felt like I'd rubbed salt in them. I hadn't been able to find much on the family beyond the perfunctory information I already knew. Names and some dates and awards the king had doled out to loyal subjects. I found nothing about the politics governing the court and nothing about the odd public disappearance of the queen at events she would be expected to attend.

When I asked the librarian about any updated texts, she sent me a withering glare before hissing out how we had one of the finest selections of books on the royals in the country.

Strike two for me today.

I sighed, stretching my arms out across the table, fingertips brushing against the last volume I'd grabbed.

Myths and Legends of Ancient Faerie.

It might be worth a try. Why not? One last book then I'd call it a day.

My fingers flipped through the leather-bound volume without really settling on a page. There were old drawings done in black-and-white ink, most of the pages faded around the edges. Monsters and creatures. What were the Fae afraid of…clearly some kind of demon, if the illustrations were any indication, demons with fangs and fur and death in their eyes?

I scooted closer and leaned until my nose nearly touched the page. The knowledge knocked around in my brain before settling with a clang. My stomach surged once before dropping hard.

Not demons, no. *Wolves.* Beasts walking on two legs and donning the skin of humans. Skinwalkers or shifters, I wasn't sure. It didn't matter. These were the evils, the terrors stalking innocent Fae for no good reason.

I flipped to the next chapter and stopped at the scrawled script next to a woodcut of a wolf howling at the moon.

"The Faerie Prophecy." Author unknown; first published by Oxana the Sightless during the Age of the Red Dawn.

Hmm, interesting. I'd read somewhere how King Ty's reign began around the same era, though no one knew for certain, the date merely an approximation. The Age of the Red Dawn, jeez. Who came up with these names?

I leaned closer still to make out the fading words and mouthed along with them.

At breaking light of black moon morn
A shifter child shall be born
An innocent and pure of heart
Born to rip the Fae apart

Born to rip the Fae apart
A wicked end, downfall's start
And falling into endless night
Shall bathe the blood with sweet delight

There was more to the text, but goose bumps rose on my skin and I slammed the book shut, my eyes burning from squinting too long. I focused on getting my breathing in check. *A shifter child...*

Now I understood, in part, why the Fae hated shifters. If any of them put stock in this "prophecy," then they believed a shifter child would tear apart their cozy world. They were skeptical of all shifters because of it, and generations of fear had bred a deep hatred of my kind.

Fairy tales, the same snarky voice said loudly in my head. I couldn't get her to shut up. *It would be ridiculous to hate an entire people because Oxana the Sightless had a vision thousands of years ago.*

Still, the reading rocked me. My fingers trembled as I put the book back on the shelf where I had found it. Flashing a weak smile to the librarian on my way out, I made my way down the hallway and into the dim hush of night.

I needed air.

I should have left the book alone instead of trying to find information. It's not like I didn't have anything else going on, more important and pressing issues to tackle.

But what did it mean, a "black moon morn"? I wondered as I walked. The words stuck with me. Could it have meant an eclipse? Didn't *most* prophecies reference an eclipse? It seemed to be a common element in all cultures.

The whole thing just left a bad taste in my mouth and I wanted to forget everything I'd read. It was stupid to worry about, really. I'd found the poem in the middle of a book on myths and legends. It wasn't real.

It's not real.

Shuffling alone through the chilly night—thankfully there was no moon at all on this night, therefore no threat from moonlight—my mind turned back to thoughts of Mike. As usual. Mike and the prophecy, Mike and the dead students. Mike and the prophecy and dead students and a werewolf detective—

Footsteps sounded behind me. My ears twitched, noticing the sound, and when I turned around to see who was walking, there was no one there.

"Hello?" I called out.

The wind picked up around me but there was nothing on the breeze to give me any information, no scent carried to me. Not that I could do anything with my senses dulled by the potion spell.

Had I imagined it? I wondered if it was because of the potion or because I was finally losing my mind and seeing things. Or rather *hearing* things.

If I still had my wolf senses, I would be able to know one way or the other. I'd be able to take care of myself if there truly were someone following me. Now, I couldn't afford to take any chances.

Something snapped behind me. I ran.

The books I'd checked out were heavy in my arms and weighed me down to the point where I thought about ditching them. Then I heard the pounding of heavy boots gaining on me.

Over my shoulder, I caught a glimpse of a man in black running after me. Real, very real! My fear skyrocketed until I could taste it, like licking the inside of a copper pipe. I made the split-second decision to duck into the nearest doorway. I didn't realize until I was inside: I'd chosen the one hallway I'd tried to avoid my entire duration at the academy.

The hallway lined with mirrors.

Dammit!

I had nothing to cover my face, nothing to hide my reflection. The spell broke the moment I glanced over and saw myself reflected in the mirror. Again, it was like being doused with icy water. The wraith staring back at me from the glass had my long auburn hair but her eyes were wide, dark. Terrified. Her skin looked bleached to the color of bone and her shirt stuck out at odd angles, hanging loose on her thin frame.

At least I knew, as soon as the spell failed, I'd be able to use all of the resources available to my wolf half. Heightened senses, extra speed. I could let my wolf rise to the surface and do what she needed to do. No, not fight. Fighting would be a bad idea when I had so many books and clothes weighing me down, so many eyes ready to pop around a corner and see what I'd diligently hid these last few months.

I had to protect my wolf half. We had to run. We had to get away to safety and only then could we figure out our next move.

Despite the discomfort of having the spell break away, my muscles warmed, and when I widened my nostrils, I caught the scent at last.

Male. Young male. And angry. Driven in a way I could not fathom.

I had found the killer and he had me in his sights. Too bad he didn't understand the person he now messed with. I might look small and innocent, but I packed a wallop.

Courage surged through me.

With the hour late and no one around to see me, with the man steadily gaining on me, I threw caution to the wind and ran, faster than a normal Fae. Faster than a normal human.

Shifter speed.

And my heart nearly stopped when my pursuer did the same.

24

The man following me was a shifter.

I knew it the way some people knew when rain would come. No matter how fast I ran, he kept pace with me, down one hallway and up another. My breath came in short gasps and when I inhaled, I smelled wolf. Wolf and testosterone and a burning desire to catch me. To the point where my desire blotted out any other emotion including self-preservation.

He didn't care if anyone saw him.

I had to do something, and fast, because I couldn't keep running all night. Eventually someone would try to stop me. Eventually I would tire and the man behind me would catch up.

I couldn't think. Couldn't draw air into my body.

Run, run. Hurry!

I pushed my legs as fast as they would go and listened to the heavy echo of my footsteps. Heard the way the man did the same. His footsteps approached closer yet, a slap of leather soles on stone.

And glancing over I saw my salvation.

A fairy sconce on the wall.

I skidded to a stop beside the sconce, remembering what Melia had told me about the secret passages.

Look for the fairies. They guide the way.

I jumped up to reach the sconce, thinking to pull some kind of hidden lever and open the door. But there were no secret levers here. There were only words. Words of power to get me inside the tunnel.

What were they? Oh my God. This was a *terrible* time for me to forget.

I pressed my palm against the wall.

Losing precious seconds, I tried to remember the incantation phrase. Too many wrong attempts. I heard the man getting closer, heard his boots echoing closer and louder.

Tavi, think!

"*Elaphrium*," I whispered.

At last I managed to get out the right words for the spell and the stones melted away, revealing the pitch-black interior of the secret tunnel. I made it inside with seconds to spare and said the words a second time. The stone closed behind me and, though muffled, I heard the man pass by the other side without noticing my disappearance.

A dull ache flared across my back. It spread to my biceps and down the sides of my chest. I must have been tensing harder than I thought, because everything hurt. I took a moment to try and get my pulse down from heart attack territory. Shaken to the core.

The killer was a shifter.

No one but a shifter could have kept up with me, especially not when I let my own wolf out to play. And he'd stunk like one of my kind.

He *had* to be the killer, because no one else on campus had a reason to chase me, to single me out. Because I'd gotten the top spot and like an idiot left myself open for an attack by walking alone at night. Reason enough, right?

Still, why would someone put in time and effort to kill off probationary first-year students? It didn't make *any* sense to me. I leaned my head against the stone and winced, clutching my books tighter to my chest. Dear God. Someone wanted to kill me.

Did this mean there were more shifters hidden at the academy? And if there were, then how did they avoid detection? The only other one I knew about was the detective assigned to the case. Wilson. But he hadn't given me any other vibe beyond disgruntled and maybe a little pissed off. Also, the scents didn't match. He certainly hadn't seemed like a killer.

Then again, appearances could be deceiving.

Losing track of time, I caught my breath then followed the hidden passageway back to my dorm room, and climbed into bed still shaking. No one commented on the cobwebs decorating my hair. Not even Persephone, much to my surprise. She stared at me long enough that any other night I would have felt uncomfortable. Tonight, I just didn't care.

Ducking my head to hide, I crawled under the covers and fumbled around until I found the two remaining vials of potion from Barbara.

One left, now.

I thought about it as I swallowed the contents down the hatch, watching my skin crawl and shift and dull my shifter nature, like crawling beneath a hot, wet wool blanket. The potion didn't take my fear with it, sadly. No, *that* was left to me in its entirety. Apparently, my body and mind wanted me to have the whole experience of being afraid.

One vial and too much time until the end of the semester rolled around. I needed to at least make it to next weekend, when I had days off and could leave the campus.

With what car?

I'd junked the Toyota and wrote it off as a loss. Maybe I could ask Mike—

My jaw locked. *No.* I refused to ask him to drive me anywhere, let alone bring him near Barbara. Or the rest of my pack. He'd have too many questions. I didn't want to be beholden to him, anyway.

I fell into a dreamless sleep and woke with the sun. Melia found me soon after I showered.

"There's a party the upperclassmen are throwing tomorrow," she began excitedly. She'd cornered me in my dorm so I had less of a chance to tell her no and make an excuse to escape.

I shrugged into a clean shirt, Melia standing near the windows with her gaze purposely averted. "A party for what?" I asked.

"To celebrate not getting cut from the school." The way she said it told me I should have known already. "The upperclassmen throw one every winter around this time. It's kind of one of those things that's grown and grown until even the staff know the Friday night after the lottery is reserved." She pushed herself onto the desk beneath the window, tucking her knees under her chin. "You know how it goes."

"I guess I do," I joked. I didn't want her to know. I was afraid. Afraid to be around so many people with a target painted on my back. "A party could be fun."

She rolled her eyes. "Of course it will be fun. This is my fourth one and I can tell you it's a pretty low-key affair but there's always something exciting. Basically, we all use this to blow off a little steam and socialize. It's like a break from the rigors of classes. There will probably be alcohol. It seems like most of the upperclassmen have the off-campus hookup and use it to dazzle the rest of us."

I liked how even though she was in her fourth year Melia didn't lump herself in with the rest of her upperclassmen. "I like the way you think."

I grabbed my hairbrush, running it down the length of my still-damp hair. My school blazer hung on a peg near my bunk. After braiding the strands, I reached for the jacket, sliding my arms home.

"You'll come?" she pressed.

What could it hurt? Maybe it would give *me* a chance to blow off a little steam. And surely no one would try to come after me in a room full of people. There would be too many eyes, too many witnesses, too many bodies to get in the way of making a clean kill.

Which made the party one of the safest places I could be, really.

"Yeah, I'll come."

I managed to squeak through classes on Friday even with my attention fractured in every direction. Later, with the moon riding high and me ducking low to avoid its light, I followed Melia into one of the upperclassmen common rooms wearing our "casual clothes." She had on black leggings, offset by a rich purple sweater hanging down to mid-thigh.

I felt like a bum in comparison. I'd gone with a light-gray long-sleeved t-shirt and a black skirt, plus my ever-present ratty Converses.

She pushed open a door on the second floor to reveal a brightly lit circular space decorated in verdant greens and natural browns. A plush leather sectional sat in the center of the room facing a massive fireplace with a mantel made of carved wood.

"I've never been in here," I murmured.

Melia nodded. "This is the common room for my dorm. Nice, right? I forget this is the first time you've seen it. You always want to study in the library, you never hang out with me here."

"I'm sorry," I replied automatically.

We made ourselves comfortable, a pair of upperclassmen pressing drinks into our hands before moving off to the rest of the party. *Talk about service*. Taking a sip, I welcomed the little rush of heat from the spiked punch while I kept an eye out for familiar faces. Well, two familiar faces.

Mike and Roman were not among the crowd.

My brows drew down and I took a long sip. Was it wrong to be bothered that Mike wasn't here? I really thought he'd want to celebrate the achievements of our class, not be petulant and standoffish. He'd made it through the lottery the same as the rest of us.

I guess it irked him how I'd done better than him. More than I thought it would. Or *should*.

Still, I was determined to have fun with or without him. I followed Melia deeper into the room, stopping to say hello to several people I knew from my class.

I did have fun. One drink turned into two. There were lots of people to speak to, more than just the perfunctory congratulatory conversation. For the first time since arriving at the school, I was included. The feeling of fitting in warmed a knot of ice inside of me I hadn't known I was carrying around.

Standing in the center of the conglomeration of fellow halflings, I was at ease.

Even with Dawn and the rest of my shifter mates back at home, I'd never felt like I really belonged. I'd always been on guard against the chance someone would pry too deeply into my past. That they would look at me and see something wrong with me.

Here, no one saw anything. Yes, I still had things to hide, and yes, if someone looked too closely they would discover darkness and lies, but...

I clung to the *but*.

Melia and I danced together until my legs burned and sweat beaded along my brow. She took a break long before I did, seeing a boy she liked and dipping out to flirt with him while I continued to move, to sway. *She deserves it*, I thought to myself, turning in a smooth circle. She deserved to find a guy to flirt with, to snuggle with, because she was an amazing person.

Hell, I was an amazing person too! Soon I would find my own guy to flirt with, someone appropriate. My brain conjured a picture of Mike and effectively soured the rest of my good feelings toward dancing. Mike didn't *want* to flirt with me. He didn't even want to be around me.

Finally, I got too hot, my head swimming and my vision fuzzy, and decided to take a break of my own. I stumbled toward the door to the balcony, still holding my drink. There were several balconies jutting off this floor of the castle and this one was more decorative than functional, only large enough to hold a handful of people at one time.

I craved the fresh air. I wasn't sure how it felt to be drunk, never having indulged this much in the past, but from the delicious warmth curling in my stomach to the fuzz between my ears, I thought I might be close to it tonight. *Safe*, though. The party continued to rage behind me and there were people everywhere. People who would watch my back and make sure nothing happened to me.

I leaned against the cool railing, letting some of the heat from my body drain away with a sigh. I deserved this, I thought drowsily. I deserved a night of fun where I didn't have to worry about mirrors, or garlic, or crystal balls.

Where I didn't have to worry about Mike and his bad attitude, or hooded killers chasing me down the halls.

I didn't have to worry about dead students or wolves on the hunt tracking me down in the service of Kendrick Grimaldi.

My face melted down into a scowl at the appearance of his name in my head. He didn't belong there. Not tonight, not ever. There was no way he could find me, not even if he put his best trackers on my scent. I was long gone. A ghost in the wind.

I felt someone move up behind me and smiled. "How's it going with Barry?" I asked Melia. "Are you making any headway yet or is he still being stubbornly resistant to your charms?" My words slurred slightly. I didn't care.

But I certainly *started* to care when I turned around and the face I saw wasn't Melia's. It wasn't a face at all but a black hood and mask covering the man's features.

The killer had found me.

25

I reacted without thinking—pure adrenaline—moving to the side and slamming my fist into the man's throat. I kicked out with my leg and hooked his right knee with my left.

The guy went down. I had the element of surprise on my side because he hadn't expected me to retaliate with any physical force. Scream, probably, but not try to break his nose off his face.

Before he hit the floor, I spun around, going for the doors now closed behind us. My fingers clamped onto the metal handle and jerked it forward.

It cost me seconds I didn't have, not with the space too small to maneuver. Especially when the doors wouldn't open.

Locked.

The man caught me around the ankle and jerked. Instead of giving in to the motion, I stubbornly planted my left leg and mule-kicked with the one he held, hammering my foot into whatever part of him I could reach. His chest, as it turned out. He tried to pitch forward, to adjust his weight and balance to avoid the kick. Then swung his arms up to grab me around the midsection.

I heard his labored breathing. Kept one hand on the door and reached back to knuckle-punch him with the other.

Everything stopped when his teeth bit into the side of my thigh. Ripped clean through the fabric of my skirt and sliced through skin, puncturing deep enough to draw blood.

I screamed then, wincing at the flash of pain. In the darkness, I couldn't see well enough to figure out my next move, not against the muscular build of the man attacking me.

A sweep of his hand knocked me to my knees and I landed hard. Bones jarred. My teeth clacked together. He moved with me without releasing his teeth from my thigh.

My head pounded and my ribs ached with every inhalation, pushed down on my stomach. Luckily, nothing seemed to be broken.

I cupped my hands together in front of me, muttering an incantation under my breath. I didn't have a chance of winning with brute strength. Not against a wolf like this and not with my spell intact, the moon hidden behind a sky overcast with clouds. But I could use magic—*somewhat*—and odds were good he could not.

I twisted long enough to send the spell flying, and a blast of magic hit the man square in the chest. He stumbled back and knocked against the side of the building. I caught the flash of yellow eyes through the fabric of his mask a second before he charged forward again. I raised my forearm to shield and his teeth bit deep. Blood dripped down from the marks.

Anger warred with fear. This guy thought he could come here and use his *wolf* against me?

I struggled to form a second spell, one to levitate him away from me and send him flying.

I wasn't fast enough.

With a growl, the man scooped me up. And tossed me over the balcony.

The night air buzzed around me on my way down, down.

There wasn't a chance to think. Not a moment for the full realization of my fall to reach me. I hit the ground hard, only one story but enough to hear a bone snap in my arm accompanied by a fierce rush of fire. My head bounced off the grass and for a moment I saw nothing but black as I struggled to breathe.

The clouds shifted. The full moon gazed down at me, a familiar sight I'd been avoiding since I arrived at the academy. And my spell broke in an instant.

But after the blow to my head I didn't have enough logic left to realize the full implications. The scent of my own blood filled my nostrils and my stomach churned. I couldn't do anything other than struggle to draw air into my body, struggle to stay conscious. I lost the fight soon enough and the sounds of footsteps came closer and closer.

He's here to finish the job...

I was alive.

I *thought* I was alive, anyway. The world slowly came into focus with a swell of agony that brought my jaws clenching together. Soon reality shifted and merged into familiar blue skin I hadn't seen since my first night at the academy.

Nurse Julie blinked at me, her gangly arms hanging at her sides. Not the killer, then.

"Oh, you're awake."

She unwrapped the blood pressure monitor with a snap of Velcro and set it down on her station.

"Where..." I tried to say. My teeth felt loose and I

struggled to form the words, running my tongue over my lower teeth to check for anything shattered there. The last thing I remembered was lying on the lawn, expecting death.

"Don't try to talk right now, Tavi, just take it easy," she warned. "Another student saw you fall off the balcony and immediately ran to get me. I brought you here."

I sat up with enough force to send another swell of pain rushing to my head and I nearly howled, pushing my palms against my eyes to keep the world from spinning.

"Miss Alderidge, did you not hear me say to *take it easy*? Do you have a death wish? You plummeted over a balcony, broke your arm, and gave yourself a pretty nasty little concussion," Nurse Julie said stiffly. Her wings rustled in agitation. "Do. Not. *Move*. Stay down until I can get you checked out. Now hold still or I'll be forced to strap you to the table."

I laid my head back down on the thin pillow, blinking through the pain as Nurse Julie took my arm and prepped it for IV.

"Oh, *God*!" I bolted upright a second time, ripping at the IV needle.

"Miss Alderidge, calm yourself!"

I was in direct overhead light. With Nurse Julie administering pain medication through the IV. And my last potion spell had broken while I was out cold.

I was both halves of myself, thoroughly, without the spell to protect me. Which meant she saw my true nature and still treated me, had probably taken my blood and tested it to make sure ...*what*?

I panicked. The nurse knew. The jig was up. I was going to be kicked out of school.

"I have to go," I managed, swinging my legs over the side of the table despite the mild concussion and the dizziness that would have brought an elephant to its knees.

Get out, get out, get out. I had to get out of here and quickly, before the Headmaster came for me, to send me back to Uncle Will.

To send me back to Kendrick.

"Miss Alderidge, please." Strong hands fell on my shoulders to steady me. "There's no need to worry. Try to relax."

It took me the longest time to recognize her smile. Even longer to know what it meant and why she was looking at me with such focus. In comfort, in camaraderie.

"You're not the only one who can go furry in this joint. Oh, stop looking at me. No more despair on your pretty face," she continued with a waggle of her brows. "That's how you get wrinkles. I won't be telling anyone unless I want to out *myself*, too."

She wouldn't...wait, *what?*

I slowed my hysteria enough to lean back and take her in for the first time. The blue skin, the wings. And...a werewolf shifter? The two pictures didn't compute to me.

"I don't understand," I said stupidly.

"Oh, honey. You think you're the only one in the world looking for a way out of bad circumstances?" Nurse Julie sighed, drawing over her wheeled stool and placing it so she and I were closer to eye level. "I know all about pack relations and the strict guidelines placed on females. Trust me, I know."

"But you don't look like a shifter," I tried to tell her, wincing when she took my non-broken arm and ran some gauze soaked with disinfectant over the wounds. They would heal soon enough. Once I got my strength back and some food in my stomach.

"You mean the wings? The skin?" She shrugged her shoulders and those wings rolled out to their full length, nearly touching each wall and reflecting the light in shades of rainbow brilliance. "Yes, they were a gift from my father before he ran off. Some species of Fae are notorious lotharios. He was one of them, and he left me with my mother, never to be seen again. There really aren't a lot of options for females in the pack, especially for someone like me, because the blue skin isn't something I can will away with magic. The wings I can make appear and disappear whenever I please, at least. My mother and I had to go to some crazy lengths to find a potion strong enough to hide my skin color."

A snap of her fingers and the wings disappeared in a whiff of smoke. Another snap and they appeared again.

I thought of Barbara, the unorthodox apocalypse-prepping witch with *her* snapping fingers. Asking her for a potion like mine seemed small in comparison to finding a way to change the color of your skin. What had Nurse Julie or her mother promised to get the spell?

"How did you get here? I mean—" I cut myself off, shaking my head and instantly regretting it. I really shouldn't be moving.

Nurse Julie smiled at me. Kindly. Openly. "It's not prying, really. I came from a pack in Iowa. Most packs operate on an old, outdated traditional patriarchy. There are too many rules oppressing women and no one willing to make the necessary changes. Especially for those of us who are seen as less than because of our bloodline. And *women*. Don't get me started. And they all hate halflings, whether you're half human or half something else, *anything* else. You want to hear my story?"

"Yes, please," I managed.

She finished addressing the cuts and abrasions on my free arm. They would more than likely heal in a few hours. "I'll share mine if you share yours, young lady. My only request, if you will. But…let's see if I can sum this up for you." Julie slapped her knees, her attention turning inward, then said, "My mother wanted the best for me, truly, but the decision wasn't hers to make. Once I reached a certain age, my alpha made a match he thought would benefit both me and the pack. It wasn't his fault. He didn't know about me, about my dual nature. My mother made sure to keep my half-Fae nature a secret otherwise I would have been killed on the spot. The prejudice extends to both sides, you see."

"Yeah, so I've learned."

She paused, drawing in a breath. "I didn't want the match. Why would I want to tie myself to a man who, if he knew the truth of who I was, would hate me? Would make it his business to ruin my life and maybe even kill me? I was desperate to get out. I would have attacked anyone who came at me. I ran. I ran until I realized. I didn't know where I was going and I had no other options available to me. I didn't even say goodbye to my family."

"You found yourself here," I supplied.

I watched her gather the dressings for my broken arm, keeping it contained to a soft cast until the bone could reset on its own.

"It seems most who are lost eventually find themselves on the doorstep of the Halflings Academy. Out in the open, we are sitting ducks. There are too many weapons pointed at us. Now, I wish I'd slowed down enough to think it through. I haven't seen my family in many, many years and I miss them greatly. But if I go back, I would not be welcome. Odds are good I'd still be killed on the spot."

"You've never gone back?" I asked. "Not even once to see your mom?"

"No, I haven't. I miss my mother dearly but I never want to go back. I imagine *you* did the same thing I did." Nurse Julie shot me a look from under her brows. "You packed up and you bolted, for whatever reason I'm sure you'll tell me about. I live at the academy and I love my life here. I've managed to work the magic to completely suppress my shifter side while I'm here. I'm sure you will find your new life too, in time."

We sat in silence for a moment, her staring at me and me staring at my hands. She had found a way to suppress her shifter side fully? I wondered how she did it. If maybe her distinct Fae heritage gave her some kind of edge the rest of us hadn't discovered yet.

I told Nurse Julie the barest minimum about my story, an eerily similar echo to the one she'd told me. I kept Kendrick's name out of it in case she'd heard of him. And when we were done, she stood, gathering up the IV and tapping the vein in my arm. The needle slipped through the skin and she wrapped it with gauze and tape to keep it in place.

"Your fated mate doesn't know where you are?" she asked.

I shook my head, the movement tiny. "No. And if I do everything right, he never will." Then swallowed a scream when she jostled the soft cast.

"Sweetheart, your arm is broken. You landed pretty hard on it and the radius is snapped in the middle. There are some cuts from the scuffle and I treated those, set the arm. While you're here, no one will be able to come in and see you. Let your wolf nature heal the rest. Bones take a little bit longer to heal without magic."

"Yes, I know. Thank you."

"There's more." Her eyes darted around, looking everywhere but my face. "It's disturbing. I wasn't sure I should tell you—"

"What's the matter?" I interrupted. "What is it?"

"You have bites on your body. Werewolf bites."

26

A wolf had bitten me, one of my own kind. Nurse Julie thought she was delivering some kind of terrible news to me. But I already knew and had made tentative peace with the knowledge.

"It's okay. I had a feeling he was one of our own when he chased me down the hallway the other day. Have they found the man responsible?" I wanted to know.

Nurse Julie bit the inside of her lip and I had my answer. "The students saw you fall but no one saw who attacked you. If they did, no one has said anything to me. Then again, I rushed you right over here once I realized…you know…what you are. I didn't want anyone else to figure it out and the more time you spent in the open, the more likely the outcome became."

"He was on the balcony with me. Pushed me right over the edge because he knew I was going to wallop him with a spell. You're right: he's a wolf." I shifted and ground my teeth to keep from crying out from the pain.

Healing abilities, sure, but this kind of damage would take me a bit of time to repair. I knew for a fact the school had a policy about broken bones. Another one of those lessons to make us strong. The nurses could treat our superficial wounds but not with magic. Any serious damage had to heal on its own or we would have to find a way to heal ourselves.

Advanced magic, I remembered Roman saying. Something they didn't start teaching until the upper years.

What if Kendrick's pack had found me and this wasn't the school's killer but a new attack? Surely my fated mate had dispatched his cronies to search for me once they discovered I had vanished. What if one of them had actually tracked me down to the academy?

Or what if they were killing students to get revenge for me running away?"

"Tavi, whatever you're thinking, *stop*. It isn't going to help you." Julie reached out a hand and pushed the hair away from my face in an oddly maternal gesture despite the blue skin. Her fingertips were soft and warm. "I know about wolf culture. The boys might be petty but they wouldn't harm innocents for no reason, even if they are Fae. And there are two other dead students in this case. Let's sit here and try to use our heads. Okay? Who else would want to kill you?"

I shivered. "Well, I just got the top spot. The last two students who died...they were in line for the top as well," I told her, sharing the idea that had plagued me.

She stared at me through wide eyes and I read the shock in them. She clearly hadn't considered it, thinking the two deaths random. "Are you sure?"

"I think I'm sure. How much longer is this going to take?" I used my chin to gesture to the IV. "I need to go." I wasn't going to let this stop me, and I certainly wasn't going to let the man get away with hurting anyone else.

"Sweetie, you need to relax. This isn't a game. You have a serious injury. Someone *pushed* you off a *balcony*. You need fluids, and your arm is going to take a long time to heal. Not to mention—"

She tried to push me back down. I understood where she was coming from, but I didn't have the time to waste. And my wolf had taken enough shit lately.

I growled, ripping the IV out of my arm with a flash of gold-tinted eyes. It felt good to be whole again. "I'm leaving now."

My voice wasn't my own. It belonged to her, my wolf. She was pissed off. She'd been silenced for too long, pushed around, thrown into situations where she hadn't had a choice, and eventually silenced entirely thanks to the potions. She wasn't about to let anyone else tell her what to do.

Nurse Julie fixed me with a stern look, the tension in her brow melting into frustration, and I knew if she had a choice her wolf would have risen as well. To challenge mine. "Well, fine, if you're going to act snarly, then at least give me a minute to get you set up with a new potion. You can't leave like this, Miss Wolf. Someone is going to see you for who you are and then we'll both be in hot water."

"I have one more potion vial in my dorm," I retorted.

"Then give me a minute to get it for you. You can't risk someone seeing you right now. Especially when you appear to have a little trouble controlling yourself. Get those canines in check, missy."

Did I have a choice in trusting her? No. Not even a *hint* of a choice. I ran my tongue along the length of my sharpened canines before willing them to return to normal.

Julie left me alone while she went to my dorm for the last vial.

It just didn't make sense to me, I mused, tapping the fingers of my good arm against the edge of the table. An attack on me, I understood. But then the odds were clearly in the attacker's favor. Coming after me during a party, when I was surrounded by people? Out in the open?

It was almost like he'd been desperate.

It would have been better, smarter, to wait until I was alone or on my way back from the party. The hallways were starting to empty out with the purgings, so it was certainly less crowded now.

And why bite me? Then again, the man didn't know I was a wolf and his bites would leave me unaffected. Had he thought to inflict extra damage?

I winced. Once I left the city and my family behind, I'd thought heading down this unfamiliar road and hiding at the academy would be the least of my worries. I didn't think I'd have to deal with a murderer on campus.

Who would have guessed?

Nurse Julie returned with the last vial and I guzzled it without hesitation. The familiar burn began low in my chest and stretched along to my extremities. My vision went blurry and for a moment I thought I would faint. Then everything disappeared, the movement under my skin calming and the familiar spell setting in, dulling my senses and pushing my wolf back into the darkness. I felt the caress of her claws on the inside of my mind, not too kindly, before a familiar kind of numbness set in.

"There you are," Julie said proudly. Her wings flickered once before lying still against her back. "You're as good as new. Your arm will follow suit shortly enough."

Wincing and cradling my broken arm to my chest within the sling, I walked slowly to my dorm and found the place empty. I guessed the party was still in full swing. Not much time had gone by between the fall and my visit to the nurse's office. I wondered who had found me, and whether they would come forward to make themselves known. I'd like to thank them.

I didn't want to even try to climb the ladder up to my bed and instead moved to the seats near the window, avoiding the moonlight. Avoiding moonlight, mirrors, garlic, *everything*.

"Hello hello?" The familiar voice called out from the doorway seconds before a wild brown head popped around the corner. "There you are!"

"Meli?"

I couldn't stand up to greet her even if I wanted to. The exhaustion had set in and once I sat down, my body decided it had had enough.

Melia stalked forward with her tongue clucking and her index finger raised and wagging at me. "Where did you go?" she teased. "I turned around and you were gone! I looked everywhere for you and then figured you came back here. Looks like my hunch was right." She sighed. "And not like Barry was making any kind of move on me."

I gestured toward the sling. "I had a little accident."

Her smile dropped in an instant and only then did I realize she'd forced it into place. "Yeah, I know." She sighed again. "I'm sorry. I went to the nurse's office and must have missed you by seconds. I was just trying to be positive."

She'd come looking for me? I'd made the best kind of friend, I realized then. One who would stay by my side.

"I'm glad you're okay. I can't believe you fell off the balcony."

"I didn't fall. I was pushed," I told her. "A hooded man attacked me and tried to kill me."

"*What?*"

Her screech would have caused birds to fly from trees. Luckily, we were alone. Luckily, she believed me without question.

"The man bit me." I kept the *werewolf* part to myself. "I tried to get inside to the safety of the party but the doors wouldn't open. He tossed me over the balcony like I weighed nothing at all."

"He *bit* you?" Melia leaned back on her heels and stared at me for the longest time. "If he bit you, then you might be able to find out who he is."

"Huh? Wh-what do you mean?"

"I mean, the odds are good even after the nurse cleaned the wounds, there is a trace amount of his DNA still left in your body where his teeth sank in. And if we can access it, then maybe we can glean some information about him by using divination," she said, her eyes sparkling.

I knew she'd had as much to drink as I had, or more, but damn, Melia had a good head on her shoulders.

"I can't touch crystal balls. I have…an allergy to quartz," I protested.

"But you're so good at divination." Um, no, I wasn't, but I wasn't going to burst her bubble. "Even without the crystal ball—which happens to be the best way to find out—you might be able to see the man in visions. I doubt Tarot would work, and neither will runes or the pendulum because they don't operate the same way. They are definitely more interpretive than accurate because those tools are only as good as the interpreter."

As she went on, I gave some thought to it. Did I *want* to know? Did I *want* to see the face of the man who had attacked me and tried to end my life? Yes. And no. I was terrified the face I'd see looking back at me would belong to Kendrick Grimaldi. What if he'd found me? He would never let me go. He would certainly rather see me dead than live with knowing I'd run from him.

"We should get to the divination lab," I said, struggling to stand. "Immediately. I can sleep later."

"Hold on now, not so fast." Melia reached out a hand to stop me. "You're in no condition to be breaking into the divination lab. You *do* need to get some sleep because you look like body snatchers just dug you out of a fresh grave."

"Gee, thanks for the pick-me-up, Mel. But no deal. We need to use whatever DNA is left before it's too late. We don't exactly have a lot of time to sit around and relax."

We stood facing each other, my shoulders hunched with fatigue and taking precious inches away from my height until I stared at her collarbone instead of her face. She sighed. "Okay, I know better than to leave you because you most certainly won't relax no matter how badly you need to. But you're not going alone, either. I'm going to come with you because two heads are better than one. I can't risk another attack on your life. The guy is probably still out there and you're the top student now."

"Fine." I just wouldn't touch the crystal ball. I could try and make the spell work without the physical contact.

"Do you need help?" Melia looked ready to scoop me into her arms and carry me toward the divination lab herself. She might have been able to, as well. The Fae were very strong.

I chuckled though it sounded more like asthmatic wheezing. "I'm okay. Thank you, though."

I grabbed a hoodie and slung it over my shoulders as best I could. We walked side by side down the darkened halls, each of my steps strategically placed to avoid the shafts of moonlight coming through the windows. If Melia noticed anything strange about the way I moved she didn't say so. I knew she could never understand why I avoided the moonlight without telling her everything.

The party felt like it had happened years ago. How much difference a few hours made. Broken bones and new revelations.

It didn't take long for us to reach the door of the divination lab and I pushed it open with a creak of wood, inhaling the familiar scents of tea and bergamot.

If I could move past my fear and do this correctly, then I might have a solid lead tonight. And this would be over. I'd made sure to slip the detective's business card into the pocket of my hoodie. Once I had a face, I could give the information to Wilson and let him handle the rest. He might not believe me but I had the sling and the bites to prove I'd been attacked. The rest would be up to him.

Then it would be done. No one else would be hurt and I'd be safe.

My arm ached and I tried to move past the pain. *It will be over soon.*

"Let's go to my workstation," I told Melia. I'd feel more comfortable there.

She looked smaller in the shadowed hush of the room. As though she'd shrunk in on herself instead of standing tall, the way I always expected her to look. "Do you have your crystal?"

"Yes. It's in the drawer with the rest of my things. I haven't touched it since the first day when it was covered with velvet." We moved up the risers toward the second tier where Mike and Roman and I worked on a normal day.

Melia did the honors, removing the crystal ball from the drawer and balancing it on its pedestal. Finally, she removed the velvet cloth. The crystal ball gleamed with an inner light. I sat down and moved my free hand toward it, close but making sure to keep from contacting the surface.

"Clear your mind," Melia reminded me as she settled at my side. "The energy connections are already there. Think about the bites, think about the attack, the way the man moved and the sensations he gave you."

"The will to live," I muttered. "I've never felt more like I had to fight for my life." Okay, maybe I could think of *one* other time.

"Place the whole of your attention on the masked man

and nothing but him. It will create a link to him and should be able to give you a glimpse of his face."

"Without the mask? I've only seen him with his face covered."

"We can only hope," she said as she crossed her fingers.

I took a deep breath and closed my eyes for a moment. Trying to center myself when everything inside of me felt like a whirlwind I couldn't contain. When I opened my eyes, I focused my gaze on the depths of the ball.

The only thing I hadn't been able to do in my divination class. And still I'd managed to pass, managed to get to the top spot. I tried to focus on the man and the way he reached out to grab me after I kicked him. The way his black hood and mask obscured any recognizable features. I tried to focus on the feeling of his body when he tossed me over the edge of the ledge.

After a few minutes of focus, the interior of the ball still remained empty. Blank. *Do not pass GO and do not collect two hundred dollars*, I thought ruefully. Maybe my exhaustion was blocking the way.

"I did tell you I've never been able to conjure an image from the ball, right?" I reminded Melia.

She blew out a breath, clearly unwilling to listen to my excuses. "I know you say you have your allergy thing, but it's going to work a whole lot better if you touch the ball. You need the connection; it's the only way we'll be able to find out who this guy is. One touch and then you can heal later."

"I can't," I told her with a pleading gaze.

"It's just the graze of a fingertip to establish the connection—"

"No, I really *can't*." My eyes went supernova with pleading. "You don't understand. This isn't just something I don't *want* to do. There are going to be serious repercussions if I touch this quartz." I didn't have any vials of potion left. I needed to be extra careful—super duper extra careful—until I had the chance to get back to Barbara the witch for more.

"Tavi," Melia replied with a shake of her head and a tone full of exasperation, "I have literally never heard of a quartz crystal allergy. I know you say you have issues with it but I doubt a few seconds of touching quartz is going to do any serious or long-term damage. Don't you want to catch this guy?"

"Why can't you just understand? This is something *I can't do*?" *Dial back the hysterics*, I warned myself.

"Because it's ridiculous!" she exclaimed. "You want to catch this guy or not? You want to do what you can to stop him from hurting you and hurting other people? He's already killed two students! Two! And he tried to kill you! He needs to be stopped. Just touch the dang crystal."

"*No.*"

Before I had a chance to react, Melia grabbed both my hands and brought them to the crystal ball, broken arm included. I yelped with pain, and then gasped with shock, jerking away an instant too late.

Too late. I'd touched the quartz. The last of the spell fell away with the familiar dousing of icy cold water, leaving my skin shivering and my stomach heaving. Leaving me exposed.

27

Numb with shock, I stared at Melia, but she was staring at the crystal ball. The interior of it had filled with black swirling smoke.

It did not show me the hooded and masked man. It showed me *nothing* except the black swirling smoke. As complete disappointment began to sink into me, the smoke changed. In a flash of red and orange light, the interior of the crystal ball burst into flame. The sphere began to hum and vibrate as if it were a bomb about to go off. How—

Melia and I jumped back in tandem and knocked into the rear desks in our attempt to get away from it.

"Down!" she yelled, and a moment later the crystal ball exploded. Quartz fragments ricocheted across the space, raining down on us in a shower of fire and splinters and sparks.

We had both dropped down to the floor with our arms covering our heads for protection. Only one arm for me and I felt the shards of quartz slice across my exposed skin. My broken arm barked in pain from the jolting.

"What the hell happened?" She was screaming to be heard above the explosion still reverberating. "What is going on?"

"I'm sorry!" I apologized immediately. It was all my fault.

"Why are you sorry? What did you do?" she continued to screech. *"This is not normal!"*

I shifted to try and cover her bare skin before the shards of crystal pierced through and drew blood. Feeling responsible if she got hurt. Tears slipped from my eyes as the shower of sparks at last came to an end. "I'm so sorry, Meli. I wanted to tell you. I wanted to tell you everything but I didn't think I should."

My shifter senses returned with a rush of pleasure, as though my inner wolf was eager to be free. Eager to lord her freedom over my Fae half so soon after being stifled yet again.

I can't be contained.

Out of vials. What was I going to do? This was bad. Very, very bad.

My breathing hitched and my heart nearly beat out of my chest in a rush like hyperventilation. Panic filled me. Out of vials and no way to get to Barbara for more. No information on the hooded killer either, so...all for nothing.

Instead of anger, as I'd expected from my friend, she sat still for a moment and considered me. The crystal shards made their final descent to earth, the sudden silence strange and heavy around us. "What is going on?" she repeated, softly this time. "Tell me what happened, Tavi. Please. I need to know."

Oh, this was going to sting. And her reaction could go either way at this point. She could understand...or she could end our friendship. The weight of that settled in my chest like an elephant sitting there.

I took a deep breath to try to dislodge the elephant there. "I'm not who I say I am," I began hesitantly. "And that's why I couldn't touch the crystal. You saw what happened." I hiccupped on another deep breath, rocking back until my spine pressed the desk behind me. "I'm so, *so* sorry. You're not hurt, are you?"

"No, but you clearly are. And I think it's about time for you to tell me what's happening so I can stop worrying," she said, biting her lip. "Why do you look different? Tavi…you *smell* different."

On another hiccup, I spilled everything. Everything I'd tried to hide, the potions and Barbara and the real reason why I had applied to the academy. I told Melia about Elfwaite and Kendrick, about my birthday party and my father's murder. Everything.

She listened with blank expression and no questions, though I saw a shadow form behind her eyes. A new tension, a stiffness to her shoulders. Frightened of me? Or frightened for me?

The latter would be more than I deserved for lying to her for so long. For deceiving my only friend.

"The shifter who attacked me tonight is more than likely a member of the Grimaldi pack who decided I was better off dead than alive," I said, adjusting my legs to get more comfortable. The exhaustion riding me so hard for the last few hours had disappeared. "But I'm not sure. Not really. I didn't think it would be a problem yet. I also didn't think it was a shifter doing the killing. It seems I was so wrong."

Melia didn't miss a beat. She reached out and took my free hand in hers, brushing aside fine splinters of quartz like diamond dust along my palm. "I don't care if you're half wolf," she told me softly. "As far as I'm concerned, you're *Fae*, and you *belong* in Faerie. You're one of the kindest people I know and you've always been there for me when I need a friend. You work hard, you accept everyone, and so what if you have no fashion sense?" The sentiment drew out a mutual if ragged chuckle from both of us. "But it sounds like you need more help in this situation than the Fae can give you. The old prejudices are no joke. On both sides."

Tears burned my eyes and I swallowed them back. Yes, I'd made the best kind of friend, I told myself again. The kind who stuck around when times got tough. I was lucky. So lucky.

"You are going to need some shifters to help you on this one," Melia continued decisively.

Um...*no way*. "I can't go to them," I insisted. I tightened my grip on her hand. "You don't understand. Uncle Will is never going to forgive me for what I did. Odds are good he doesn't even know Kendrick sent his goons after me. I doubt they're working together on this one."

Although...maybe they were and maybe my *uncle* was the one hunting me.

Acid reflux burned my throat. I didn't want to go down that particular dark path.

The entire issue was wrapped up tightly in shifters and we both knew it. The man who'd chased me the other night had had shifter speed. The one who bit me tonight was a werewolf. Whatever was happening to the rest of the first-year top students, it stank of shifters.

At least Melia shared my opinion.

I'd thought I was the only half-shifter at the school, an assumption that had turned around and bitten me in the ass. Or rather thigh. Close enough. Nurse Julie had the same issues I did. And now, sitting and thinking about it, I was pretty sure my divination teacher had a secret to hide as well. She'd felt like part of my pack. I didn't have the sensation about anyone else.

There was always Detective Wilson...

"Do you think it could be another student?" Melia mused. She squeezed my hand almost to the point of pain.

I straightened. I'd initially thought it to be another student doing the killing, then dismissed the theory when I became the target, figuring it was personal to me only, what with Uncle Will and Kendrick Grimaldi and all that going on. "How do you figure?" I asked.

"It makes sense if it's another student. Why target the top students if you have no skin in the game? I mean, I'm sure your fated mate has people looking out for you, but there's no reason for whoever attacked you to have killed the other boy and girl. Unless there are *two* killers, which means it's someone who has more to lose. Someone who is hiding like you are."

I shivered. "It does make sense. Why didn't I think of it before?"

"Because you're too close to the heart of it. This is *personal* for you. I'm guessing it's personal to someone else as well. We just have to figure out who and find a way to stop them before they kill again. Because you're still alive and they probably aren't too happy about it."

I couldn't help the dry chuckle. She wanted *us* to stop this? Once upon a time, if someone had suggested I'd one day play a key part in catching a murderer, I would have laughed in their face because it sounded ludicrous.

After everything... "No, it's definitely not going to go over well with them to know they failed," I muttered.

I thought about Detective Wilson's card in my pocket. Melia was right; we needed outside help. There was no way we could handle this alone. The pack had mighty muscle behind it. *Any* pack, not just the one I'd belonged to. Did I chance bringing in someone who might rat me out to my family?

Another rock and hard place moment.

"Will you lend me your phone?" I asked Melia before I had time to change my mind. "I need to make a call."

She looked surprised but the look faded quickly as she tilted her head. "At this hour?"

"He'll be up. Trust me."

I watched her dig into her back pocket and punch in the code to unlock the screen before handing me the sleek black cell. It was a simple matter to type in the detective's number from the card.

As I had suspected, he was awake.

His brusque voice answered the call after three rings. "This is Wilson."

"Detective Wilson, this is Tavi Alderidge. I need your help."

I kept the details to a minimum, describing the attack and telling him of my suspicions. The scratch of a pencil sounded in the background as Wilson took notes.

"Don't do anything rash. Hide until morning and don't let anyone see you. I'll meet you at the gates at sunrise. Do you understand me, Miss Alderidge? Your life is in danger if what you say is true."

"It's true," I assured him. "I'll be there."

"Good."

He hung up with a decisive click and I stared at the screen for a moment before ending the call on my end.

"There you go," Melia said, having overheard everything. Her brown eyes searched mine. "Think you can make it until the morning?"

"I hate to ask you this. You've already been so helpful. Do you think I could stay in your room?"

Instead of answering, she grabbed me in a hug, and I didn't have the heart to tell her the gesture hurt my broken arm.

"Girl, you don't even need to ask. Come on. Let's get a little sleep while we still can."

Melia made room for me on her bed and we snuggled together under the blankets. It was a different sort of acceptance, I realized now. I thought being surrounded by people at the party had been a major change for me. A milestone of growth. But sleeping with Melia's arm around me, *without* my potion spell hiding my truth, it was a different sort of realness. One I would have never expected and one I knew I would be eternally grateful for.

She saw the real me and she didn't run. No, she stood beside me and offered to help.

Most people simply weren't built like Melia.

It was more than luck pairing me with her as my mentor. My last thought before falling asleep was: perhaps destiny or fate or whatever luck governed the universe really did have my back.

I met Detective Wilson at the gate in the morning still wearing my clothes and cast from the night before, the sun beginning to peek through the trees with a golden glow, illuminating frost and tiny icicles. A knock on the iron with a small touch of magic had the gate swinging open to accommodate his car without me having to push.

He drove through and with a glance over my shoulder to make sure we truly were alone, I bid the gates to close again, accompanying the request with another pulse of magic to seal them against anyone else The twin iron structures topped with the academy logo swung slowly closed and locked behind the car.

I gestured to the left with my good hand, toward the small lot with empty spots. Wilson parked among the other vehicles and walked toward me with supernatural grace, looking every bit the predator. His breath expelled in a great white cloud in front of his face. Taller and more imposing than I remembered, and his steely eyes speared through me as he asked for a quiet place for the two of us to talk.

I led him to the library and the private study room accessible only to the upperclassmen. I'd never been inside before but Melia had given me her code, stating how the rest of the students would be too tired from partying all night to bother using the room and we'd be safe to talk there. I locked the door behind us and fixed it with a ward spell too. My paranoia had to be good for something, and with the wolf in me fully exposed, at least I wouldn't have to avoid moonlight now. Or mirrors. Or garlic. Or quartz crystal.

Just everyone else in the castle.

Detective Wilson stood by the window, studying the swirling woodwork of the old oak molding. It wasn't until he turned around, staring at me fully, that he stopped moving. Literally ceased all movement and turned into a living statue. His nostrils widened and he drew in a deep breath.

"Well," he began in his gruff voice. "You've been hiding things from me, Miss Alderidge. Do you care to explain?"

He'd caught my scent with ease. My *true* scent. I tried not to shuffle my feet or fiddle with my clothing. Anything betraying my nervousness. I had nothing to be nervous about, I reasoned. I had information to help him close this case. It would have to be enough to keep him from turning me in. *Quid pro quo.*

"Yes, I have been hiding things."

"What are you?" he barked.

I wasn't wearing my spell, and my paranoia had ridden me for so long, forcing me to act as though nothing were wrong, it almost felt good to come clean. Again. To at least make the decision to trust someone.

I didn't give him the same story I'd told Melia or Nurse Julie the night before. Detective Wilson got the abbreviated version limited to *need to know* details without the emotional backstory. But it was refreshing to get it out there to someone who was like me. Someone who understood the details of wolf pack law the way he would.

Wilson would not condemn me and return me to my uncle, not when he heard what I had to say. I had to believe. The more I spoke, the more the knots inside of me eased until the words came easier.

I finished my story as Wilson took a seat at the table with his hands folded in front of him, fingernails neat and trimmed, and a black stone ring around his right thumb. The intensity of his gaze did not mellow the longer he stared.

"As I'm sure you're aware," he began gruffly after I paused for breath, "this isn't the first time a shifter has used the academy to escape a pack. Pack culture is patriarchal and notoriously hard for women in general. Especially anyone who is even the least bit different. Most halflings are killed on sight."

I took the seat across from him. "Nurse Julie told me the same thing last night."

The corner of his mouth quirked but I saw the attempted smile did not reach his eyes. "I can tell you from experience. My own pack, the one I left before I transferred to my current position, lost a bunch of good kids because of their hatred. A few of them were half-Fae."

"Wait a minute." I peered back at Detective Wilson. "You make it sound like it's more usual than *not* for half-Fae, half-werewolf children to be born."

Detective Wilson swallowed a laugh, shaking his head. Looking at me like I was a stupid kid. "I wouldn't say it's common. But it happens. I'm sure you've heard about the promiscuity of the Fae, so definitely not unheard of. I can tell you I lost a very good friend from my pack because he was different. Not half-Fae, but gay and half-pixie. You can imagine how well *that* combination went over with the pack elders. I've been searching for him ever since. I take whatever cases come through the academy because I'm still hoping to come across information about him."

"Look, Detective Wilson." I placed all my cards on the table. "I've had a few experiences lately leading me to a certain truth. The killer is a shifter."

His eyes narrowed. "How do you figure?"

I told him my suspicions, stopping only when he interrupted me with a rude swear word. "I knew it." His hand curled into a fist and beat once against the top of the study table, jolting the pewter candle holders in the center. "I knew there was something screwy about this case. I *knew* it."

He had good hunches, then, and I had to wonder just how far Headmaster Leaves had gone to stymie the detective in these recent cases.

"Do you have any idea what to do?" I asked him.

"I'm still thinking. You're telling me the shifter is killing off top students and you're next. You honestly believe what you're saying?"

I gestured toward my arm, still in a sling although I sensed the bone had knit itself back together during the night. "He tried to kill me by pushing me off a balcony. He's going to come back and finish the job very soon. I know it."

"Well then." Wilson paused, leaning far back in his seat and crossing his feet at the ankles on the tabletop as though he owned the place. "I think I might have a plan."

"Tell me," I demanded.

"I have a feeling you're right and he'll strike again. You're going to help me catch this perp." He continued through my squawked protest: "We'll use you as bait."

28

I needed *allies*.

After spending the morning bouncing theories and opinions off Detective Wilson, that was the takeaway message.

We needed people who could be trusted to help with the sting and takedown. I vehemently disagreed with Wilson calling in members of his pack to help but he insisted. He knew who to trust, and made a few phone calls to get those people to the academy property. He assured me he knew a way to get around the headmaster's involvement. How to keep things under wraps until we caught the guy.

Yeah, right. Wilson hadn't been able to so far, right?

I didn't have many people I could trust with the truth here. In fact, there were only *two* I felt safe sharing this secret with. Melia and the shifter nurse, Julie, and I didn't want to include either one of them in a potentially dangerous plan. I briefly considered Professor Marsh and then decided against her involvement. She was too close to Leaves.

Detective Wilson insisted he would do everything in his power to keep us safe and I had to let him do his job.

I knew he meant what he said. I could sense the vehemence in his tone. The conviction in his every move. Still…

It was a big risk.

I knocked on the nurse's door and walked inside without waiting for her to answer me. The woman never slept, apparently, because I found her at her desk scribbling away on a student's file that she snapped closed the moment she saw me. Large eyes blinked in surprise.

"Have you reconsidered your ridiculous plan to catch a killer by yourself?" Nurse Julie asked. Then laughed loudly. "No, I can see it in your eyes. There's no getting you off of this idea even if I tried. What do you want from me, Miss Alderidge?"

"I want your help." I closed the door behind me to keep the rest of the world from disturbing us. Then I flipped the lock. Reinforced it with another pulse of magic. At least the magic came easier now than it had before.

Julie swiveled around on her stool and stared at me, her eyes narrowing until I almost lost them in her blue skin. "Hmm. You're not wearing your potion spell. Didn't we just fix you up yesterday? What happened?"

I shrugged. "I'm out of vials. Apparently, I have terrible luck with them and I've broken the spell more times than I'd anticipated. Which means I'm out in the open now because I don't have an opportunity to go back and get more. I have no choice."

"Oh, you foolish child." Julie clucked her tongue, grabbing the file and standing to return it to its place in a cabinet on the opposite wall. "*Seriously* foolish child. Give me a moment. Do not leave this room under pain of death."

She stalked out through the door, shattering my magic with a thought, and returned a moment later with an eerily similar glass container to the ones I'd had in my wooden case.

I stared at it without blinking, then swallowed hard. "You...where did you *get* that?"

"My own stash I've learned to make," she said haughtily as she shook the vial. "Where do you think I got it? I told you, I'm in a similar situation. Here, take this. I gather all the ingredients myself. When this is over, I'll teach you how to make your own. And you will never have to deal with another witch in your life. It's much better, trust me."

I swallowed a smile along with the potion. It didn't taste like burnt garbage and battery acid the way my old potion had. In fact, after I finished the whole of it, an aftertaste of flowers filled my mouth and I licked my lips to clean them.

Wow, *so* much better than the sludge from Barbara. Worlds apart.

My skin wavered, shivering as the potion took effect, then settled along my bones. No dizziness. No stomach pains. It was a far cry from the effects I'd gotten used to with my own potion, where I felt like dying every time I downed a vial. And my wolf...*she was still there*. Under the surface and suppressed, but not numbed.

I breathed a sigh of relief. No more debt to that loon. "Oh, my God. Thank you."

"There. Are you satisfied now?" Julie asked. "I assume you came for the potion?"

"I wish it was."

She scowled at me.

After explaining the situation to Julie and extracting her agreement to do whatever she could, I left feeling lighter than I had since before my eighteenth birthday. Even going so far as to smile at whoever I passed in the hall.

We had a plan in place. A plan to end this ridiculous situation once and for all without anyone else getting hurt.

At least I hoped no one would get hurt. In the dorm, I removed my sling, flexing my hand to test my strength. The bone had knit itself back together all right, healing with unnatural speed thanks to the hours I'd spent without the potion. *Good.* I would need every kind of advantage to get through what was coming.

Bait. Detective Wilson wanted to use me as bait.

I pushed any lingering doubts and fears aside. I wasn't helpless. Not in the least. Thinking back on my last interaction with Kendrick, where he'd had me trapped in the hallway, I'd felt like a victim. One who let the situation overwhelm her instead of standing up for herself and her boundaries. I had felt like I didn't have any kind of options.

Weak, my mind supplied.

But I wasn't weak. I had power. I had a plan.

I didn't see the others until dinner. Melia already knew the setup, as she and I had spoken before lunch, and soon it would be time to put the rest of it into action. Against my better judgment, she had a part to play, although I knew she would have flipped her lid if she found out I had a plan that didn't include her.

Not like I could even eat. Nothing wanted to stay down and my stomach churned in anticipation. According to Nurse Julie, I still had to be wary of garlic while taking her potion, so I stared down at my habitual salad in distaste. God, I wanted a burger. A big juicy burger with extra cheese and a side of fries that hadn't been doused with garlic salt.

"Where are the boys?" I asked Melia through a mouthful of lettuce, forcing myself to chew and swallow. "Have you seen them?"

She jerked her head backward, indicating a different table. "They're over there. I guess Mister Pain in the Butt is too good to sit with us again. Doesn't matter anyway."

I ignored the crack forming in my heart. Mike was still

ignoring me. To the point where he didn't want to sit at the same table. Wow. Talk about taking things too far.

"However! If you're going to spread the word," Melia said in a hushed whisper, leaning forward so I could hear her, "then do it now. Don't wait any longer. The moon is rising. It's almost time."

The first part of the plan was about to commence and we didn't have time to waste.

Good. I was eager to get it over with. At least I wouldn't have to finish my salad.

I agreed with her statement with a sharp nod. "Hey Meli, I'm going for a walk." I made sure to raise my voice to be overheard.

She blinked at me, the response exaggerated. "By yourself? Are you sure it's safe?"

"I need air, a little breathing room. No worries. It's a nice night." I sighed and knocked my tray aside for emphasis. "I'm not hungry anyway."

It wasn't a lie.

"Fine, whatever you want," she agreed easily, using her fork to arrange the macaroni and cheese around her plate. "I'm going to hang out here for a while and then try to talk to you know who."

"Barry? Good luck, girl," I told her.

I felt the invisible tingling caress of her magic from across the table. A goodbye. And good luck to me as well. I pushed away and walked toward the exit, seeing Mike and Roman out of the corner of my eye.

I looked rough. I knew it, and had fended off more than my fair share of well-wishers asking me if I was okay and telling me to get better. It played right into the plan. News had spread about my fall from the balcony and though I'd healed, I'd amped up the shadows under my eyes, the slight hitch in my gate, and kept the sling in place despite no longer needing it for my arm.

Let them think I was still weak. It would help with tonight's mission.

Mike might have been ignoring me, but he noticed the bruises. And he noticed the arm sling. Out of the corner of my eye I watched him rise from the table, his fingers gripping the tabletop until his knuckles turned white.

Seconds later, he ran up to me with Roman right behind him. "Tavi, are you okay?" he said immediately. The voice of concern. "What happened to you?"

"What do you care? I'm sure you already know." I kept my gaze pointed straight ahead and left the noise of the cafeteria behind me. "Would *you* be okay if you were pushed off of a balcony?"

His eyes went full moon wide and he tried to grab me, to force me to stop. I shrugged him off with a sharp hiss, as if he'd caused pain to my injury.

"What? No, impossible. You weren't pushed. That's, ah, that's not what I heard."

"It's quite possible, let me assure you." *Don't look at him, don't look at him.* I had to keep the mantra going because all I wanted to do was turn to him and drink my fill. He was touching me again. "I broke my arm, thank you very much. So be careful."

"Tell me what really happened," he demanded, lengthening his stride to keep up with me.

"Tavi, talk to us," Roman piped in, a step behind. "We're worried about you."

"Oh, sure you are." I didn't have to force the anger into my voice. All I had to do was think about how they'd sat at a different table tonight. *It should have been me*, Mike had said after the results of the lottery. Yeah, I didn't have to work at my frustration at all.

"You look terrible—" Mike cut off when I swiveled to glare at him. "I mean, no, that's not what I mean. I'm just saying you look a little beat up."

"Thank you so much for your observation, Michael." I brushed him aside, the haunting worry in his gaze following me. "I'm going outside for some air. Please leave me alone."

The boys fell away and I continued my walk alone. Alone outside with my not-broken arm and no weapons. But I knew I had allies waiting nearby, my favorite blue-skinned nurse and werewolf detective, plus extras working for the police force, all prepared to help me when the masked killer arrived.

And he surely would. This was the perfect time to make a move.

I stopped on the front steps of the castle with my hands cupped in front of my face to warm them against the early winter frost. I fought against the chill crawling along my skin. Turning my face to the moon, I noticed with a jolt I no longer needed to fear the moonlight. Garlic yes, but not moonlight. I could walk outside under the dark night sky without protecting my skin.

It felt like a homecoming.

The nurse's potion was very different from the one I'd received from Barbara. She hadn't given me any other objects or situations to avoid outside of those I already knew. I wondered if I'd be safe from quartz now or if I'd still have to worry about divination—

God, when Marsh found out what I'd done to her divination lab, with the broken shards of crystal... Or maybe she already had. I was going to be in for a world of hurt. And stripped of points. A *lot* of points.

There went my number one status. Ah well, easy come easy go, right?

My breath blew out in a white cloud of mist in front of

my face. The night was cold, winter setting its claws into the land as December rolled around. The thin school blazer I wore did nothing to protect me from the chill.

I thought about the moon and how I'd missed her. *My lady*. Although my shifter senses were still dulled under the effects of the potion, I could feel my wolf beneath my skin. A part of me stretching lazily and relishing the buttery-soft silver rays from overhead.

I didn't have the luxury of those kinds of thoughts. Not now. It was showtime.

I drew on the constant low level of anxiety I'd harbored since arriving at the academy, using it to add an aura of fear to my person. The killer was a shifter. He would be able to smell my terror. It would draw him.

Yes.

My sneakers crunched along the partially frozen grass of the front lawn as I stepped away from the relative safety of the castle. Outside of the light cast from the lanterns along the exterior wall.

It didn't take long for our guy to make his move.

Footsteps sounded behind me, muffled to try and keep me from sensing him. They drew closer. I heard them and turned slowly to see a man approaching me, tall and thick across the shoulders with suitable menace in each step. A one on one shakedown. I knew what he wanted, I knew he was stronger, and I knew he wouldn't stop until I was gone for good.

"I knew you would show up," I told him. Turning fully to face him and seeing the same mask, the same build as the one who'd knocked me around last night.

The last of my fear disappeared. This ended now. I wasn't sure and I couldn't see through the thick material of the mask, but I could have sworn I caught the hint of a smile, like an animal before a fight. This was about to get ugly.

He didn't speak. Just continued to stare at me.

"Are you going to try to hurt me again?" I asked. "I say *try* because you obviously didn't get the job done last time."

The taunt bounced off of him without eliciting a response. How long would it take for Detective Wilson to come out? Where was the rest of his team?

Seconds ticked by and nothing happened.

"You have a lot of nerve, coming after me where people could see you. Aren't you worried someone will come outside and catch you?" I tried again, raising my voice to make sure my backup could hear.

Wilson, come on!

I glanced around toward the side of the castle where the team was supposed to be waiting. They were. I noticed three figures standing directly in front of the stone foundation, facing away from me with a blue nimbus around each of their heads. I tuned in to the stench of magic around us.

Glamoured.

My backup had been glamoured, an unbreakable spell until the caster decided to end it.

"Oh, no." My stomach dropped.

Yeah, I had no backup. I rubbed my hands on the sides of my hips, trying to wipe away the fatigue and anxiety of knowing I was alone. Trying and failing.

"Who are you?" I burst out. "What do you want?"

I'd never been more shocked in my life than watching the killer remove his mask.

Especially when I saw Roman's shining eyes staring back at me.

29

I couldn't breathe. The air caught in my throat and I clawed at it. *Oh, God.*

Bile rose to burn my insides. It wasn't possible.

Mike's best friend...had been killing people? Roman was *my* friend too. He'd been there since day one, laughing with us, studying with us, eating every meal across the table from me with a smile on his face.

How had I not known he was a shifter?

He caught the look of shock and horror on my face and chuckled.

"Oh, come on, Tavi, you have to understand," he began, taking a step forward. "Being here is a big deal for me. I need to protect my interests. There are certain things you don't know about me and the life I've lived. You think you're the only one who has to take a potion to hide their true nature? Like you're something special?"

Roman was much larger than me. He had eight inches of height and more than one hundred pounds of muscle on me on a good day, when I was in fighting shape. Now I'd lost weight with my inability to eat anything other than salad and fruit.

I'd felt the snap of his teeth break my skin. Oh boy. Memories slammed into me about the pain from those bites. What would he do if he got his hands on me this time?

"You're not special," he stated. "I know a dozen half-shifters who have tried to escape using the Fae Academy. Dozens more who tried to fight their way into Faerie."

Me? Special? *Nope, not at all.*

"If you're a shifter, then how did you and Mike even meet each other?" I asked to stall him.

Roman shook his head and took a step closer. "Ah, now that is a question you should have asked earlier on. It might have given you an edge for tonight. I knew there was something about you I'd need to watch for. Knew it the second Mike told me he'd helped a girl with her broken-down car."

"I must be special enough to leave a lasting impression on the prince." I summoned a smug smile I knew would irk Roman, no matter how Mike and I weren't on speaking terms.

"Sometimes, when you are powerless, you fall for things that are bad for you just to feel like you have a little bit of control," Roman taunted. "It's a classic move. You have a pretty face and a decent disposition. You aren't one of those simpering tarts falling all over themselves to win his favor. Of course he'd be drawn to you. Like a drug addict."

"I thought we were friends, Roman." I knew I had to keep him talking. To keep him distracted while I worked to find a way to break the glamour keeping Wilson and the others trapped and immobilized.

"Keep your enemies closer and all." To him, it was simple. "I had you in a spot where I could watch you. You didn't become a threat until you somehow managed to make it into the top ten. Then I knew I had to act."

Roman was cocooned in magic. I sensed it the closer he got to me. Some sort of protection spell he'd set up before our interaction. Keeping him safe…from me? Keeping him safe from anything.

Sweat drenched my face despite the chill in the air, a product of stress and adrenaline. I shifted my balance and spread my legs to stand my ground. I was the damn top first-year for a reason. I had to believe in myself.

I wasn't going down without a fight.

"Why are you doing this?" I demanded.

"It's not even about me, not really. I mean, of course I had to make sure I kept my place. But no one deserves a spot at this academy more than Mike," Roman insisted, conviction evident in his gaze. He took another step forward, closing the distance between us. "I'm doing what I have to do to make sure *he* stays."

"Wait, what?" Confused, I said, "Mike is the crown prince. He doesn't even *need* to be in the academy. He's full-blooded Fae and heir to the throne. Why would he have to be here?"

"Oh, but he does need it. It's imperative. You just don't get it. Mike is too damn honorable to fight dirty, to scrabble and claw to stay at the top. It's up to me to make sure he stays. He has to earn his place and makes it through to next year. And I'm sorry, Tavi, but your sob story and mysterious background isn't enough for me to think you deserve it more than he does. So, you need to die. It's the simple truth. You've jeopardized his position enough already. He's lost focus because of you."

Roman clucked his tongue as his words skittered down my spine like a spider. Then his fingers flexed at his sides and the tension between us went nuclear.

I wasn't talking to my friend anymore, if he'd ever been

one to me. I was talking to an enemy. And only one of us would walk away from this.

I didn't wait for him to continue his speech. All was not well at the Halflings Academy, and now I was more confused than ever. Magic sang through my bones as I called a spell to levitate Roman away from me without doing any physical harm.

The spell snapped like a striking snake. I sent him flying with a blast of power, all the way backwards into the side of the castle hard enough to knock loose bricks and rubble down to the ground.

Strange, it took him less than a second to get to his feet and charge me on a howl.

Yeah, *not good*.

My heart pounded and my ribs ached with every inhalation. Gradually my brain churned, slowly at first, trying to come up with a battle plan.

I was on my own, but I didn't need to act like it. Roman had severely underestimated me this entire semester. Now it was time to show him why.

Roman's spell rocked against me like a shotgun blast before I could dodge it. The rest of the air left my lungs in a startled cry and my heart squeezed itself into a tiny ball as his magic rushed over me. I bent over, cradling my chest, the pain holding me captive. My eyes rolled back into my head.

"Come on, Tavi. Tell me you didn't learn *that* spell?" Roman taunted. "Aren't you the *top student*? Do you know how hard it was to pretend I needed your help with levitation?"

I used the pain, drawing it into my veins, into the vessels and the capillaries until my whole body tingled with it. With unreleased magic. I threw it back to Roman with a yell and exhilaration lifted me up. Like I had suddenly grown wings.

Yes, I had magic too, asshole. And I was going to use it to crush him.

The blast hit him square in the chest but this time Roman stood his own ground with his arms out to the side. He rushed me again, one leg sweeping out to knock me off my feet. He grappled with me, using his momentum to slam a hand into my supposedly broken arm. Despite the healed bone and the added protection of the sling, it still hurt like hell.

I screamed. The sound pleased him. But he was close enough for me to grab his sweatshirt and smash my forehead into his face.

Blood burst from his nose. "You little bitch!" But he didn't fall.

Roman roared again. He lunged forward and struck with claw-tipped hands, like the blow of a sledgehammer to the sides of my head, whatever potion he'd used to hide his nature allowing him to shift.

Then the jerk *tripped* me. He knocked me back, his muscles sinuous and strong, pushing me across the grass and onto my back. Seconds later he dropped directly on top of me, his knees pressing into my sternum.

Then the world decided to crawl sideways.

"What's the matter? Having trouble breathing? Can't get up?" Roman continued with the taunts, his thighs tightening.

I raised my legs and hit him in the back with my knees. It gave me just enough room to wiggle out from underneath him. He jerked his head, trying to shake off the sudden pain in his kidneys from the strike, then reared back and prepared to slice me open.

I rose to my knees, slammed my fist into his throat while hooking his thigh with my ankle. Roman toppled. Before he hit the ground, I scrambled back, spinning in an attempt to get away and clawing at the dirt to gain ground.

Roman stared at me, his mouth open, then slid forward and grabbed me around the hips to pull me back. I yelled as my fingers dug into the ground.

"Do you really think you can win?" His voice was low and growling. "I mean, honestly, Tavi. Do you think you have the upper hand here?"

Winning definitely wasn't on my mind. *Surviving*, however…

A tingle of awareness shot through me and I knew we'd gotten closer to his glamour skill during the struggle. The undercurrent of his magic ran deep. It would take time to find a back door to it. To break through his spellcasting so I could find a way to release Wilson and the others under his magical thrall. It was time I didn't possess.

"Let me go, you asshole," I managed to get out. When I turned around to give him my most intimidating glare, his eyes glowed amber in the darkness.

Asshole wolf slimeball. The same type as Kendrick, the type who thought they could do what they wanted without a care for who they hurt along the way. Maybe Roman believed he did this for Mike but there were other ways to help your friends succeed. Ways that didn't involve *murder*.

Roman muttered a spell under his breath, sending me twisting into the air and landing hard on my back for the second time. I skidded a few feet before a tree broke my path.

I saw stars. It was a different kind of pain than the one in my arm, and different too from when he'd pushed me from the balcony.

The stars didn't want to go away. I still saw them when I turned over on my side, coughing. They were scattered across the lawn and glowing sharply. A contrast to the dark dampness of the grass.

But the one closest to me wasn't a star.

It cost me precious seconds to understand; the glimmer I

saw was a piece of quartz from the exploded crystal ball. I was wearing the same clothes from last night, so shards must have fallen out of my clothing, stuck there even hours after the explosion.

Instinctively I reached for it, reaching for anything I could potentially use as a weapon. After my fingers closed around the chunk of quartz, I realized might not have been such a good idea at all. Would it break Nurse Julie's potion spell? On second thought, breaking the spell would release my own inner wolf and put me on a more level field against Roman. Because until I could discover a way to break the glamour enchantment, I was on my own.

A heartbeat, then another, and then...the familiar icy coldness. But it was taking too long. Would I have time for the full effect to take hold before I had to fight off Roman again? And if not...what was I going to do with a piece of rock?

Roman leaped into the air, his eyes glowing and a growl cutting across the night. He landed on me and pinned me to the ground. Leaving me no room for escape. The ax was about to fall.

I clutched the crystal and jammed it as hard as I could into the exposed skin of his neck just as Roman tightened his grip, his hulking shape on top of me and holding me down.

The crystal fragment still had fire inside it. The same fire that had caused it to rupture in the first place. I could feel it pulsing in my hand. My only hope of surviving was that somehow the quartz crystal would have an effect on Roman, at the very least weaken him enough for me to get away.

Then his teeth ripped into my throat and the world exploded.

30

The stars disappeared. Both from the sky and the ones I'd seen like chunks of diamond scattered across the lawn. Everything disappeared under the tearing of those fangs through my skin. Through veins and arteries until the warm rush of blood pooled beneath me and I could no longer feel my arms or legs.

I felt nothing.

Roman and I were falling together. Out of reality, out of existence. He continued to rip at me maliciously until I didn't know where I left off and he began. Was he drinking my blood? Anger built up inside of me, straining for release, before disappearing under a wave of pure agony.

Every part of me went icy-cold. I tried to focus and couldn't, tears leaking from the sides of my eyes. Darkness encroached at the edges of my vision until I lost myself on a tide of pain, no longer present. No longer able to fight back.

I was dying.

A pop sounded. Muffled. Far away.

Someone help me...

I didn't want to die alone. I waited for visions of my life

to flash before me and remind me of all the things I'd done wrong, all the things I'd miss when I passed from this life to the next. I'd never dreamed it would end like this.

My pulse beat roughly in my ears. I wasn't sure what I heard. Until suddenly everything came to a screeching halt and Roman collapsed forward, his jaw releasing from my throat and hot blood, both his and mine, flowed over me.

A commotion broke out around us.

His body fell to the side just as hands reached for me and when I blinked, though he was distorted, Detective Wilson stood over me.

I watched his mouth moving but I didn't hear the words. I heard nothing beyond my pulse until Nurse Julie gathered me up into her arms.

I was hallucinating. They couldn't be here. They were glamoured. I felt the force of their words although I wasn't sure I made them out.

It's going to be okay.

"It's going to be okay."

Julie held me for the longest time as men swarmed the lawn. Wilson's men, as he'd promised, those on his staff and those from his pack he trusted.

They'd come for me at last. How?

My head was spinning.

"Stay steady, dear. We've got to stem the flow before you bleed out. Try not to move. Tavi, do you hear me?" Nurse Julie rasped.

I glanced over toward where Roman lay in the grass near me, saw his unblinking eyes staring straight at me, and I caught a glimpse of the shard of quartz I'd managed to strike him with, still lodged in his neck, dripping with blood mixed with the crimson decorating the lower portion of his face.

Dead.

Somehow, I'd gotten away with my life.

"Come on, let's get you out of here and get you cleaned up." Nurse Julie pulled me to my feet with a flutter of her wings. "Stay with me, now. I've got you."

Every inch of me hurt but I didn't protest, teetering on the edge of consciousness. When I couldn't walk, she lifted me easily and turned, carrying me off. I lay cradled in her arms, trying to see but everything blurred again. I rested there, nearly blind, each step sending a jolt of pain through my ravaged body. But I didn't cry out as she whisked me inside the castle straight to her office.

"Stay with me," she repeated.

"I'll try."

Was that my voice? It didn't sound like me.

I lost myself to the pain. Was I awake? Asleep? The last thing I remembered was Julie's concerned expression before I passed out entirely.

※

"Using the crystal against Roman was a stroke of genius on your part," Julie told me later, once the blood had been cleaned, my wound dressed, and my newly re-broken arm reset again. "I swear, you continue to surprise me. How did you know it would disrupt his magic enough to release the glamour enchantment?"

I struggled to sit up by myself but when it proved impossible, I let Nurse Julie help me into a seated position. "I didn't know. It was the only thing available to me. I didn't have a choice."

"Well, it worked. It weakened him just enough so Detective Wilson was able to stop him."

I shook my head and winced. "Wait... You mean I didn't kill him? With the quartz, I mean."

"No, honey, you didn't. Detective Wilson shot Roman. And just in time, too."

My head still spun but at least I didn't have Roman's death on my conscience. "He meant to kill me."

"And almost succeeded, judging by the damage, but you did good, kiddo. Unfortunately, touching the quartz negated your potion spell. Here's another vial for you." She reached into her drawer and withdrew a potion for me to take. "You really do go through these like candy. We are going to have to work on it. Now go get some rest. We'll meet again tomorrow. I can teach you how to whip up your own batch. And I know this is a needless warning, but don't touch another quartz crystal again. I'll have to tell your divination professor to provide you with an obsidian ball if you want to do any more scrying. Marsh keeps a few in her office."

"Thanks." I offered her a weak smile and swallowed the potion. "I owe you."

"No, sweetheart. You owe me nothing."

We were interrupted by the clearing of a throat and Nurse Julie and I turned to the doorway in tandem.

"I hope you're lucid enough for me to come in and ask you a few questions, Miss Alderidge." Detective Wilson looked softer than normal, as though someone had shaken him out and smoothed away the rough edges.

I gave him the same smile I had given Nurse Julie seconds earlier. "Sure. Let's get this over with," I told him. Better now than later.

Nurse Julie made a perfunctory protest about how I'd been through enough and needed rest, but she stood and offered up her swiveling stool to the detective anyway. He thanked her with an inclination of his head but didn't sit.

"I wanted to let you know. Roman did not survive the gunshot wound. Your secret will go no further than those in this room," he told me softly. "We will keep your true nature hidden."

Roman had been my friend, or so I'd thought. We'd spent countless hours together talking and laughing. Now he was dead. I tried to search inside myself and find the remorse I knew I should feel. Somehow, I found nothing beyond a cold edge of satisfaction. The situation was finally wrapped.

"Too bad two students had to die before he was stopped."

Detective Wilson grimaced. "It's unfortunate, yes. But at least we stopped him before he could commit a third murder."

"Are you going to tell the headmaster about me?" I wanted to know.

Detective Wilson scoffed, turning his head away to give me a view of his strong profile. "Your headmaster is a prejudiced piece of crap. It would go against everything I believe in to reveal your secret to him. So nah, little girl. I'm going to be cheering you on from the sidelines. Continue to kick serious ass and get your Faerie citizenship so you can get the hell out of here."

I held my hand out for him to shake, his callused fingers wrapping around my much smaller ones. "It's a deal."

※

After I was sewn up and bandaged and sent on my way, I met Melia outside of the office. When I looked over at her hastily covered sniffle, her eyes were wet and tears trailed down her cheeks.

"Meli, what's the matter?"

"Oh my God, Tavi. Just…just—" And she stopped, hugging me to her chest as only Melia could. "I'm so glad you're all right."

Though my one arm remained in the cast, re-broken

during the ordeal, I hugged her close with the other one. "I know, me too. But if you don't stop crying then you're going to make me cry too, and I already look bad enough."

She laughed through the tears. "I'm glad you didn't die. You're my best friend."

I rested my head on her shoulder and drew in Melia's unique and familiar scent, like a flower in a thunderstorm. "You're mine, too."

Melia swiped at her cheeks. "Headmaster Leaves wants to see you in his office right away."

I groaned. "Great. I guess it couldn't wait til morning, could it? I'm dead tired."

She wrapped an arm across my shoulders. "Come on, I'll walk you there."

We made our way to Headmaster Leaves' office and I took a seat in front of his desk. I listened to him as he commended me for my bravery in assisting a law officer with the takedown. Obviously he didn't know the full story and thanks to Detective Wilson he never would.

His soliloquy on my strength, courage, and powerful magic included an admission on how my actions would not bring back those who had passed, but he was proud to know I was one of his students.

Once I would have nearly preened with his praise. It was exactly what I wanted. Someone validating my place here. Someone in authority telling me I belonged and I'd done a good job.

Now it amused me, this prejudiced werewolf-hating loser praising my virtues while he had no clue who actually sat across from him.

Good. I wanted to keep it that way.

"One more thing before you go, Tavi." Leaves fixed me with a stern look not in the least softened by his smile. "I took a glance through your file to find information on your family, to contact them about your heroic actions. I didn't see anything. Most of your personal info is blank. There's no permanent address, no phone numbers—"

I hurried to interrupt him, heart thumping. "I'm sorry, Headmaster. My, ah, my father is a very private person. He doesn't like me giving out our numbers."

"Well, we're going to need a way to contact your father if you're to continue here at the academy."

"Oh, absolutely. I'll have him call you. Thanks again!" I pushed away from the desk and bolted for the door, leaving Leaves stuttering behind me.

Close one. I'd have to be super careful going forward. Leaves couldn't find a way to contact my uncle, or this whole thing would be blown.

I exited his office expecting Melia to still be there waiting for me. I certainly didn't expect to see Mike.

Something fluttered in my chest. I stopped, taking him in for a long moment before speaking. "What are you doing here?"

He just stood there, swiping at his nose with the sleeve of his shirt. His eyes were red, shoulders slumped forward, and hair all askew. If I didn't know any better, I would have called his look downright *devastated*.

Had he heard about Roman, then? Had the news spread through the school already?

"Hey. Can I walk you back to your dorm, Tavi?" he finally asked me, his words watery as if there were still tears yet to be shed.

My heart melted for him. "Sure."

I started toward him and he stepped aside to let me walk past. Almost as though he couldn't stand to be so physically close to me, which confused the hell out of me. But after a few steps he caught up and our footsteps fell into an easy rhythm as we walked side by side.

"Are you okay?" Mike asked, his voice cracking slightly.

"I'm alive," I answered simply. "About the best I can tell you right now."

"Tavi, I'm so sorry I didn't believe you when you told me you'd been pushed off the balcony. And I'm sorry I wasn't there for you when you needed me. I was acting like a jerk, and you didn't deserve any of it."

I tried to shrug and found the motion awkward with the soft cast and sling over my shoulder. "I've got some bumps and bruises. Nothing you could have prevented."

"You have to believe me when I tell you. I didn't know about Roman. *I didn't know.* He kept a lot from me."

His insistence nearly broke my heart. "I know you didn't. Roman told me."

Mike stopped in his tracks. "What did he say?" he asked, his voice strangled, eyes glassy.

"He said you were too honorable to do anything about your situation, so it was up to him to do it for you."

Mike sucked in a breath and shook his head, his normally bright-gold hair gone dull. "He was my best friend," he said slowly. "We'd known each other since my first visit to the mortal world. I can't believe he was—"

It hit me then: Mike couldn't have known Roman was half wolf-shifter.

"—a murderer," Mike finished.

"We can't always know everything about a person," I said softly. Thinking about Uncle Will and how if I had my way he'd never know where I was. My heart lurched. "And I think it was *because* he was your best friend that he did what he did. He cared so much about you, he wanted to make sure you earned your spot in the academy. Even if it meant picking off those he saw as serious competition."

We approached the door to my dorm and I stopped, not ready to go in just yet. Wanting the two of us alone for as long as I could manage. There were still a lot of unanswered questions. "*Why* do you need a spot at the academy, Mike?"

Instead of answering, he kept his gaze on his shoes, mouth zipped closed.

I sighed. If he wanted things to be this way… "We all have our reasons for being here, and maybe we don't want other people to know them. But maybe we should work together instead of standing against each other in competition. And one day, when we feel safe enough, maybe we can share our secrets."

I wanted to tell him, I realized. I wanted to tell him everything about me down to my last secret, even when he had the power to destroy me entirely.

Mike only smiled. "I agree. One day." Then he bent and placed his lips on my cheek. And the simple action rocked my world to the point where everything tilted and I knew, nothing would be the same again.

My mouth rounded in an O. I didn't let him see it.

"If you're up for it, do you want to meet at the library tomorrow? Five o'clock?" he asked. "We still have a few tests coming up before winter break and Christmas. I mean, I don't want you to push yourself if you're not feeling well, but things haven't been the same without you, Tavi, and I could really use some normalcy right now."

How could I say no? "I promise I'll be there."

I watched him leave, Mike glancing over his shoulder at me before he turned out of the hallway. My heart fluttered at the sight.

Oh, crap.

The *last* thing I needed to add to my crazy life right then was falling in love with the future king of Faerie. Yet that's exactly what was happening to me. My head was screaming at me to run but my heart didn't seem to care.

I didn't want to stop it. No matter how dangerous.

No matter what Kendrick Grimaldi would do to *both* of us if he found me.

The End

Continue the Fae Academy for Halflings novels with *Faerie Gift.*

For author updates, sign up for Brea's newsletter
www.breaviragh.com/newsletter

ABOUT THE AUTHOR

BREA VIRAGH is a USA Today bestselling romance author based in the Blue Ridge Mountains. She is a proud Gryffindor, a graduate of Brakebills, and a member of Fairy Tail. When she isn't writing and daydreaming about her newest project, her hobbies include binge-watching HGTV, scouring thrift shops for goodies, and maintaining her alpha status among her puppy and three cats.

Read More from Brea Viragh
www.breaviragh.com

Printed in Great Britain
by Amazon